LIFE GOES ON

LIFE GOES ON

THE KURTHERIAN GAMBIT™ BOOK 21

MICHAEL ANDERLE

DISRUPTIVE IMAGINATION

Copyright © 2018 Michael T. Anderle
Cover by Gene Mollica and Sasha Almazan
https://www.gsstockphoto.com/
Cover copyright © LMBPN Publishing

LMBPN Publishing
PMB 196, 2540 South Maryland Pkwy
Las Vegas, NV 89109

Version 2.2 March 2023
eBook ISBN: 978-1-64971-588-3
Print ISBN: 978-1-64202-021-2

THE LIFE GOES ON TEAM

Mike Pendergrass
Sherry Foster
Daniel Weigert
John Ashmore
Thomas Ogden
Erika Everest
Edward Rosenfeld
Veronica Torres

Thanks to our JIT Readers for this Version
Timothy Cox (the myth)
Diane L. Smith
Dave Hicks
Deb Mader
Dorothy Lloyd
Peter Manis
James Caplan
Mary Morris
Rachel Beckford
Veronica Stephan-Miller

If I missed anyone, please let me know!

Original Editors
Stephen Russell
Lynne Stiegler

This version edited by
Lynne Stiegler

**Thank you to the following Special Consultants
for Life Goes On
Jeff Morris - US Army - Asst Professor Cyber-Warfare,
Nuclear Munitions (Active)**

To Family, Friends and
Those Who Love
To Read.
May We All Enjoy Grace
To Live The Life We Are
Called.

And a special call out to Joshua (D'artagnan) Anderle
Who was half the reason I even wrote that first book, Death Becomes
Her.

CHAPTER ONE

The massive Leviathan-class superdreadnought hung in space, slowly moving through the black depths above the planet. Silent, but not immobile.

Well over seven thousand times a second, the AI updated the attack plans should her Empress need to call on the abilities of the warships to rain fire on the planet below.

It was intended to be a peaceful visit, ArchAngel knew, but she developed contingencies as she eavesdropped on the communications.

She was *always* prepared.

Ixtali News Agency Duonto

"This information has been confirmed." The news reporter gripped his microphone as he looked at the drone camera. "The two massive Etheric Empire warships above our planet are here on a planned visit, bringing Empress Bethany Anne to speak with our political leaders."

He turned to his right, his four mandibles signaling that he was just a touch uncomfortable.

He had heard the rumors of the Empress' incandescent rage over the new Federation efforts, especially the many requirements they were trying to place on her people.

And for what it was worth, he sympathized.

However, he could also sympathize with the other governments, as well as the Ixtali. The Empire itself was too powerful to create even a semblance of equality among the proposed Federation's members, so the negotiations were rather rough with those in the Empire itself—including the most divisive issue, which he was sure would set the Empress off.

They wanted her to step down.

QBS _ArchAngel II_, above the Ixtali Planet

Bethany Anne put a hand to her forehead and closed her eyes. "Just shoot me now, and let me leave this fucking job already!" she murmured. Opening her eyes, she looked at herself, or rather, the visage of the AI ArchAngel on the screen in front of her, and asked, "Are you sure?"

"Yes," she responded. "Two different groups are working to break up the meeting, either while or after you speak with the Ixtali council."

Bethany Anne made a face and glanced at John, who merely shrugged his shoulders and smiled back at her.

Same shit, different planet.

"We have a call from a private line," ArchAngel informed Bethany Anne, who raised her right eyebrow. "From Legate Addix," ArchAngel qualified.

"Well, that tears it." Bethany Anne turned and started toward her weapons closet. "This will be an armored visit."

The AI opened the door before she got to the room. As she stepped inside, she answered, "This is Bethany Anne."

The Ixtali's voice came from the speakers. "Empress, I apologize for going outside normal protocols, but there are a few issues here you might want to be aware of before you come down."

"Speak to me, Addix," Bethany Anne replied as she opened drawers. She turned and pointed at John and then to a new set of drawers she'd had installed.

She turned back to her search, so she didn't notice the unasked question on John's face as he started opening the drawers.

"Oh," he murmured as he pulled out a couple of knives. "Someone has been shopping at the blades and cutlery store and not sharing the spoils," he whispered as he selected two for himself.

When he turned around, Bethany Anne was naked, about to pull up her under-armor suit. He quickly turned back, raising his eyes to the ceiling as he shook his head.

Damn that woman! "What happens on the mission stays on the mission," he subvocalized, listening to her dress behind him. She had been tweaking him since way back in Florida.

He'd complained to his wife Jean about it a few decades ago, but she just patted him on the cheek with a knowing smile on her face.

He'd had no clue what Jean had meant by that, and that had made the response scarier than it should have been.

When he heard the expected zipper closing, he turned around. She was putting on a skintight suit that did little to hide much but changed her skin color from white to a Lycra-looking black.

He rolled his eyes. At least he wasn't staring at Baba Yaga.

Does this make me look fat? she sent straight into his mind as she carried on the conversation with the senior legate. He glanced around the room to confirm nothing seemed amiss and then headed out of her arms locker.

Well, it was much more than an arms locker, really.

You might have gained a pound, he sent back, chuckling under his breath as he imagined her eyes trying to burn a hole through the back of his head. He smirked. She would be trying to figure out where that pound was for a week.

Priceless!

"ArchAngel?" John called over his own link to the AI.

"Yes, John?" He could hear her through the bone conduction speakers in his head.

"Please close the arms locker door," he commanded, and the door behind him immediately started closing as he took up a protective position outside.

"Closed," she confirmed. "Why?"

He smirked. "I don't want to hear her bitch about weight gain after the call with the senior legate."

Bethany Anne stared at the broad back of her friend as he stepped out.

If only she had laser eyes!

"Bastard!" Bethany Anne murmured. John took up a protective position with his back to her as the door to her room closed.

"I'm sorry?" the senior legate replied over the speakers in her suite. "I don't think I know that word."

Bethany Anne rolled her eyes as her focus snapped back to her call. "I have to apologize." She turned and opened the drawers where her latest armor setup was stored. "It was a personal comment," she admitted as she pulled out the core chest and back protection. "Who will need their ass kicked, and why?"

QBS *Ranger Prime*, On-station near the QBS *ArchAngel II* over the Ixtali Planet

The Empress' Rangers had fought many battles, either by themselves, with their support staff, or with their ships inside and occasionally outside the Etheric Empire. For many of the last decades, major law enforcement problems inside the Etheric Empire had been significantly reduced, and that could be traced to one ship.

The QBS *Ranger Prime.*

Ranger Prime was the largest law enforcement ship any political group in any system near the Etheric Empire had in their possession, and the ship made a statement.

The statement was, "Don't try to play pirate in the Etheric Empire. They don't fuck around."

The Skaines had learned a few valuable lessons, not the least of which was to never believe it was safe to try and rip-off a quick score. When an Etheric Empire superdreadnought whose *raison d'être* was to focus on piracy and other law enforcement operations might arrive at any time, there wasn't shit they could do if it showed up but hope they could make a run for it.

Only huge system-level governments could foot the costs of building and manning warships. The Skaines as a group used them.

However, the Etheric Empire was already at war, and their damned Rangers had requisitioned one of their elite and largest capital ships for themselves.

And the Empress had gone along with it.

During the Battle of Yerrluck, the Skaines had tried to box *Ranger Prime* and destroy her. For this engagement, fifteen percent of the Skaines' total military force had been concentrated in one location.

Fifteen minutes after the battle had started and the Skaine trap had been sprung, the QBS *ArchAngel II* and the QBS *Reynolds* arrived.

One-third of the Skaine ships had been decimated before the surrender message could be verified.

Barnabas often used the ship as a silent reminder to criminal organizations who were fighting amongst themselves to refrain from killing civilians in the process.

Ranger Prime would arrive without a word and slide through the atmosphere to park a few thousand feet in the sky over a city.

Most of the criminal organizations had heard that after the arrival, they had six hours to fix the problem—or else. If they hadn't notified the ship by then that they were working on a deal, a message went out to explain that the warring factions had three hours to make peace.

Barnabas didn't believe in allowing his Rangers or their support teams to take risks, so his people went on-planet wearing EE-LEA, "Etheric Empire-Law Enforcement Armor."

One of the most poorly-kept secrets was that the Rangers' LEA was military-grade armor with a fresh coat of paint.

Something criminals could rarely afford, and what they *could* buy was never as good as what the Rangers wore.

At last count, over one hundred and twelve peace agreements had been signed on *Ranger Prime*.

Barnabas walked onto the bridge, which was as he liked it.

Calm, quiet, and civil.

Even during the heat of battle, rarely did the personnel on the bridge feel any anxiety from their leader.

He was over a thousand years old and had worked for centuries perfecting his ability to remain composed. Barnabas was the quintessential example of "cool under fire."

He allowed very little to bother him.

Unfortunately, just a short time back, he had gone on an operation with Tabitha and Peter where he had tasted a little freedom from the normal restraints he engaged to keep his emotions in check.

And it had felt good. *Really* good.

. . .

Leviathan-class Superdreadnought, shadowing the *ArchAngel II* above Ixtali

Barnabas' face was a mask of calm as he sat down in the captain's chair on his bridge and contemplated future steps for his Rangers.

It had been decided that the QBS *Ranger Prime* would go with Bethany Anne to Earth and be listed in the records as having left.

Barnabas pursed his lips, thinking about…other options.

"Ranger One?" The EI's face was a copy of Barnabas'. It didn't use much creativity in communication.

"Yes, Prime?" Barnabas cocked his head to the right.

"The Empress has requested your presence for an operations effort. No Rangers on this mission, volunteers only."

Barnabas pushed on his seat's armrests and stood up. "How many volunteers does she need?"

"Right now, she says the more, the merrier, but at least five."

Barnabas thought about who was aboard and smiled. "I'll have seven."

"She asks that you suit up, but it might be a few hours before the operation starts. She says to let you know the *Shinigami* will arrive to convey the volunteers."

Barnabas spoke over his shoulder as he left the bridge. "Understood."

Ixtali Planet, Capital City, Convention Hall

The large convention hall was full. The Ixtali leaders walked down the stairs from above, then across the floor before stepping onto the podium that held their table. Once they were seated, they looked at the audience, and the room hushed.

The atmosphere was electric. The last few times the Etheric Empress had visited this location, nothing had happened.

This time, there was an undercurrent of expectation.

There were video documentaries of her first trip to Ixtali and the deaths that had occurred when the rebels had tried to harm her. However, it was so far in the past that the stories had grown to be damned near unbelievable.

The convention hall was accessed through twelve doors. Four were larger, and one, a double set, was considered the main entrance. Rising two stories, the twin doors were gilded in bronze metal and decorated with serif sigils inlaid in silver metal. It was through these doors the Etheric Empress entered.

In armor, with her helmet on.

Hushed whispers crisscrossed the auditorium as she took her first few steps down the stairs. She had four flights to descend before attaining the floor.

She went down five steps before she started air-walking. With each step she would descend a little, but it wasn't long before she was easily a full body-height above the stairs themselves.

There were five guards below her. The one in front was a female.

Gabrielle, send someone back out and have them ready to close and lock the doors when I get to the podium, if necessary.

Yes, ma'am, Gabrielle replied, and from beneath Bethany Anne, an armored guard turned and went back up the stairs.

Gabrielle looked around. *How many are we looking at?*

Just one at the moment, Bethany Anne replied.

Where?

I'll take care of her, was the response.

You're taking all our fun.

I keep as much as I can, but I'll give you guys the rest.

That's nice. Gabrielle continued scanning the crowd. *You still need to tell me where.*

Fine, Bethany Anne warned, *but if you snuff her before I get a chance, I'll be doubly hard at Tuesday's workout.*

You can be harder? Gabrielle asked. *Unholy hell, have you been going easy on me?*

Do you wish to find out?

There was a pause. *Yeah*, Gabrielle admitted. *I need to know if I have to up my game more.*

Sucks coming back sometimes.

Not as much now as the first time, Gabrielle replied as they approached the floor. *Last time I spent hundreds of years trying to not do much martially. This time I thought I wanted to enjoy motherhood and then family life, but I finally realized it was just an excuse. I had an aversion to the pain of training.*

And now?

I rather enjoy it again, Gabrielle admitted. *Plus, the look on John's face when I get inside his guard is sweet. So, where is my mark?*

Bethany Anne didn't look behind her. **First row, fourth Ixtali on your left. She is wearing a red necklace with a purple flower of some sort as a pendant.**

You mean the one who looks like she wishes she could shoot lasers from her eyes?

You can't fault her for that. Bethany Anne sniffed as she walked toward the podium. Darryl and Scott followed Bethany Anne, while John went around the podium to stand guard on the other side. **That's a cool-ass ability I'm trying to figure out how to implement.**

You mean, TOM cut in, **so you can also figure out how long it takes to regrow your eyeballs?**

As Bethany Anne ascended the podium's steps, her weight decreased so as not to damage the Ixtalis' stage.

Darryl and Scott broke off to flank the podium.

That's just you being melodramatic, Bethany Anne replied. **Think positively.**

Okay, he replied dryly. **I'm *positive* you will have to regrow your eyeballs and potentially your eye*brows* 'cause you're a stubborn ass.**

Oh, now you are adding eyebrows to the mix? I'm starting to think you're just trying to scare me because you fear me having laser eyes...and don't think I didn't catch you saying I'm stubborn.

I'm inside you. Why would I fear laser eyes?

One day you won't be, and you are a conniving little male.

I'm alien.

You're male.

Your point?

You're probably afraid I'd laser your butt.

I'll make sure I wear laser-resistant briefs.

What would you make them from? Bethany Anne wondered. *Some sort of diffraction material?*

Um, no, TOM replied, thinking it through. If you mean what I think you mean, that would only disperse the beam that was burning a hole in my ass.

Well, that's a positive, right?

Only if I didn't mind having my whole pelvic area being cooked to five thousand degrees by the diffracted laser beams bouncing around in my boxers, burning the shit out of my willyworm.

SHUT UP! She laughed mentally. *I've got to keep shaking hands here!*

TOM kept quiet but put an extra mark by his name. He had flat scored with that last comment.

Gabrielle had stayed at the edge of the floor a few short paces from the Ixtali Bethany Anne had pointed out.

What do you want done with her? Gabrielle sent.

Mmmm, Bethany Anne replied as she took off her helmet to greet the personages and a glove to shake the appendages of the Ixtalis. *She seems to think she missed her opportunity since I had the armor on. Let her go for now, and tell Eric to stand down for the time being.*

We have other fish to fry, Bethany Anne finished.

CHAPTER TWO

Barnabas ignored the ship that was slowly coming to rest near him as he spoke to one of his Rangers.

"Not this time," Barnabas told him. "You have worked with both me and Lance, and since the Rangers are going to drop out with the Empress, I think your future is with—"

"Lance." Johnnie sighed and held out his hand. "Barnabas, I can't thank you enough for letting me play Ranger, but I can't go forever without seeing my mom."

Barnabas took the hand. "Being a Ranger was a good cover, wasn't it, Johnnie?" They both smiled. "At least it kept your mom off Lance's back for the most part."

"She never did forgive _you_, though," Johnnie admitted. "You actually ate up all the goodwill you created by showing me my dad's video, and then some. She wanted Admiral Thomas to win."

Barnabas shrugged. "Lance and I knew your weakness for sugar," he admitted. "Have you given any thought to your time now? You will have to change your persona to keep going."

Johnnie ran a hand through his hair. "I've thought about it, sure," he admitted. "I think I'll go with 'Sean.' That's the other thing my mother might have named me."

Barnabas grinned. "Sean Bond?"

Johnnie chuckled. "Absolutely not!"

Barnabas tried again. "Sean Powers?" he asked, but Johnnie shook his head emphatically. He went back to Johnnie's question. "No major requests…just run this ship as a Ranger. You can't be involved in this altercation, and we need someone with an active badge on the ship."

He looked at his young protégé. "Sean Royalty?" Barnabas offered a last suggestion, but this time Johnnie didn't even answer. He just smiled, waved goodbye, and walked toward the hangar's exit. Johnnie called over his shoulder, "Sean Royalty? That has possibilities!" He waved to Tabitha and the Tontos as he passed them and exited.

Barnabas nodded as Tabitha and her five remaining Tontos walked up. "Everyone ditch their Ranger ID?" he asked.

Tabitha winked. "Yes, oh Wise One of the Ages," she lied as she stepped onto the ramp, her coat swirling as she headed into the ship. Hirotoshi and Ryu nodded sharply, as did Katsu, Jun, and Kouki as they passed him.

This time everyone had their Jean Dukes.

He walked up after Kouki, and the ramp started to rise as he entered the ship.

"Barnabas," the AI's voice, a little guttural to his ears, came through the speaker system, "would you mind coming to the bridge?"

"No problem, Shinigami," he answered.

Six pairs of feet followed him.

It seemed that the Japanese vampires and their esteemed leader wanted a chance to see the AI in person.

It was a large ship, and he admitted to himself that he would love to grab one of these. Had Bethany Anne allowed a second to be made?

If not, who had the plans?

When they got to the bridge, the team fanned out. They had no problem with a bridge that looked more like a nice living room, or perhaps a comfortable meeting room in an office.

With a circular sofa.

A face came up on the screen—Baba Yaga, but with Bethany Anne's teeth and younger skin. "Shinigami." He nodded as he took a seat.

"Ranger One," the AI replied as she looked around. "Ranger Two and Tontos, welcome to my ship." She placed an external video stream on the far-right screen. Kouki and Jun had to lean forward a little and look sharply right to see what was going on. "We are leaving *Ranger Prime* and will be cloaked the whole time."

Tabitha pointed to the screen. "That explains that guy in the upper right-hand corner scratching his head."

Inner Chambers, Ixtali Cabinet

"So that's the sum of it," Bethany Anne told the fifteen highest-ranking members of the Ixtali Cabinet. "The one group is housed here," she told them, pointing to a blue location on a map floating above the table. "They want to go back to the old ways." She pointed to an orange-highlighted area. "And we have this group, which wishes to secretly bring enough of their people into positions of power to operate the government in the future. They want to start using your information services to tap into the fractious efforts of the different polities coming together to create the Etheric Federation. Since you guys are currently part of the Empire, I'm going to be a bitch about that."

A senior Ixtali on her left leaned over and asked what that meant. Bethany Anne answered, "It means I'm going to be a hardass." He looked back at her, still confused. She willed her eyes to flare red and glow. She pointed to her face. "Pissed off!"

His mandibles signaled he understood now, and her eyes returned to normal.

"With your permission," she continued, not that her tone indicated she was asking as she looked toward the members, "we will take down both locations simultaneously. We will have interrogation-capable talent with each team."

"Where will you be during this operation?" the third-from-the-left Ixtali asked. Bethany Anne thought his name was Gril, but she might have been mistaken.

She smiled. "Kicking in the front doors, of course," she told him as she reached down and grabbed her helmet. "Why do you think I dressed this way?"

Gril wisely kept his thoughts to himself.

Minutes later, the fifteen members were sequestered so that no information could get out "accidentally." Bethany Anne and her people left.

It was time to win their hearts and minds—one way or another.

QBS _Shinigami_

Barnabas reviewed the compound's layout from the data provided by Bethany Anne's team, tapping the screen as Tabitha, Ryu, and Hirotoshi looked on. "So," he pointed to the top floor of the three-story schema, "we have an underground location, and no idea if they have bolt holes."

"I can help with that," Tabitha answered. "I'll toss a couple small spy spheres..." She tapped her lips. "Okay, maybe four of them. I doubt we need to worry about the first floor. We should be able to clear those three rooms within seconds."

Barnabas tapped his head. "We need them read and cleared if possible."

"We can do that." Ryu and Hirotoshi nodded. "Enough to call them clean or dirty. If clean, we will zip-tie them."

"And dirty?" Barnabas asked.

"Shoot them first," Hirotoshi answered, "then zip-tie them."

"It would be easier to separate the bad apples," Tabitha agreed.

"What, with the blood and all?" Barnabas asked.

"Actually," Ryu answered, "we usually can tell by the screaming, but puddles of blood work just fine, too."

Tabitha shrugged. "Sometimes it takes us a while to get back to them, so they either get hoarse or have fainted from blood loss."

"I...see," Barnabas answered.

Ryu turned to Hirotoshi. "What is the bet?"

Tabitha looked at her teacher in anticipation. "Yeah, Pops, what do we get?"

Hirotoshi shook his head. "No bet today. Just try to keep up with Barnabas."

Tabitha waved him off. "Easy-peasy."

Only Barnabas noticed the slight curve of lip Hirotoshi displayed as they broke up from their discussion.

QBS *G'laxix Sphaea*, Above the Headquarters of the Strom

"This is the captain speaking," a Yollin voice called as the ship winked out of existence on the landing pad on top of the Ixtali convention hall. "While I would love to go with you, my task—whether I want it or not—is to be a glorified taxi driver."

Bethany Anne looked at Kiel as they checked each other's packs. "Is he serious?"

Kiel locked down his right arm's armor before looking back at her and shrugging. "Only a little. Kael-ven was miffed he didn't find you first, so he is grumbling a little. Talking about getting into armor to do the door-knocking."

She looked toward the bridge. "I've got half a mind to tell him to do it," she mused.

"Only problem is," Kiel replied as he locked down his torso

plates, "we don't have any bottom armor for a four-legged Yollin. His important bits would be unprotected. It could become a game of tackle-torture for the Ixtalis, and completely ruin his chances of ever becoming a father...again."

Bethany Anne turned back to him and raised an eyebrow. "I thought he was done with kids after his stint on-planet? Wasn't the last time he went home to his ex and their three grown kids, and I quote, *'an existential effort to singularly befuddle him into an old folk's home?'*"

"He was a bit of a curmudgeon to them," Kiel admitted. "By the end of the evening, he had told his pacifist son to grow a spine, his politically-minded daughter to marry a Marine, and his literati son to read some of the classics. When said son explained he had, Kael-ven told him he meant *human* classics. He was pleasant to his ex-wife's husband, and pissed her off by slipping him a thousand-credit note to help him with his drinking problem."

Bethany Anne thought about that for a moment. "I didn't know Gleerah's husband *had* a drinking problem."

"He didn't at the time," Kiel explained. "Kael-ven told him he was paying it forward."

Everyone around Kiel had finished suiting up and was listening to the story. Bethany Anne chuckled. "What did Gleerah say about the money—or did she know?"

"Not at first," Kiel admitted. "Her husband kept the note and waved goodbye until Kael-ven was far enough away, although our esteemed pilot did hear her yell a hearty 'you piece of bistok shit!' as he closed the door to his Pod."

"And Kael-ven's reaction?"

Kiel drew in a deep breath and blew it out. "It took three days to get him to stop smiling."

The green light in the hold went to yellow as Kael-ven's voice came from the speakers. "This is the captain speaking. Would everyone near my soon-to-be-erstwhile Marine leader please take a step back? I'm going to open the ramp door and jettison him for failing to tell the story correctly."

The chuckles went around as Kiel looked up at the nearest speaker and asked loudly, "What the hell did I get wrong, you old goat?"

"One mark until we drop on the compound, and to answer your question," Kael-ven paused a moment, then finished, "I smiled for a total of *five* days straight!"

Bethany Anne, Gabrielle, John, Eric, Darryl, and Scott laughed as they walked toward the ramp. Kiel shook his head, then followed Scott and asked, "Where's Peter?"

Scott turned around. "Got the short straw. He had to stay on the *Meredith Reynolds* to make sure he did a few more training videos for the recruits who will come after we leave. Wants to make sure he passes down his knowledge, and that there is institutional memory for those who gave it all during his tenure."

"Like Todd?" Kiel asked.

"Especially Todd." Scott nodded. "He set up a whole room of Todd's mementos and a lot of Todd's training videos, so he isn't forgotten while Peter is out roaming the universe."

Kiel nodded.

Sometimes you couldn't do enough to thank someone who chose to give you the chance to continue breathing at their expense.

The ramp lowered and the seven of them headed into the night, stepping off into the air and floating down to start their attack.

Back on the bridge, once he confirmed everyone had dropped, Kael-ven hit the button to raise the ramp. The craft silently lifted into the sky, making sure it was out of any lanes of traffic. It wouldn't do to be hit by a stray personal flitter and scuff the paint.

It would be even worse for the personal flitter.

. . .

QBS _Shinigami_

The craft barely made a ripple as it glided through the traffic in the dark. Two personal flitter pilots thought they had seen a white face in the night, but there was nothing there when they looked again.

Barnabas watched the external video. "Are you _trying_ to get us seen?" he asked the AI. "I've noticed one for sure, and perhaps two pilots who looked in our direction."

"Not exactly," Shinigami answered. "I'm working on showing only part of the ship in a low-risk environment."

"Well, stop it," he told her. "Now is not the time to seed hints about the ghost ship."

"Uhh," the AI's face popped up on a nearby screen, "how did you know what I was up to?"

Barnabas glanced at the AI and started, "Shinigami, do you think you are the first youngling I've had to school?"

Tabitha, who was behind Barnabas, turned her attention away from the screen. Ryu and Hirotoshi looked at her, and the rest of her team's lips curled up slightly as they listened to them talk.

"Just because you're an AI," Barnabas continued, "doesn't mean you won't necessarily show traits of immaturity. Unless you screw up this operation for us, you will have many years to create a badass reputation."

"Understood, Barnabas," the AI responded, and the vampire logo faded into the night.

The team was locked, loaded, and ready to walk out of _Shinigami_'s hold when the AI's face appeared. "You know, I could just puck the fuck out of the ground."

Barnabas turned to look at her on the nearby screen. "Why would we do that?"

"Minimal casualties for our side," the AI answered.

"We won't have any casualties," Barnabas replied. "Trust me."

"Wow, take all the fun out of my night," Shinigami snarked as her avatar disappeared.

What in the seven hells, Barnabas thought to himself, *did Bethany Anne do to this AI?*

———

Gabrielle checked the image against her HUD's specs and set the seven dots for those on her team. Normally Bethany Anne wouldn't have been included on the op, but even Lance understood that she was working to become a figurehead, so why not?

It had been John who had suggested Gabrielle get back into gear as captain again. Her martial skills were increasing, and she needed to get her mind back in the game.

It felt a bit like old times.

She tagged the AI-only line on her HUD. "ADAM?"

"Yes," he replied.

"Do you have comm engagement?" she asked.

"Affirmative."

"Any chatter I need to know about?"

"None. No one currently suspects an attack. There *have* been two references to a three-person operation waiting for Bethany Anne to appear outside the Ixtali convention hall," he added. "That information was routed to the appropriate authorities, who are busy getting their people to locate and subdue."

"Sow confusion into the communications as you can. We are going live."

"Understood."

She changed to the main channel in time to hear Kiel.

"Anyone got an invite?" he asked over the personal comm as the seven dropped out of the darkness, their antigrav armor slowing them in the last four seconds. This compound had seven floors, with heavy security around the first three—which sucked for the security team on the roof who were easily targeted by those who floated down from above.

Bethany Anne tagged four locations in the HUD, and Gabrielle marked one for each of the four Bitches, waited a moment for them to lock on, then issued the take-down command.

Four red marks changed from circles to Xs.

Seven pairs of armored boots landed softly.

"All right, everyone, we have a simple plan. If they have a gun, they die. If it looks like they are ignoring commands, they die."

"If they are breathing?" Scott asked.

"If they look at you funny, they die," Gabrielle replied. "If they look like they are non-combatants, zip-tie them."

"Would have been easier," Bethany Anne admitted, "if we still had the ability to turn off their embedded chips."

"I didn't think they had those anymore," Kiel commented as the seven quick-timed it to the roof entrance.

"They stopped two generations back," Bethany Anne reminded him as she walked up to the door and knocked very softly. She scanned the other six full-armor helmets that stared back at her. "What? I knocked. I'm being polite!" She grabbed the handle and pulled; the lock barely slowed her down.

She stared at the door she had yanked completely out of the frame. "Oops."

CHAPTER THREE

Planet Ixtali, Glory of Ghosts Compound, Third-floor Basement

Guhdiss bowed his head to the master and turned to walk back toward his seat in the rear. There were ten rows with ten seats each on either side of the main walkway, and only three seats weren't filled.

He kept his hands inside his robe, as he had been instructed to do in the first meeting. Now they were having their sixth and final meeting.

It was time to accept the chip or bow out of the Glory.

There were always one hundred adherents brought into the Glory, and his group was the second to make it through the mysteries. The goal of the group was to grow to ten thousand strong, working in all parts of Ixtali society to bring back the glory of generations past, when all societies' leaders bowed to the power of their people.

And they trusted no one, especially the Etheric Empire, to protect them as a race.

Neutrality was their right, and neutrality was their way. It had been this way in the past, and it would be this way in the future.

Only the true believers would be willing, Guhdiss was told, to accept the Chip of Ascension. It was the only way the Glory could make sure their people were safe now and into the future.

The first row stood, and the master, his face hidden in the darkness of his hooded robe, intoned the Invocation of Acceptance. To his right was the Master of Truth, and to his left was the Master of Secrecy.

The first row turned to their right and walked up to the Master of Truth, the first person taking the small chip in their own hand. Once all ten had their chips, they raised them and recited a creed, accepting the truth of the future and their obedience to both the cause and their brothers and sisters in the Glory.

Then, one by one, each handed their chip to the Master of Secrecy, who inserted the chip into the base of an injection gun. The adherent faced the audience, and the Master of Secrecy placed the injection tool at the base of the first neck.

"Do you accept the truth of the power of the Ixtali people?" the master asked.

"I do," the first adherent replied, his mandibles frenetically moving in anticipation.

"Do you accept the power of the truth in your personal life, for those whom you will help while they sleep, unaware of the sacrifice you make for their offspring and their offspring's offspring?"

"I do," the first adherent answered again.

"Then accept this into your body as a physical sign of your adherence to the Glory. The Chip of Ascension forever bonds you with those in front of you, together agreeing that the future of the Ixtali people is the perfection of your own walk into the next stage of life."

The last of the first row was intoning his acceptance when the explosions started above them.

All three masters eyed the double doors at the back of the

room. The Master of Secrecy pulled two pistols from inside his robes, and the Master of Truth unsheathed a sword.

The master simply kept his hands in the folds on his cloak. "Be still. We are safe in the temple. These doors are locked for a reason. There are adherents to the Master of Secrecy above us who will protect the sanctity of our convocation and the location of this temple with their lives."

More explosions occurred, this time closer. Dust flew, and parts of the ceiling dropped to the floor.

Then Guhdiss heard people screaming in pain.

"Well, fuck all!" Tabitha spat as the latest Ixtali grabbed his spilling guts after her sword sliced through his abdomen, shredding his robes. "Would someone tie up that old man?" she snapped. Barnabas opened the door to the next room and walked through.

Nothing seemed to touch him.

For every Ixtali she killed, Barnabas killed three. He used whatever was around him to take out those he attacked.

There had been two guards posted outside the front doors of the compound when they arrived.

Barnabas had bowed to them. Tabitha could see the confusion in their eyes, which lasted until Barnabas' eyes flared red.

Before they realized their mistake, both were dead. One had his skull caved in, the other had the ceremonial long knife from her belt shoved upwards through her neck into the base of her skull.

Then Barnabas simply walked through the doors.

It had been like scenes from an old movie where martial arts masters went through the fortress of their enemies ever since. Barnabas had figured out enough to tell everyone that it was a lost cause and to just kill whoever they found.

So they had.

She had downed at least eight herself. The Tontos had taken out a few she had wounded but not killed in her attempt to keep up with Barnabas.

Hirotoshi had smiled the whole time like he was having a religious experience.

"Who the fuck *is* that guy?" Tabitha asked as they walked into a room with two more dead Ixtalis. One had been shot with a Jean Dukes—the exploded head was the clue. The other had had a piece of a wooden chair forcefully shoved through his rib cage and was coughing his last as her group walked in.

Ryu delivered the kill, then nodded at Hirotoshi. "I'm taking credit for that one."

Hirotoshi shook his head and kept walking. A moment later, Barnabas came back to them. "One moment. I needed a bigger door-knocker."

"Locked?" Tabitha asked.

An explosion rocked the room beyond them and a gust whipped through the door Barnabas had just emerged from.

"Not anymore," he replied, walking back through the door.

Tabitha pointed her sword at Ryu. "Who took my boss and left this maniac? Was it you?" Ryu smiled but shook his head. She pointed to Hirotoshi. "You?"

Hirotoshi shook his head. He told Tabitha as he proceeded through the door, "I think you need to spend some time learning about the monk's past. If you had paid more attention to his energies, you would have realized the veil has been torn."

Tabitha followed the two of them into the next room. "What the fuck does a veil have to do with that guy?" she asked, her voice getting lost as another explosion went off in front of her.

Bethany Anne nodded, and Gabrielle called to John to step inside and take the front. Eric followed, then Bethany Anne and Gabrielle. Darryl, Scott, and Kiel were tail-end Charlies.

John kicked open the door to the seventh floor and walked into a shitstorm.

Glory of Ghosts Compound, Third-floor Basement

Guhdiss and those near him tried to remain as calm as the masters at the front of the room seemed to be, and everyone watched the double doors.

Behind the ornate decorations on this side were plain concrete covers to match the basement walls.

The explosions stopped, the screaming stopped, and after a few minutes, Guhdiss' heartbeats slowed down.

Then a slow, methodic pounding started, echoing through the temple.

BOOM, BOOM, BOOM.

The reverberations had barely died down when they started again.

BOOM, BOOM, BOOM.

Guhdiss glanced at the masters. The Master of Secrecy had aimed both his pistols at the doors.

Guhdiss started trying to push his way to the wall. He wasn't sure what kind of ammunition was in those pistols, but if it threw shrapnel of any sort, anyone near the door would be hit.

BOOM, BOOM, BOOM!

This time Guhdiss could see the double doors shake with each hit. He placed his hands over his ears to deaden the sound.

That was when the doors exploded. At least twenty of the Glory's believers were killed when the wood and rock blasted into the temple.

The Master of Secrecy fired his pistols, but half a second later, his body was blown back against the wall behind them. His chest exploded and painted the wall with blood before his body slammed into it and slid down it.

The Master of Truth was next, head shattering in gore and body flopping backward. The master himself remained silent, his arms still inside his robes.

A red-eyed human walked in with a pistol in each hand and looked at the carnage before focusing on the master. "I believe," he announced, "the existing political structure is happy with the future of the Ixtali people. They do not need you to think and decide for them."

"How would you know, human?" the master ground out. "Your kind stole the glory of our past and herded us like bistok into this future, ripping away our power for your own use!"

"No," the human answered, walking in farther as others of his kind backed him up. "It was your people who would either be friends with the Empire or destroyed by us. Your forbearers chose to join the Empire and have flourished, protected, ever since. Now you wish to re-engage old practices, where you can snuff out a life on a whim." He shook his head. "I doubt you even have a chip in your skull, old one."

"I am righteous!" the master screamed back. "I am *TRUTH INCARNATE!*"

"I doubt that," Barnabas answered. "ADAM?"

"Yes?" a voice answered from speakers on the human's armor. "Have you broken the code for the suicide chips?"

"What was there to break?" ADAM answered. "They never bothered to change it."

Barnabas glared at the master, whose mandibles were grinding together. "Then on my authority, execute."

Nine of Guhdiss' brothers and sisters in the front row dropped, their eyes glazing over as they fell dead to the floor.

Barnabas spat in the direction of the master. "And yet," he hissed, "you stand."

Those still alive and capable of thought turned to look at the master in shock.

Guhdiss was the first to speak the truth.

"He has no *chip!*" he yelled.

Headquarters, Seventh Level, the Strom

Six people jumped to the side as flechettes streamed through the open door. John crossed the threshold as Eric dodged to the right behind him.

Gabrielle went next, following Eric to the left, then Bethany Anne entered, tailed by Darryl, Scott, and Kiel.

There were five Ixtali bodies in front of them in different death poses. Blood splattered the walls as the seven passed through the halls.

"Clear!" John called. Eric passed him as the seven went through the corridors. Bethany Anne and Gabrielle could tell if there were bodies in the rooms, but the Bitches wanted the Mark One Eyeball to view every room they passed.

You never knew what might lie in wait for your team, and the team knew that not all troublemakers were organic.

"Not clear!" Darryl called just before his armored body was blown across the hallway to crash through the opposing wall into the room Scott was checking. "Inorganic!" he choked out.

Bethany Anne had already passed the door, so it was Gabrielle's turn to twist her pistol to eleven and run into the room with Kiel behind her. She went left as he went right.

In the middle of the room was a four-armed robotic sentry that had to have just been activated, since it hadn't even been disconnected from the recharger. Gabrielle tried to shoot out the connections where the arms intersected the body while Kiel worked on the body.

Kiel ignored the head after he destroyed the two video cameras that had been facing him and started spraying rounds up and down the body as he moved forward. Gabrielle had found protection, so Kiel put out his leg and kicked off a half-wall, trying to not get into her line of fire as she shredded the killing appendages.

"Isn't this fun?" Kiel spat and pushed off another wall. "TAKE COVER!" he yelled as he crashed into Gabrielle.

She wondered what Kiel was doing, and then the security bot exploded behind him and shrapnel lanced his back.

He clutched her armored body and hunched over her protectively, then twisted to hit the wall with his shoulder. The two of them erupted through it, flames licking them both.

"*WOOOOO!*" he whooped as they rolled over before slamming into the wall opposite.

"Status?" Bethany Anne asked.

Kiel coughed out, "One security bot KIA."

"One Yollin that better get off me!" Gabrielle pushed Kiel off her, throwing his armored body high enough for him to land on his feet, prepared to defend them.

"That was fun!" Kiel exclaimed.

In front of him, Bethany Anne's eyes flared red.

ADAM, shut down this site, she commanded.

The building went dark.

"That is not possible!" the older Ixtali hissed. There were four others in the secure meeting room watching the video feed. He turned to the female on his left. "Feeglie, when will our people get up here?" he demanded.

Then the power went out, and a lone blue light came on.

Feeglie's voice was a grating hiss as she answered, "When they can rush up four flights of stairs."

"We will be fine in here," he answered. "Just stay put."

She turned on him. "We can't *go* anywhere, you idiot!" If she had known exactly where he was, she would have punched him. "The doors are electrically locked, and the motors that open them also need power!"

"No," a third voice interjected, "we can move them manually."

"Not with the Empress and her people outside!" Feeglie shook her head. She had tried to bypass the long road and had signed on for a new future and a new government.

What she had signed on for was her death.

Bethany Anne *pushed* fear as she searched for life on the floor, stepping down the hallway as her team came up behind her.

She turned left at the next juncture, her HUD allowing her to see easily. The fire control system had kicked in to shut down the fire the security bot had started.

She took another twenty steps and turned left toward a wall, ignoring the massive doors to her right. She holstered her pistol and stabbed her Etheric sword into the wall, willing the power to flow through her and into the stone.

Which started to sizzle, then crack, and finally to melt.

Feeglie sniffed, then turned to her right to see a point of red light pierce the wall and continue another six inches beyond.

"She's here." She sighed. "This game is over."

Feeglie never felt the plasmium bolt that entered the back of her head, causing her face to explode and coat the wall in front of her.

"There is always hope while you still breathe," Karel spat as Feeglie's body dropped to the floor. "She was a doubter." Karel stepped behind the table, holstered his pistol, and tried to lift the edge. "Someone help me turn this over!"

Three others rushed over and heaved, and the heavy table crashed onto its side as the four took positions behind it. "Whoever comes through, fire!" he demanded.

Four hands aimed their pistols, waiting for the wall to crack open.

Bethany Anne waved Gabrielle over. "Class is in session."

"What, now?" Gabrielle asked, shocked.

"I want you to feel the Etheric—the draw and the flow. Continue energizing this sword."

Inside her helmet, Gabrielle's mouth dropped open. "Bethany Anne, we are on an op. Not the best time to be practicing."

"Consider it a pop quiz, with a really bad fail result," Bethany Anne told her. "Now, grab this with me.

Gabrielle stepped up next to Bethany Anne, who had moved her hand up the hilt to allow Gabrielle a place to grab. "You feel the energy?" Bethany Anne asked.

"Yes," Gabrielle answered. "Shit!" Her hand tingled.

"Open yourself to the draw. Feel the energy's movement, and duplicate it. You got this," Bethany Anne encouraged her.

Gabrielle narrowed her eyes in concentration as she reached into the flow. She thought about the truth of the Etheric as she understood it—a dimension that had a form of reality which the nanocytes within her engaged to create energy or other properties that operated on her body to make changes. She willed the nanocytes to move energy without using it.

"Ohhhh, *fuuuuuck!*" she whispered when Bethany Anne released the hilt. The surge of power threatened to overwhelm Gabrielle.

She was pleased to see that the sword didn't falter, but she believed her hair would start glowing.

"Grenades?" Bethany Anne held out a hand to John.

"Seriously?" John looked down at her. "You're going to co-opt my weapons now?"

"Fine!" She smiled and pushed him, and he disappeared. She took a step and followed.

CHAPTER FOUR

Warn a guy next time! John sent when Bethany Anne appeared in the Etheric. He was about ten feet away.

Don't be so stingy and I'll think about it, she replied as she walked over to him, then leaned forward to look into the room for a split second.

She grabbed John's arm and pulled him five feet to the left. *We don't want you to appear seven stories in the air.*

That would be a surprise drop, John agreed. *So what's the plan?*

Bethany Anne sniffed. *Well, I wanted a few grenades and you didn't want to share, so I'll just send you.*

Send what? John asked as he felt her foot plant itself on his ass. She pushed.

Kiel looked at his HUD and informed the group, "I think we have a few undesirables coming up the west stairs."

Scott started walking toward one of the green signs at the end of a hallway. "Someone want to help?"

Darryl trotted to catch up to him. "Got any grenades?" He chuckled as the two approached the stairwell.

"Grenades are not friends," Scott commented.

"You didn't answer my question," Darryl replied.

"Of course I have a couple," Scott answered, and his armor opened along his thigh to allow him to grab two small silver balls before it closed again. "They aren't the *other* guy's friends, but I happen to know that John doesn't share, so I always carry a couple just in case."

Darryl chuckled as he grabbed the door handle. "Three, two, one!" He pulled it open. Scott peeked in quickly, then stepped in and shrugged. He waited until the footsteps got closer, then tossed the two round spheres against the far wall. They banked off it and started bouncing down the next flight of stairs.

Scott stepped out of the stairwell and started jogging back to the group. Darryl had just caught up when the first *whump* occurred, and after a second louder *WHUMP* the door behind them flew off its hinges and bounced down the hallway to land just five feet behind them.

The scene inside the room was tense. The four Ixtali were waiting for the red sword to finish opening the wall when all hell broke loose.

An armored human appeared in the air and crashed into their barricade. He came to rest on top of the two at the end.

Crushing bones in the process.

Before the two who were still standing could turn their guns in his direction, their heads exploded.

"Dammit, Bethany Anne!" John groused as he tried to get off the two Ixtalis, who were yelling in pain. He holstered his pistol.

"You broke my bones!" one yelled at John.

"Probably," John answered as he stood. The guy was trying to get up, so John stepped on his lower leg. The snap of bone was audible in the quiet of the room. "Nope, definitely," John raised his voice above a fresh bout of screaming. "I'd say 'My bad,' but your other option is dying."

The other Ixtali was unconscious.

Private Residence Outside Ixtali's Capital

Two black Pods screamed through the air, using the clouds to stay out of sight to the best of their ability.

While authorized, the travelers preferred to remain anonymous.

After maneuvering behind a large homestead, the first Pod descended the last few feet, then snuggled under one of the tree-type plants.

The Pod opened, and Bethany Anne and Ashur jumped out. The second Pod landed next to her and John stepped out.

When she strode up to the back of the house, the door opened, and Addix stood there with a smile on her face. "Good evening," she greeted, stepping back to let her guests in.

"May I enter?" Ashur asked, his voice coming from a small collar around his neck.

"Certainly," Addix answered, her mandibles signaling her pleasure. "I am not affected by your fur."

Ashur followed Bethany Anne through the door while John wiped his boots on the mat, nodded, and entered last.

The door snicked shut behind them.

Bethany Anne was wearing a flowing red top and deep-purple slacks, and John had on the latest version of their suit armor.

Casual yet protective.

Bethany Anne turned to Addix and bowed her head slightly. "I wanted to come by and thank you personally, and ask if you had any requests for me."

Addix laughed. Her hoarse breathing sounded labored, but it was a byproduct of her speech. "Requests of *you*, Empress? Hardly." She waved to the furniture, and Bethany Anne walked over and leaned against something that seemed sort of comfortable. Bethany Anne wasn't sure how an Ixtali would use the furniture and frankly had no desire to find out.

"If I were a few years younger, perhaps," she replied. "Well, actually, I have a question."

Bethany Anne waited, raising her eyebrows to signify she was listening.

"How did you do this?" Addix asked, making an intricate wave in front of her face.

"What?" Bethany Anne asked. "I'm not sure what you are asking."

"Make me younger. Make me live to the ripe old age that I have?"

Bethany Anne chewed the inside of her cheek before answering, "We have the technology to make this happen. To help rejuvenate bodies."

"Is this why your people are so plentiful?" Addix asked. "You never die?"

"Oh, no," John answered, the two ladies turning to him. "We just go at it like bunny rabbits, trying to figure out how to increase the... Increase..." He looked at them. "I'm going to shut up now."

Addix's hoarse laughter caused Bethany Anne to smile. "You," Addix pointed to John, "can't keep your mouth shut, can you?"

"Oh?" Bethany Anne's eyes narrowed as she looked at John before glancing back to Addix. "When was the last time this occurred?"

"When I met with your General," Addix replied. "I will tell you the story the *next* time we meet."

Bethany Anne suppressed her desire to look at Addix in

confusion. Instead, she asked her internal secretary, *ADAM, do I have a scheduled time to meet Addix again?*

>> You do not.<<

Well then... Ohhhh, she's a crafty one! Bethany Anne thought about her options for the fleetest of moments.

Bethany Anne let the statement drop and instead asked, "Addix, what are you going to do now?"

"I have no idea," the Ixtali answered. She moved to one of the pieces of furniture and reached behind her, lifting the back of her robe and then moving up the side. Bethany Anne could only imagine that her spider-like legs were climbing up the furniture under the robes. "I feel young in mind, but even your vaunted technology can't stop age forever." She settled her head on one of her hands. "If I had the time, I would pay you back five times over for what you have done for my people, so you asking me if I want a favor is simply ludicrous to me."

Bethany Anne glanced at John, but it didn't seem like he was going to interject anything this time.

She pursed her lips. "Would you consider leaving Ixtali?"

"For?" Addix asked, leaning forward a bit.

"I'm thinking that I have a planet that could use your particular skills—the Ixtali ability to handle secrets and uncover the unknown. The position requires someone I trust to operate independently and wield quite a bit of authority."

"Empress, I'm honored," Addix replied, "but at best, I've got a couple of years left. Maybe five, if I push it."

"That is for me to worry about," Bethany Anne answered. "If you are willing to take the job, I doubt you will be back. And if you do come back, it wouldn't be in a way that anyone would know who you are."

"I would be changed?" Addix asked.

"You would be a ghost. No one would believe it was you."

"What the hell," Addix answered. "I've done all I can on this world, and I've buried all the family who knows who I am. If I quit visiting the others, I become just a rumor for family gatherings." She paused a moment in thought before returning her gaze to Bethany Anne. "What shall I do for you, Empress?"

Bethany Anne shrugged. "You will help by learning to ferret out those who would do evil, to hide the biggest secret in existence, and to make sure those who need help find you." She put up a finger. "Oh, and you will have to drop your last name."

"For?" Addix asked once more.

Bethany Anne smiled. "How do you say 'Nacht' in Ixtali?"

QBBS *Meredith Reynolds*

Lance had barely sat down at his desk when the voice of his daughter interrupted his thoughts.

"How the hell are we going to hide our people?"

Lance calmly looked up. Bethany Anne was staring down at him. "Don't you knock anymore?" he asked, pointedly glancing toward his door.

She looked at it too. "I didn't come in the door. What do you want me to do, walk to the door and knock on it from this side?"

"Or wear a bell," Lance agreed.

"*Hell*, no." Bethany Anne leaned in and kissed her dad on the top of his head. "How are you, old man?"

"Wondering what the hell you got me into," he huffed, then locked his hands and put them behind his head, leaning back. "I heard you got back from Ixtali last night. I didn't think I'd see you so quickly. I assume your question refers to all of the personnel from the military drawdown?"

She nodded. "Yes."

He shrugged. "Well, some will wish to leave the military. That will take care of forty percent right there." Lance looked up at the ceiling. "We are going to give you another twenty to thirty

37

percent." He glanced at Bethany Anne, who had sat down in the chair in front of his desk. "Right?"

She nodded again. "Yes, take or give a few percent. We can operate on as few as ten percent, but if we got into a battle that could seriously hamstring us."

He leaned forward, placing his hands on the desk. "I think plenty of people in the military want to find out what you are going to do next. Plus, going to Earth? Many will want to go on that trip anyway. It's being billed as a once-in-a-lifetime opportunity."

Her eyes unfocused, but she agreed. "It's being billed like that because that's what it will be."

Lance broke her out of her thoughts. "The hard part is, we are going to have to hurt some people."

"What? Why?" she answered. "Who are we going to have to hurt?"

"A few people who can't know the future. Can't know our plans, because those damned Noel-nis will be tracking them—I guarantee it. Some of our top people will be pissed when they are let go." He left the rest unsaid for a moment.

"Because," she picked up the thread, "if we tell them early, they won't act naturally or be pissed off enough." She slumped back in her seat. "Dad, I don't know about that."

"What if I told you we had to battle thirty thousand Leath, and we expected to lose five thousand at a minimum?" he asked.

She eyed him. "You did," she told him flatly. "That was the battle at Leer's Gate 404 over in Section...uh..."

>>**Forty-two.**<<

"Forty-two," she finished.

He shook his head and pointed a finger at her. "You had help."

She held up two fingers close together. "Only a smidge. I couldn't remember if it was forty-two or fifty-two, but ADAM clarified."

He put his hands flat on the desk. "With this plan, there are going to be less than a thousand at risk, but it will save millions and allow us to hide what is really going on. The challenge will be telling them later. We will lose some, but I don't know how to make the black ops work without doing it this way." He shook his head. "Perhaps other, wiser heads need to give me ideas." He thought about ADAM helping Bethany Anne a moment before. "Wow, needing ADAM to help you along with your memory!" He tsked. "Getting old."

Her eyes narrowed. "I'm not getting old, I'm in vacation mode."

He tapped his desk. "You haven't abdicated yet, or stepped down, or whatever the hell they are calling it." Lance shook his head. "How can you be in vacation mode?"

"I have less and less responsibility on my shoulders," she clarified, "so it feels like a vacation."

"You know about vacations, right?" Lance asked. He continued when she raised an eyebrow. "You do twice the work leading up to it, four times the work coming out of it, and you are blamed for anything that goes wrong while you are gone. If everything goes right, the person who covered for you accepts all the credit."

"That would be you," Bethany Anne pointed out.

"Oh, I expect to blame you for decades." Lance smiled.

"Wonderful," she snarked as she stood up. "I'll see myself out."

Lance eyed her. "You saw yourself in. I don't know why this would be any different."

"Wait until you don't know I'm around." She grinned as she reached the door. "Then, *wham!*" She winked. "I'll scare the shit out of you when I appear!"

"You better not, or I'll give my job back to you," Lance groused.

"Oh, hell, no!" She shook her head vigorously. "I'll be good," she declared as she stepped through the door. "I *promise!*"

The door clicked closed behind her.

"I doubt it," Lance replied to an empty office.

Outside in the hallway, Bethany Anne considered her next meeting. *ADAM?*

>> **Yes?**<<

Please ask Stephen to meet me in my suite. I have something for him to do.

CHAPTER FIVE

QBBS Asteroid *R2D2*, R&D

The design of the working space for the team could be traced back decades. Whether they were here on *R2D2*, back on the *Meredith Reynolds*, or on the base in Colorado, they shared common DNA. A table for the team surrounded by whiteboards or their digital equivalents, and a fridge nearby, allowing for Bobcat to call the meetings to order.

Bobcat stepped away from the table, heading for the little bar they had built.

"Where are you going?" Tina asked.

"This calls for a beer," Bobcat answered over his shoulder.

"This is an important discussion!" she snapped.

"Then three beers!" his voice floated back, body hidden behind some of the whiteboards.

"William?" Bobcat called.

"Two!"

"Two?" Bobcat's voice shot right back, confusion evident.

Tina stared at him. William smiled as he added, "I've got to watch my figure!"

"Oh, true dat!" Bobcat replied. "Marcus?"

"One," Marcus answered.

Tina looked at the two men sitting with her at the table. "Is there no question so important you guys won't drink during the discussion?"

"A minor amount of alcohol is not going to affect the clarity of my thought," Marcus answered.

"Yes," Tina agreed. "You are only drinking one."

Marcus nodded to William. "Remember, alcohol absorption and body weight."

William nodded, patting his belly. "That's why I'm cutting a third of my intake."

Bobcat walked past the whiteboards holding a homemade six-bottle container and pulled out one for himself before setting it on the table. He took a seat, and Tina looked at him. "And Mr. Three here?"

Marcus reached over to grab his beer. "We have scientifically proven Bobcat isn't affected until…" he started to answer, then turned the beer around to read the label. "Wow, lower alcohol content." He turned to his wife. "Approximately twelve of these."

"Twelve?" She stared, astonished once again at the man across from her. "I've been around you for long enough that I'm not even sure why I have this issue anymore."

Bobcat shrugged. "Probably from stuff you saw back on the *Meredith Reynolds*," he answered. "Stupid teenage boys doing stupid things due to alcohol. Few rise to our level."

"And what level is that?" Tina asked.

"Godhood," he replied and took a sip.

Tina leaned forward, and snatched a bottle out of the six-pack, opened it, and took a sip.

"Hey!" Bobcat complained. "That was *my* beer!"

"You never asked *me* if I wanted one," Tina told him. "I presumed you could mind-read."

His eyes narrowed as she smiled at him. Bobcat pushed

himself back from the table. "Okay, before we get started, I've got to make another beer run."

"One!" Marcus called.

"I'm good," William offered.

Tina looked at her bottle. "One!" she called, then turned to Marcus. "How do they get the berry flavor in this?" she asked before taking another sip. "This is phenomenal!"

"It's Mountain Tiger brand, and to answer your question, we don't have a clue," Marcus admitted. "Keldara bastards took top honors last year at the annual Yollin Beer Festival."

William shook his head. "Bunch of mercenaries," he grumbled. When Tina looked at him, he continued, "No, really. They are a bunch of mercenaries called the 'Keldara' who have a base in the mountains. They grow this one fruit—"

"Berry," Marcus corrected.

"Whatever." William continued, "They grow this berry that is astringent as hell if you try to use it."

"You tried to use it?" Tina asked.

"Of course," Bobcat replied, slipping another four bottles into the container before he sat down. "We've tried to use every human-ingestible ingredient on Yoll. Even my wife can't figure out what they are doing. It chapped her hide to be beaten last year by Mother Lenka."

"Are they human?"

"Some," Bobcat answered. "Mostly human, lots of Yollins, and a couple of Shrillexians, of course."

"Where there are fights," William reasoned, "you find Shrillexians."

"Like bees and honey," Marcus stated.

Tina ignored them. "So, that's the tiger part?"

Bobcat took a sip and shrugged. "I think so. There aren't any tigers on Yoll, so maybe they hope to import a few genetically enhanced ones, or hell, someday bring some from Earth."

"Will Bethany Anne allow that?" she asked.

"Possibly," Marcus confirmed. "They are in the final stages of construction of a huge ark to facilitate bringing back vast amounts of diverse terrestrial genetic material. Some will never be introduced anywhere, just frozen for the future in case they need to reseed Earth."

Tina's eyes widened. "That's…ambitious."

"That is the story of our life," Bobcat agreed. "And the latest chapter is titled, *How Not to Blow Up Family and Piss Off the Friendlies.*"

William added, "Subtitled, *With Seven Hundred and Seventy Megajoules of Focused Laser Beams.*"

Tina nodded. "That would leave a mark."

Marcus shook his head. "No mark. Complete atomic destruction into so many constituent parts you couldn't find enough pieces to put them together and say 'Look, here's a mark!'"

"It would completely ruin your day," Bobcat agreed.

"Plus," William added, "it is way more than enough that even something like the *ArchAngel II* would be dead in an extra couple blinks of an eye."

"Bethany Anne would be a bit peeved to be killed by her own BYPS system."

"So how do we make sure that doesn't happen?" Marcus nodded. "That is the question."

"And not an easy one to answer." Bobcat sighed. "I've spoken with ADAM, and AIs are dead out. If this goes on for too long, an AI could go crazy, or in any case, there is a large enough chance to make it too risky."

Tina thought about that. "What is too large a chance?"

"Somewhere less than one-tenth of one percent," Bobcat admitted. "That could mean it happens once in a thousand years, but if it did?" He put his hands together, one still holding his beer, and exploded them out. "*BOOOOM!*"

"Plus, we need to deal with the ones near Earth." William leaned forward and put his elbows on the table. "I'm sure the closer to a body they are, the bigger the chance for issues to occur. When one of them drops from the net, it needs to engage some sort of heavy manual override so it doesn't blow the hell up."

"Security password?" Marcus suggested. "I'm just starting this ball rolling. It won't work because the enemy just needs to learn it and *poof!* All of the BYPSs turn and aim toward Earth and fry the hell out of it."

"Earth kabobs," William supplied.

"More like a marshmallow for s'mores." Tina looked at the ceiling. "No, that isn't the right metaphor either."

"Genetic?" William kicked in.

"What happens if the genetic material either dies or is stolen?"

"We need a guard post," Tina stated. She was staring into the distance when the weight of the three pairs of eyes caused her to look around. "What?"

Bobcat rolled his bottle. "Keep going."

"Guard post?" she asked, and he nodded. "Well, I was thinking that we need someone or something which can answer the door, or maybe forward the call."

"That…" Marcus thought out loud, "might work."

"We can't just have an AI or some people sitting around with their thumbs up their butts for a hundred years."

"No, not there," Marcus answered. "We need to figure out how to make a long-distance call through the Etheric."

"I thought we couldn't travel that far?" William asked.

"We can't, exactly. However, I was reading about some research Anne is doing that might apply," Marcus told them. "She was playing with inter-Etheric communication and alter-waves, but she had a hiccup and then went off on another adventure. By the time she was finished, she was focused on another research project. I picked up what she had in her notes."

The four of them were quiet for a minute before William asked, "Are we going to become the next AT&T?"

"Who?" Tina asked.

"Old American company that helped wire and then wirelessly enable telephone calls back on Earth," William supplied. "I mean, that's what we are talking about doing, right?"

"Fuuuuuuuck." Bobcat downed his beer, then grabbed another and swallowed half the bottle. When he finished, he used his beer bottle to point to the remaining beer. "You'd better drink up."

"Why?" Tina asked as she reached toward them. She grabbed one for herself and another for Marcus. "What did you realize?"

"I realized," Bobcat answered, "that we have a shot with this idea."

"That's good," William supplied as he sipped his only beer. "Right?"

"What do you think our timeline will be?" Bobcat asked.

"How much time do we think we need?" Marcus shot back.

"Fat chance," Tina answered. "I see what Bobcat is saying. Someone better grab more beers."

"Why?" Marcus asked as Bobcat nodded to Tina and stood up, heading for the fridge one more time.

"We only have three more Mountain Tigers," he called back to the table.

"*Mine!*" Tina yelled. "Well, at least one!" She turned to Marcus. "Because we have exactly as long as it takes Bethany Anne to figure out how to get our asses to Earth and Michael.

"That could take a decade," Marcus argued.

William snorted and nodded to Marcus. "You, sir, are thinking like a scientist."

"Of course," Marcus answered. "I *am* a scientist!"

Tina shook her head. "I give us maybe a year, but more probably six months." She downed her bottle as she reached out to take the beer Bobcat offered her before he sat down. "We better order more Mountain Tiger," she added.

Bobcat nodded, then looked at the clock and patted William on the back. "Don't you have a date tonight?"

William's color drained as he looked up at the old-fashioned clock, then grabbed his tablet and checked his calendar. He relaxed a moment later, wiping sweat off his brow. "You ass!" he told Bobcat. "My date is next week!"

QBBS *Meredith Reynolds*, Empress' Suite

Stephen walked into Bethany Anne's front meeting room and snagged a Coke from the fridge. He sat down on the couch to drink it as he waited for her to come in.

The door opened behind him just five seconds later. "Sorry I'm late," she told him as Ashur padded in behind her.

"I've seen more of you than usual," Stephen commented to Ashur. "What's up?"

Ashur dropped to the floor, and Stephen would have sworn he sighed. "Babies," Ashur told him, his voice coming from his collar.

"You expecting?" Stephen asked. "Or rather, is Bellatrix?"

"No, thank the makers of the universe. She wants more, and I'm dodging left and right," Ashur replied. "She knows that Bethany Anne running off like she did bothered me, so I can get away with staying glued to her side—at least for now."

"It's my penance," Bethany Anne agreed, sitting down on the couch across from Stephen. She leaned down to pet Ashur's head. "Seems dogs *do* know how to create a guilt trip."

"Desperate times call for desperate measures, my Empress," Ashur replied. "A little to the left... Yeahhhhh, right there." He cocked his head to the right, allowing Bethany Anne to continue to scratch him. "Why would anyone want to give this up for another set of trouble with four paws?"

"I have no comment," Stephen replied to Ashur and looked at Bethany Anne. "You called?"

"Yes." She leaned back, taking her hand off Ashur's head.

Ashur looked at Stephen. *"You bastard!"* he bitched before he laid his head on the floor.

"I have plans for my planet," she told him.

"Yes?"

"I brought Addix back from Ixtali. I want to leave a group on Devon to make sure it is properly developed and ready to be a rest stop for my teams as we traipse around the galaxy. I need someone to manage it for me."

"Addix?" Stephen replied. "I assume you mean someone other than Lerr'ek, our Zhyn friend?"

"Yes." She nodded as she got up and walked to her fridge and pulled out a Coke with her left hand. Using her fingernail, she popped the top off and caught it with her right hand, casually tossing it into the small can on the countertop before returning to the couch.

"Lerr'ek is doing fine, but long term, I think he will want more action. Plus, he is too squishy."

Stephen looked at her funny. "Zhyn aren't usually described as 'squishy.' Scaly, hard, blue, but never squishy."

Bethany Anne thought about it for a moment. "I'm trying to express that he is killable. Unlike you and some of the others, he can't come back, given enough energy, time, and opportunity."

"You don't trust him enough to upgrade him?" Stephen asked.

"He has some honor, but his fear of Baba Yaga drives him at the moment. He's in for his ten, and then his option is to leave and go do something else somewhere else."

"He will have to be mind-wiped if that happens."

"Yeah." Bethany Anne sighed. "I hate that, but Devon needs to disappear into the history books.

Stephen took a drink. "Addix can make that happen."

"Oh?" She raised an eyebrow. "How?"

"Think about it. She has access, I suspect, to all the Ixtali methods for data acquisition. She would be perfect to manage an operation that provides incorrect data and disburses it."

"What about Nathan?"

"He can add to it, but the responsibility would be on Addix. She will be in the middle of the storm, so to speak, and able to deal with accidents more readily."

Bethany Anne nodded, twirling her fingers for him to keep going.

"You want this all handed to you on a silver platter?"

"Yes," she replied. "I'm lazy. Get moving."

"Okay." Stephen put his Coke down. "I'm thinking that we… what?" He stopped, looking at the face she was giving him.

"When I said, 'Get moving,' I didn't mean explain more." She smiled, pointing her bottle like a baton to indicate that Stephen should stand up and leave her suite. "I meant, go check on Addix, make plans, and get moving to Devon to implement them."

"Oh, Jumping Jehoshaphat!" Stephen got up and walked to the fridge and grabbed two more bottles. "Jennifer?" he asked on his way out of the suite.

"Take her with you!" Bethany Anne proposed. "I suggest locating quarters and checking on all the projects!"

"Wonderful!" Stephen replied as he opened the door.

"Don't forget my garages!" she called as he shut the door.

Stephen walked down the hallway on his way to Medical. *Garages?* He thought about that a moment before rolling his eyes. Who called military bases where you parked superdreadnoughts "garages?"

A moment later, he smiled. *I wonder what Reynolds is up to?*

49

CHAPTER SIX

<u>**QBBS *Meredith Reynolds*, General Lance Reynolds' Office**</u>

There was a knock at Lance's door. He looked up as he chewed on his unlit cigar, then glanced at his calendar. It was clear. He looked down at his tablet again to read the rest of the reports on the status of the Gate movement, ignoring the person outside his door.

The knock came again, but before Lance could growl "Go away," the door opened and Felix Castile walked in.

"Got a minute, General?" he asked, a smile on his face.

"No," Lance replied. "And why are you in here, Felix?"

"My security code…" Felix started.

"Has been severed," Lance bit out. "Did you hear that, Meredith?"

"Yes, of course," the EI answered. "Do you need a removal team?"

Felix looked at the speaker, and his eyes narrowed in annoyance. "I'm not someone you *remove*."

"Not yet," Lance replied, still annoyed by the man. "I didn't invite you into my office, yet here you are."

Felix calmly closed the door as he spoke. "That's because I've been trying to get on your calendar for three days, General Reynolds."

"You and everyone else, Felix," Lance replied. "What's your point?"

Felix was forcing his smile at this point. "I would imagine not everyone was as helpful."

"As what?" Lance replied. "I believe you have an inflated opinion of your value to the military. Throwing three parties for the Guardians and the Guardian Marines was casual help. Perhaps placing your ships as support carriers is a next step, and physically carrying supplies onto a planet where you can smell the dust from the houses destroyed one block over is yet another level."

Felix reached down to straighten his cuffs. "Yes, well," he looked up, "be that as it may, I helped. Now I would like a little quid pro quo."

Lance's eyes narrowed, but Felix ignored the warning.

"I would like to be on the Empress' ships when she goes back to Earth. I'm not asking to be on the *ArchAngel*, although I could argue that it would be appropriate. However, I get that there are many people whose backs you have to scratch, so I won't push it."

Lance's blood began to boil as Felix continued.

"I would like the chance to bring back genetic material for commercial purposes. I would be happy to provide the Federation with a three-percent fee for every product we bring to market from research into the genetics. Now…"

Lance subvocalized, "Meredith?"

"Yes, sir?" Meredith replied in his ear.

"Figure out which is the worst removal team I have and send them here post haste."

"Yes, General," she replied.

Thirty-two seconds—and a continuous blather from Felix, who hadn't noticed—later, Lance was looking at the clock on the wall behind the man. Two Guardians rapped their knuckles on the door and stepped in, stopping Felix in mid-sentence.

"Finally! You shut up." Lance took his cigar out of his mouth, the end nearly bitten in two. "The answer is *hell, no*, you cannot go to Earth. You are obviously an idiot when it comes to military decorum, and your use of your security clearance was a breach of personal etiquette. You are a self-serving shit-hole side of swine whose mere presence makes me wish to take a damned shower. Now get the hell out of my office—which you didn't have permission to enter in the first place—and get the hell out of my sight. If you try this bullshit with Bethany Anne, expect to die in a horrible way."

Felix stared at Lance with his mouth open.

"Further," Lance stabbed his cigar in Felix's direction, "there are no backscratching ticks going to Earth. Every person has been vetted as having a need to be there if they are coming back to the Federation, or they won't *be* coming back here. Your ass doesn't count for either option. So unless you wish to get tossed out an airlock and told to walk back to the *Meredith Reynolds*, which I suspect would happen in about thirty seconds if you ever got in front of Bethany Anne, you should kiss the ground I walk on that I'm not letting you commit suicide by brown-nosing the wrong woman. Consider the absolutely minuscule goodwill you created by throwing those parties paid back in spades."

He waved his cigar at the guards. "Now get out of my face, my office, and my life."

Lance rolled his eyes as he listened to Felix's bitching, muffled by his closed door as it was, for a full thirty seconds before it faded away.

"Sometimes," Lance grouched as he resumed reading his reports, "I wish *I* could throw people into the Etheric."

QBBS *Meredith Reynolds*, Private Meeting Room, Secured Level

Bethany Anne's chin rested on the palm of her hand as she listened to those around her discuss moving the Gate and how to make it happen faster.

"Guys?" she ground out. Dan and Marcus, who had been arguing a moment before, turned to look at her. "Don't make me grab two bricks to get the ideas coming a little quicker." She smirked. "No pun intended."

Dan smirked. Marcus missed it.

She leaned toward them and nodded to those around the table. "Okay, Dan, Bobcat, William, Marcus, Tina, Dad, Admiral Thomas, Kael-ven, and those listening, I appreciate your present efforts," she paused for a moment, "but they all *suck*."

She stabbed the table with her finger. "I want to be back on Earth yesterday. Seeing as how I am here and not on Earth, I'll settle for tomorrow. When tomorrow comes and I'm not on Earth, a drop of annoyance is going to develop in my bloodstream."

She tried to smile, but it didn't help.

"I am not telling you this to threaten. I'm informing every one of you because I love you, and you know this about me as much as *I* know this about me. I'll become a royal bitch if we continue this for too long." She pointed behind her. "Michael is about a bazillion miles—"

"Actually he is—oof!" Marcus grabbed the side of his stomach closest to Tina.

Tina smiled at Bethany Anne. "Please continue."

Bethany Anne smirked. "Yes, thank you. Marcus, I don't need to know the actual miles." She looked down the table. "Now, I respect and love you all, but you are giving me *shit*," she made a square with both hands, "that is *inside the box!*"

"*I* know it's inside the box and *you* know it is inside the box, so let's dispense with the inside-the-box shit! At the current rate, I will be here for ten fucking years. A byproduct will be making your lives and my own a horrible, no good, existence. This will occur as I work to make the journey take place faster. I believe we can achieve a better state of affairs."

She pointed to those around the table. "We left our planet, kicked Kurtherian ass, and brought justice and laws and all sorts of cool shit to lots of aliens we never thought we would meet a hundred and fifty-plus years ago. All I'm asking is to grab a relatively large, priceless, unique, and somewhat delicate Gate and move it, then reprogram it to allow us to fly through it to Earth so I can get me some Michael. I will be a happier woman...after I beat him senseless."

Admiral Thomas spoke up. "Has anyone suggested not beating Michael up first?"

"And lived to tell about it?" Bethany Anne asked.

"Well, of course."

"No," she replied, "but I will take that suggestion as guidance for the future, and since I hold you in such high-esteem for your previous service, I won't tell you it isn't going to happen. But," she winked at Admiral Thomas and then whispered loudly, "it isn't!"

He waved a hand in her direction. "Okay, just wanted to make sure all options were on the table."

"He almost got himself killed, which wasn't one of his choices when saving the base," Bethany Anne replied, "so let's get me back to him quicker. That way I will have less need to take out my frustration at missing him on *him*. That will leave more time for the romantic parts all the holodramas will talk about."

"We could always destroy it," Dan supplied.

Bethany Anne looked sideways at Dan and was about to reply when she noticed he wasn't joking. In fact, his eyes had a distant look. "What are you thinking?"

"We need to hide it." Dan's focus turned to her. "Best way to hide it is to destroy it."

"Nice," Bethany Anne replied dryly. "I want the damned Gate!" She waved to the rest of the table. "Were you not listening to the BA rant just a moment ago? I can have Meredith replay it for you while I choke you for suggesting we destroy my way of getting back to Michael." She smiled. "I assure you, you will remember the second time you listen."

Dan chuckled. "Hey, you had my attention at 'two bricks.' Think about it, Bethany Anne. We need to hide the Gate."

"Riiiighht," she agreed.

"Why do we need to hide it?" Tina asked, then put up a hand. "Never mind—we don't want others finding Earth. I just need more caffeine."

"It *has* been a long meeting," Bethany Anne agreed, "but we will be here until we have a next step, and the trip taking five to ten years is *NOT* a viable next step." She waved to Dan. "Go on."

Dan looked down the table at Lance and Admiral Thomas. "If we hide it well, is that the best security?"

"It's the best *first* layer, sure," Lance agreed. "You don't look for something that isn't obviously there."

"So we blow it up," Dan continued, "in front of God and everyone, especially the news agencies. We make a big spectacle of the awesome might of the Etheric Empire."

"Fucking brilliant!" Bethany Anne whispered. "Except the part where we have to suck ass to make it work."

Dan turned back to her. "Think of it as the ultimate flea-flicker play in the history of the Etheric Empire. No one will believe we did it on purpose because we have never failed to accomplish anything we wanted in our history."

"Damn," Lance agreed, "that is brilliant."

Bethany Anne moved her finger in a circle. "So, how do we do it?"

Dan leaned back and pointed to Team BMW and the others. "That's why we have smart people in the room. I just come up with brilliant ideas. Execution for blowing up irreplaceable Gates goes on the shoulders of others."

The chuckles around the room released some of the tension

as everyone, including Dan, leaned forward to figure out how to move an Annex Gate and blow it up in front of everyone, yet have it safe and sound lightyears away.

Six hours later, the team broke up. There were tired smiles as they parted ways, hoping that sleep would help smooth out the rough patches.

No one wanted to be around Bethany Anne if this took another ten or fifteen years.

Bethany Anne had suggested they just freeze her and wake her back up if that were to happen.

QBBS *Meredith Reynolds*, General Reynolds' Office

Lance rubbed his eyes. "I cannot believe I am going to do this," he muttered. It had been a week since the meeting about the Gate, and a chance talk to Bethany Anne two days ago had reminded them both of an opportunity on Earth.

The problem? He needed a specialist.

A *Gott Verdammt* space-archaeologist specialist, so he needed to talk to Giles Kurns about joining the trip to Earth.

The man had been pestering him for too damned long to go there and dig around on the planet, but there had been no distinct need, and not having him on the trip had been a better choice than having him on the trip without a reason.

Lance considered taking a stiff drink before doing this, but what was done was done.

Giles was needed, and the aftermath of telling the man that his pipedreams would come true? Well, he hoped he didn't regret this down the line.

A couple of minutes later, there was a knock on his office door.

"Come in, Giles," Lance called in a normal voice. Giles already had several small upgrades, and hearing was one of them.

The dapper man cracked the door and nodded to Lance with

a small smile on his face. Maybe it was because he never seemed to take anything seriously that he rubbed Lance the wrong way. He was kryptonite to any good military operation.

"Uncle Lance," Giles replied, pushing up his glasses and taking a seat. "You wanted to speak to me?"

"Yes," Lance agreed, leaning back. "I was talking to the Empress a couple days ago, and she reminded me of an opportunity that needs—"

"A space archaeologist?" He leaned forward in excitement, pushing his glasses up again.

Lance's mouth quirked as if he were holding back the next utterance with all his willpower, but the word succeeded in gaining its freedom.

"Yes," Lance admitted.

"WHOOOOOP!" Giles jumped up, fist pumping the air. His old-fashioned jacket fluttered behind him.

Giles' face was animated. "What will I be searching for?"

Lance resigned himself to the inevitable. "Kurtherian tech."

"*WHOOOOP!*" He jumped into the air a second time. "*HOLY CRAP!*" He drum-rolled on Lance's desk.

Lance looked down. "Please stop that," he told him and Giles' hands stopped. He gazed down at them. They were poised to continue drumming, but he slowly pulled them away and sat back down.

"Sorry." He blushed. "Just excited!"

"I gathered," Lance replied. "Two things, young man." Lance put up a hand. "First, you are going to be working with professionals who will see this kind of thing," he pointed a finger to where Giles had been drumming, "as the mark of an immature youth."

Giles pushed himself back in his chair and composed his face.

"And second," Lance continued, "you will be working on a project that probably still has Wechselbalg protecting what we want to find. Therefore, you," Lance pointed at Giles, "are going to have to double up on your martial practice and weapons lessons."

"I understand, Uncle Lance," Giles agreed.

"Now, a new third," Lance put up three fingers. "I'm 'Lance' or 'General Reynolds,' depending on the operation. See if you can cut the 'Uncle' part out when we are in meetings. It will tarnish your ability to say with a straight face that you are a space archaeologist." Lance leaned forward and whispered, *"Favoritism."*

Giles had leaned forward too and started nodding his head. "They will think you made up a job for me."

"Yup, you got it in one," Lance agreed. Despite all the trouble Giles had created, he was a very smart person. It was generally his intelligence—coupled with a complete lack of planning—that got him into trouble. His quick wits, a significant number of fast moves, and a galaxy-sized bag of luck got him back out.

All the people in the universe who had bad luck should demand Giles give the luck back.

"What do I need to do to prepare?" Giles asked, then quickly added, "other than the martial classes and weapons practice. I understand those."

"Good." Lance pulled up his tablet and sent a message. "You need to get with ADAM about the Sacred Clan—"

"WHOOOP!" Giles' fist pumped the air again.

Lance looked up. *At least he didn't jump up this time,* Lance thought. *Small advances... Be happy for small advances.*

Giles noticed the look and coughed, pulling his arm back down. He set his arms back on the chair.

"Oh," Lance looked Giles in the eye, "and a fourth item, or your mother will crucify me."

"Don't get killed," Giles replied.

"Exactly," Lance confirmed. "You have your marching orders. Your part in this is hidden until I say so. Limited to you, your parents, obviously the Empress, and ADAM. No one else has need-to-know right now."

Giles nodded, then stood up and walked toward the door.

"Um," Lance leaned back in his chair, "Giles?"

Giles turned around, his hand on the doorknob.

"Ask ADAM about Michael. You need to know how to operate around the ArchAngel. He might kill you for being insolent, and 'Insolent' is your middle name."

Giles nodded acknowledgment to Lance and listened to the two quick sentences ADAM spoke into his ear. The blood drained out of his face.

He failed to say goodbye as he walked out of the office.

"ADAM?" Lance spoke aloud.

"Sir?"

"What did you tell Giles just now?"

"Nothing but the truth," ADAM replied. "Michael has been known to kill people who failed to say, 'Good morning' properly."

Lance chuckled. "That wasn't the Michael we left on Earth."

"And yet," ADAM replied, "it was true about Michael."

Lance sighed. "Well, let's hope this Michael isn't still *that* Michael or we may lose Giles the first time he meets him."

"I calculated the chance that Giles will be killed by Michael if you would like to know the percentage."

Lance thought about that. "No, I'd rather not. Better to plead ignorance. And remind me to speak to Bethany Anne about Giles and Michael."

"I can have that conversation with her," ADAM offered.

"Okay, please do," Lance replied and looked at his calendar. *Damn*, he had a meeting about the Gate later. He'd better eat first.

CHAPTER SEVEN

QBBS _Meredith Reynolds_, Arriving Research Pod 441

"Is she here, Meredith?" William asked, checking his collar for the fourth time.

"I'm only answering because you two have a date, and yes, she is. She is waiting in All Guns Blazing."

"Oh, no!" William shook his head. "Who's hitting on her?"

"You can calm down, William," Meredith replied as the Pod slowly descended to the floor. "The Empress is aware you're late and—"

"Oh, shit!" William grabbed his tablet. "Did I miss something for her?"

"No," Meredith answered. The Pod's door started to open, and William blinked at the two men just beyond it. "She left a welcoming team to make sure you were expedited to All Guns Blazing."

"Darryl? John?" William asked. The two Empress' Guards smiled at him.

"What the hell are you waiting for, man?" Darryl grabbed William's hand and pulled, nearly yanking William out of his seat. John started walking, and Darryl pushed William in front of him. "Bethany Anne said to get you to All Guns Blazing posthaste. Double-time it, soldier!"

William tried to keep up with John Grimes as they strode through the busy docks, took the secured entrance into the Arrivals area, and walked through the security detector.

The alarms started flashing almost immediately but stopped a microsecond later.

"Ooops," Meredith's voice came through the speakers. Everyone turned to see William being led through the special area with John in front of him and Darryl behind him.

John and Darryl were armed, which explained the alarm.

But why hadn't Meredith had it shut off before they got there? William wondered.

Bethany Anne took a couple of popcorn kernels and munched on them as she watched the three men go through the security.

"Oh. *OH!*" Gabrielle squeaked in humor. "Everyone is seeing him treated as he should be!"

Bethany Anne beamed as Gabrielle dipped her hand into the popcorn bucket. "This is good," she murmured. "Real-life romance, unscripted."

Bethany Anne shrugged. "Well, I wouldn't say it was *totally* unscripted." She nodded toward the screen. "That part with the alarm was planned."

"Oh, you are devious," Gabrielle murmured.

"That was me," TOM admitted over the screen's speakers. "Unfortunately, William is going to have to forgive me for what comes next."

Gabrielle leaned forward. "This is going to be good." She reached out, and Bethany Anne put the bucket under her hand.

"Hold this," Bethany Anne told her and walked to her suite's door, then opened it and waited two seconds.

Scott's voice called, "Tina's here!"

"Let her in, you dummy!" Bethany Anne answered. "She's missing the good stuff!"

Tina jumped over Ashur, who was lying outside the door, passed Bethany Anne, who was still in the doorway, and rushed into the suite.

"*Holy crap!*" Tina exclaimed. "I want to be an empress."

Bethany Anne just shook her head. Most women who were invited into her suite loved it.

It was a perk of Empressing, that was for sure.

"So, furball, are you coming in?" Bethany Anne looked down at Ashur.

"No," Ashur answered, putting his head back down. "It's romance. I could get infected by accident."

"Hurry, BA!" Gabrielle called. "They are almost through security."

She could hear Gabrielle handing Tina the popcorn.

Bethany Anne shook her head and closed the door, then headed back to the couch to protect what was left of her popcorn.

Or at least secure another couple of handfuls.

John got a message to slow down. He wanted to shake his head, but it might have given William a hint that something was up.

After stopping to plug in a security code—which Meredith could have done for him—he pulled open the door. Darryl stepped ahead, taking the lead position as John switched to the rear.

The big man motioned for William to go ahead of him, then pulled the door shut behind him.

This, he thought, *should prove interesting.*

"Here they come!" Tina squealed as she clapped, watching her teammate exit security. "I can't believe you did this for him!"

Bethany Anne looked at the young scientist. "Thanks for bringing it up." She nodded to the screen. "William needs to know he is special, and this is a good way to tell him that." Bethany Anne popped a kernel into her mouth. "That it will impress his date is just a nice happenstance."

"And that we get to watch?" Gabrielle asked.

"An even nicer happenstance," Bethany Anne agreed.

William followed Darryl through the middle of an exhibition in the main courtyard near All Guns Blazing, and when he saw a few of the large dioramas on display, he almost stopped.

They were all about projects he had been involved in. The first he passed was a history of Pod research from back on Earth, and then the antigravity efforts with TOM and the shipping containers. There was a picture of him, Bobcat, and Marcus in front of Shelly back at the Colorado base, and another of the three of them celebrating the Moon Base.

He slowed down, not realizing that Darryl had stopped to allow him to walk through the dioramas and relive the highlights of his past.

William knew some things were too secret to be put on display, but it was amazing just how much was here for others to learn about what Team BMW had accomplished.

The largest part of the exhibit was about the artificial sun, and how it had been created to bring energy, light, and life to the *Meredith Reynolds*.

And he was in every picture.

"I hate to rush you," John whispered behind him, "but you shouldn't let your date wait."

"Oh shit!" The crowd around him started clapping when they figured out who he was. He blushed, waved, smiled, and hurried to catch up to Darryl.

Tina wiped her eyes. "Did you see him?" she asked, her voice catching. "He doesn't realize just how much he has been involved in through the decades, and all the amazing things he's helped create."

"He doesn't." Bethany Anne took a moment to get a dust particle out of her own eye. "That man is the definition of 'team.'"

Darryl asked over the team's comm, "John, how is he doing back there?"

"I think he is pretty amazed, actually," John replied. "Those people clapping for him pushed him out of his comfort zone."

Darryl chuckled. "Well, then he is about to have an existential crisis."

Gabrielle asked, "Who came up with that one if TOM came up with the first one?"

ADAM's voice came from the speakers, "That one was mine. William doesn't think much about the true length and breadth of what their team has accomplished. I thought the realization of just how much their team—and he as a part of it—have accomplished would help his sense of self-worth."

"Anyone can have self-worth issues," Bethany Anne added.

"Even those who give everything, crawling to help just a little bit more as they bleed out on the battlefield. William has had issues in his past with relationships, so we did this to help him out."

"What is your surprise?" Tina asked, looking at Bethany Anne.

Darryl nodded to the bouncer, who waved back the line so the three men could enter.

William heard the people in line talking about Darryl and John as they passed. "That's him, right? He's taller in real life."

He smiled, remembering those who had just clapped for him a moment ago.

It had felt good to be recognized.

Entering All Guns Blazing was good too. He hadn't been here in a while. He wondered who would be in this evening and if any of the regulars were around.

That was when he saw the group of fans ahead of them. He smiled, knowing that Darryl and John had to deal with this whenever they went out in their armor to do something official for the Empress.

Except Darryl stopped and stepped out of the way, turning to William and waving him forward.

The crowd rushed him, their eyes sparkling with delight at meeting one of the famed members of Team BMW, the group that had brought them the sun as well as the technologies they used every day.

William took the pen John stuck in his hand and started signing, asking questions of everyone. "Who would you like this signed for?" he asked. He smiled and moved to the next one as the guys slowly navigated him through the crowd.

"Is that real?" Tina asked, amazed. She turned to Bethany Anne. "I mean, you didn't hire them?"

Bethany Anne shook her head. "That would have been fake, and it would have bitten me in the ass." She pointed to the scene inside the club. "A couple of the university's history classes have a section on the Etheric Empire's technological wonders, and it just so happens that there was just a week-long unit on Team BMW and their contributions from Earth to here. Apparently they talked about how the group is very secretive and don't come out too often."

"That's because they are usually on *R2D2* focusing on their current projects," Gabrielle shot back. "They were in All Guns Blazing all the time before that."

"Not William," Tina replied. "He was there *some*, but he liked to make his barbeque pits and stuff."

Bethany Anne shrugged. "I only pointed out they weren't out in public, which was true. The fact that they have been off *Meredith Reynolds* for a while now in a secret laboratory only helps their image." She pointed to the screen, where William was smiling, signing, and slowly being guided through the crowd.

"That was the only reason?" Gabrielle asked Bethany Anne.

Tina's eyes narrowed, and she looked at Bethany Anne as well.

"Perhaps," Bethany Anne temporized. "I wanted to make sure this person William is interested in realizes he isn't just a shy, fun-loving guy who can't talk about his job. He is actually," she nodded at the screen, "a *Gott Verdammt* superstar!" She wiped another tear. "It was the least I could do for him."

Kathy opened her tablet and checked her face once more, using its selfie camera, then turned it off. Her date was supposed to be here in two minutes, but she wasn't sure she would care if he was a couple of minutes late.

She had already been treated like a princess.

She was wearing a dark-red dress with a white half-jacket and dark-red shoes and carrying a red clutch, and she looked amazing. Now she felt like she was the VIP of the evening.

When she mentioned her name at the door, Bronson the bouncer had told her to "Wait one minute, ma'am," and then whistled to catch the attention of Derek who, in a tailcoat, walked over to them. "Please take Ms. Williams to VIP."

His eyebrows had lifted. "Which booth?"

"Empress' booth," Bronson had answered.

"Are you sure?" Derek asked. He turned to Kathy. "My apologies. I didn't know you knew her."

Kathy's eyes narrowed. "Knew who?"

Bronson nodded and slipped a card to Derek, who confirmed it had the Empress' script on the outside. "Right." He turned back to Kathy. "This way, ma'am."

The club and restaurant were in separate areas, restaurant on the left and bar area to the right. They were heading toward the elite section in the back, above the main floor.

"The Empress, ma'am," Derek answered.

"I don't," she replied.

As they made their way toward the back, others started watching her and Derek. One person at the bar tapped a friend and pointed to her when the two of them reached the roped-off area.

"Well, someone does," Derek informed her as he plugged in the code to drop the security field around the VIP section. "Sorry," he continued. "Too many people try to get into her section when we aren't looking, so the Empress just had someone install a security field for us."

Kathy stopped, mortified. "This isn't just a name?"

Derek turned around. "Name of what?"

She pointed to the other three VIP areas. "You know, names of special VIP areas?"

Derek nodded to her left. "Well, in a way. You've got Team BMW, who are amazing in their own right, but they own this bar as well. Their VIP is that first one on the left. Then the Guardians' VIP here, next to the Empress'." He turned to point to the other side. "That is the Bitches' suite. Only the Empress and her select guests are ever allowed in her area. You can't get in here without her permission."

"Billy, who the hell are you?" she wondered aloud.

"Who?" Derek asked.

"Billy, the man I'm meeting tonight."

"First date?" Derek asked and gently took her elbow to help her cross the divide and slide into the huge booth. "We can take out the table, but for just you, it would look weird. I'm sure Billy will be here soon."

Kathy nodded absently as she slid into the seat. She had never been to All Guns Blazing. As a chemist, she was very aware of the molecular changes necessary to create alcohol, but the idea of tasting it had never appealed to her.

Now she wondered who her date really was.

On the virtual dating site, he had explained he was a research scientist who focused on transportation. He was a handsome black man whose eyes she had lost herself in on more than one occasion. His photos had been poorly shot, and she was concerned he had faked them.

He had assured her that they weren't fake; his buddy was crap with a tablet camera.

Kathy had arrived two hours early via the *ArchAngel II*'s special limo service and had spent thirty minutes getting into the *Meredith Reynolds*.

She'd spent most of the rest of her time looking through Team BMW's History Retrospective in the main courtyard.

"Wait," she asked Derek before he turned around. "Did you say Team BMW owns this place?"

"Yes, ma'am," Derek replied.

"Them, or their children?" Kathy asked absently. She knew from the information outside that the members of Team BMW were old.

Seriously old.

Faces-should-be-lined-with-wrinkles-if-they-weren't-already-sleeping-forever-somewhere-*old*.

"Them?" Derek answered. "You might see them from time to time, but they haven't been around for a while. They work with the Empress, and they left to deal with new projects."

"Wow." Kathy couldn't quite wrap her head around it. "They are still putting in time after all these years?" She shook her head. "That's amazing."

"They *are* pretty cool, yes!" Derek agreed. He lifted his tablet. "What can I get you to drink?"

"Water?" she asked. He nodded and stepped away.

As she looked around, she saw a group of excited youth congregating around the front. Many had small notebooks and pens in their hands.

"Are we going to go down there?" Gabrielle asked.

"Hmmm?" Bethany Anne looked at her friend. "What's that?"

"You know," Gabrielle pointed to the screen, "crash their date?"

"Don't you dare!" Tina protested, leaning forward and tweaking the back of Gabrielle's ear.

She gasped in shock when Gabrielle just *moved*. Before Tina knew it, Gabrielle had her hand in a vice-like grip, and her face expressed annoyance.

Gabrielle released Tina's hand. "Sorry!" She tried to smile it off. "I've had a lot of practice sessions with Ms. Warbucks, and you never know when she is going to tweak you."

Tina nodded and asked, "'Warbucks?'"

Bethany Anne popped a piece of popcorn into her mouth. "She's talking about me. I have been getting her fighting game back up to snuff, and now we're kicking it up a notch so she can take on Eric again."

"Eric?" Gabrielle grumped. "You made me take on Eric and Darryl yesterday."

"So?" Bethany Anne shrugged and leaned over to offer the container to Tina. "Popcorn?"

"Ooooh, look." Tina accepted the popcorn and pointed at the screen. "Here they come!"

CHAPTER EIGHT

QBBS _Meredith Reynolds_, All Guns Blazing

Kathy's eyes opened wide when she figured out who everyone was getting excited about.

It was Darryl! "Holy crap!" She pinched herself. "It's an Empress' Bitch!" There was a shorter man behind him she didn't know, but she recognized the last person. "Oh, my God, John Grimes!" she whispered. She turned her tablet on and hit the camera's video button. "They aren't going to believe this back in the lab!"

She zoomed in and caught John holding the crowd back from the person he was guarding. A hand got in the way of her video, so she switched to Darryl. She was filming him when he moved aside, and she saw who was signing autographs.

She almost dropped her tablet. It was William from Team BMW, but it couldn't be! He had to be so damned old he was... She zoomed in closer. It _was_ William!

That was when her jaw dropped and her world went upside down.

Everyone down there had turned to stare at her.

"Date at eleven o'clock!" Darryl called to John.

John glanced over. "Bethany Anne's table?"

Darryl replied, "Yup."

John whistled. "Damn, how the hell did William get that class act to show up for his pouchy ass?"

"I think he baffled her with bullshit." Darryl chuckled. "Either way, she's taking video, so look sharp!"

An armored hand directed William to turn left. "Sorry!" John's voice boomed. "We have to get him to his date."

The fans looked in the direction they were going and stared at the striking black lady in the Empress' booth.

"There it is!" Bethany Anne whooped. "She just figured out who he really is!"

"What?" Tina asked, popcorn falling out of her mouth. "Sorry! *What*? Didn't she know already?"

"No." Bethany Anne shook her head. "He was hiding who he was on the dating service."

"Wait a minute!" Gabrielle turned to look at Bethany Anne, who was busy watching the video. "How do you know this?"

"I know everything," Bethany Anne replied smugly. "Awww, that's so cute! She's trying to hide in that big-assed VIP suite, and she can't."

"Actually," ADAM supplied, "*I* told her."

Bethany Anne pointed up. "What he said," she admitted. "Look, look!" She pointed urgently. "He's about to say 'Hi.'"

"He'd better not fuck this up!" Tina griped. "If he trips, I swear I'll go over there and kick his clumsy ass!"

Darryl stepped aside but remained on guard, allowing her date to slide into the VIP area. "Kathy?" he asked, extending his hand.

She nodded and took it.

"I'm Billy."

"No." She shook her head. "You are William of *Team BMW!*" she accused him, then politely let go of his hand.

"Um, about that," he started to say, but she cut him off. "Do you really know the Empress?" she pointed to the table, "or can you get into this VIP area because you own this restaurant?"

Well, damn. This wasn't going how he'd wanted it to.

"Oh, damn!" Bethany Anne whispered. "C'mon, William, you got this."

"Actually," William sat down and put his arms on the table, "I can't. This is a special area that only Bethany Anne can use. I didn't know we were sitting here until John pointed you out."

"John?" she asked. "You mean John Grimes?" She looked up when she saw movement out of the corner of her eye. John had leaned forward and was waving at her and smiling.

"Yeah." William turned to nod in response to John's wave— not realizing he had meant it for Kathy—and turned back. "Why?"

"And Darryl?" she asked.

She wasn't surprised when Darryl turned around. "Good friend."

She leaned forward. "General Lance Reynolds?"

"What about him?" William asked. He wasn't sure where this was heading, but it was clear he was in a minefield.

This was the part that sucked about relationships. Women were too damned sneaky by half. He wasn't sure what he was in trouble for yet.

"You mentioned Bethany Anne. What would you call her to her face?"

"'BA?'" He shrugged. "'Empress,' if we are in an important meeting with others. Occasionally I've said worse, but she gives a mean ear tweak." He unconsciously rubbed his ear. "Usually I just call her 'Bethany Anne.'"

Kathy sat back in her chair. "I'm on a date with 'W!'"

"I'm not George Bush," William clarified.

"William," Darryl had turned around and got his attention, "she means the 'W' of Team BMW."

He shrugged as he looked at Kathy. "Yeah, so?"

Kathy leaned backward as Derek arrived with her water. "Do you have something a bit harder? I'm having a bit of trouble catching up."

Derek and William exchanged fist-bumps. "Things going okay with Terry?" William asked the waiter.

"She's good. Fourth year in the Etheric Academy. Thanks for putting in a good word."

"She's a smart cookie. I'm not sure how she missed the filters, but older or not, she's aced the classes."

"Thanks, William, we appreciate it. Wait!" He pointed at William but looked at Kathy. "This is Billy?"

William blushed.

"Yes!" Kathy's head bobbed up and down. "See?" She pointed to Darryl and John. "This man didn't tell me he was royalty!"

"I'm not royalty," William argued.

"Yes, you are!" Bethany Anne spat. "Don't make me come down there and prove it!"

"Yes, you are!" Kathy shot back. She pointed outside. "Did you see all that information about you and your team?"

"Yes," William admitted, scratching his chin.

"*You* helped build the *Meredith Reynolds*. *You* helped create the energy system that runs it. *You* helped get humanity off Earth!"

"It was a team effort," William argued. "I'm just a guy who was good at working on helicopters and had a friend who helped him get a job."

"Then your friend saw greatness!" She eyed him. "Was that Bobcat?"

William nodded.

"Was it he who made all this happen?" She gestured to the table.

"Oh, hell, no." William shook his head. "This was BA."

"*You ratfink!*" Bethany Anne stared agape at the screen. She pointed at the video but looked at Gabrielle and Tina. "He ratted me out!"

"The Empress did this for you?" She sounded dubious. "Why?"

John leaned toward them again and answered, "Because she likes to play Cupid, and William is a personal friend."

"Why do I feel like I've fallen through the looking glass?" Kathy asked.

"It's what happens around Bethany Anne," William answered. "I'm sorry, I can see my position and such is bothering you. I apologize."

"No, *no!*" Kathy put a hand on his arm. "I'm sorry, Billy, it's just taking me a minute to realize that the wonderful man I've been talking to is someone who has helped make the Etheric Empire what it is." She leaned toward him. "I'm turned on by smarts, and there's a whole display about your smarts right outside!"

"*OOOOHHHHH!*" Gabrielle snickered. "You pulled that one out of the dumpster, you lucky dog!"

"Not lucky." Bethany Anne sniffed. "Just good."

"*Not a dog, either,*" Ashur grumbled from where he lay. He was trying not to drool, hoping Tina would throw some popcorn his way.

"So," Kathy accepted the Coke and clinked it with William's glass, "my date is actually one of the most amazing bachelors in the Empire?"

William smiled but just looked down.

"*Yes!*" John called, not even bothering to turn his head. He and Darryl were keeping the audience at a distance.

William chuckled and looked at her. "I'm sorry. I know BA meant well, but I didn't even know she knew I was going on a date."

"No, I like it," Kathy replied. "You didn't tell me any of this before because you wanted to get to know me. Everything you have accomplished is obviously not that important to you." She nodded and took a drink. "You are humble."

"It's not any big deal. We're a team," William replied, taking a sip of his Dr. Pepper.

"Don't you like beer?" Kathy asked. She lifted her Coke. "I'm not against alcohol, I just never acquired a taste."

"Oh, I like beer fine," he admitted, "but I'm working on my figure."

Kathy leaned over. "Working how?"

William glanced down to take stock of his body and blinked a couple times.

"You still think you are hefty like you were in some of those pictures from back on Earth," she told him.

William turned to her. "Well, I guess I do."

"You aren't," she replied. "And I'm very happy you decided to reach out to me, Billy." She winked. "And if you will forgive me, I'll get over your secret identity and be happy. You're the most amazing researcher I could know."

"Damn!" Darryl called. "We have incoming!"

"Bobcat?" William turned around. "I didn't tell him I was going anywhere!"

"Not Bobcat," John replied. "Tina, Gabrielle, and Bethany Anne will come through the front door in sixty seconds."

Kathy looked at John, then the door, at William, then at the door again. "The Empress is coming here?"

William scooted closer to Kathy. "Unless you want her next to you, I'd better..."

Kathy grabbed her stuff and moved to the side, then grasped William's arm and pulled him closer. "You will protect me, right?"

William smiled.

He rather liked her holding his arm. "She doesn't hurt friends."

Darryl and John grunted their opinion.

Kathy leaned over to whisper in his ear, "Thank you for being you. I wouldn't have dated you if I had known who you were."

He looked at her. "Why not?"

"Me?" She looked down at herself. "I'm just a chemist in the Navy."

She was surprised when William stared at her, then she noticed that Darryl and John had turned toward her too. "What?"

"Someone," they told her in unison, "needs a new mirror!"

"No, really!" she told William. "I'm a chemist. Nothing to see here, move along!"

William wiggled his eyebrows and grinned. "Did I tell you that smart women turn me on?"

The bar erupted in applause when the Empress entered the establishment.

QBBS _Meredith Reynolds_, Private Meeting Room, Secured Level

Lance walked into the meeting room and patted his daughter on her shoulder. Tina had her head on the table, and he raised an eyebrow to Marcus as he pulled his chair out. "What happened to your newest team member?"

Marcus scratched Tina on the back, but she just groaned. "At William's party last night, she forgot she didn't have nano-enhancements to neutralize the alcohol. She tried to keep up with Bethany Anne and Gabrielle."

Lance looked at Bethany Anne, who shrugged. "It is an important lesson to learn. 'Know your limits.'"

Tina put a hand up, with five fingers outstretched. "Five," she got out before the hand sank back down.

"I think," William teased, "she means she went five shots over her limit."

"They were strong shots," Bethany Anne agreed, then remarked, "Let's get this show on the road." She looked down the table at Admiral Thomas. "What do we need to accomplish for you today?"

"Well, not so much me as you," Admiral Thomas agreed, "but we have to destroy some ships for the new Federation. This includes the AIs, by the way. Apparently they provide an unfair advantage."

"Which is the point of war," Lance pointed out.

"And," Admiral Thomas continued, "we have to give them confirmation that they can take back to their people to show progress on the Federation dictates."

"They want to gut us," Lance grumbled. "Some things we are getting, others freak them the hell out. Our superdreadnoughts with AIs freak them the hell out."

"Which pisses me off! There is no way I'll destroy those ships," Bethany Anne stated, "but every time I complain, the General asks if I want to come to the Federation meetings. So, how are we going to make this occur and yet stick it up their asses one more time?"

Dan kicked in, "I suggest we destroy them." He turned to Bethany Anne and grinned.

"Are you a one-trick pony?" she asked him. "Okay, I get that we aren't going to destroy them, but we have to do this in front of God and everyone to make it stick."

Tina's voice was muffled by her hair. "Do it at the same time as the Gate."

Dan snapped his fingers. "Perfect!"

"Of course it's perfect for *you*," Bethany Anne grumped. "You propose blowing shit up as the one and only practical solution to every problem we have."

"All kidding aside—" Dan started.

Bethany Anne leaned over to Frank. "Was I kidding?" she asked.

He shrugged in response.

Dan looked at her, and she waved for him to continue. "Oh,

do go on. We are going to blow the shit out of them in front of God and everyone, and yet we—" She stopped talking and her eyes unfocused. "Oh, I get it."

Dan snapped his fingers again and pointed at Bethany Anne. "Bingo!"

She started nodding. "Okay, that is going to take some seriously amazing efforts. Let's take some noodling time on this, and come back together in forty-eight hours with details." She stood up. "Nice job, Tina, working through your pain like that."

Bethany Anne nodded to everyone at the table and walked out.

Lance looked down the table at Dan. "What just happened?"

Dan pursed his lips. "If I'm guessing correctly, Tina probably said something to see if we could get this meeting done quickly—since she is ready to die—and it actually works in our favor as a method to move the Gate. However, we have a few sticky details to develop in the next meeting. Bethany Anne wants those who have the brains to use them to consider the sticky problems. The challenge is, one of those brains is not worth much presently."

Everyone looked at the pile of hair that was Tina's head, which was still lying on the table. She put up a fist. "Go, team!"

A few chuckled, and those at the table stood up. Admiral Thomas looked at Bobcat. "You guys got ideas? I really don't want to lose any of my ships."

"Possibly," Bobcat cautioned. "I think I see what Bethany Anne was alluding to, so we will work out the details."

"Keep me updated," Lance told them as he walked around the table to leave.

"Me too." Admiral Thomas nodded, and the two men exited the room together.

Tina slowly lifted her head and looked around at the half-empty room. Dan smiled at her. "Did it work?"

Dan nodded. "It did indeed."

"Good," she slowly laid her head back down on the table, "I'll just take a nap." She started to snore, her hair blowing out each time she exhaled.

QBBS Asteroid *R2D2*, R&D

William smiled and waved to the video camera before leaning forward and shutting off the connection.

Bobcat walked into the room. "Kathy?"

"Yes."

"She okay with everything?" Bobcat asked.

"Amazingly, yes." William blew out a breath. "I need a beer."

"You, sir, are a poet," Bobcat agreed and continued right past their work table to the fridge. "We got more Mountain Tiger."

"I'll take two," William called.

"Seriously?" Bobcat called back, then started rapping. "Okay, I'm bringing back a six-pack. I'm gonna drink it all down, but not like a hack. But a professional, who looks at the crowd and raises a fist, to—"

Tina called as she and Marcus arrived, "Please don't quit your day job!"

"Fine!" Bobcat told her as William turned to accept his beer. Bobcat held the six-pack behind him. "But you can't have any of my Mountain Tiger."

Tina twirled her fingers. "Rap that bit, you'll be a hit, don't take no shit from people like me." She waved her hand at him. "Now, gimme!"

Bobcat rocked his hand from side to side. "I'll give you one because I'm impressed you changed your mind so fast. I'll ignore the past, and liberate the libation for your mind so we can all unwind!"

Bobcat looked at Marcus and raised an eyebrow.

"What?" Marcus put out a hand. "Give me one. I don't rap." He accepted the beer from Bobcat and sat down. "I prefer metal."

"Spoken like a true fan." Bobcat sat down. "Okay, BYPS manufacturing 'Oh Gawd, we fucked up again,' Take Two."

"Is someone recording these conversations for posterity?" Tina asked. All three men looked at her. "What?" She pointed to William. "That stuff Bethany Anne did for William was genius. You guys really do wonderful shit."

"Spoken like another true poet," Bobcat agreed. "And yes, everything you do here is recorded."

Tina swallowed, a blush inching up her cheeks. "Uhhh, everything?"

There was a glint of humor in Bobcat's eyes. "Don't worry," he told her, "it's all vetted before it can be viewed. So, if you and Dr. 'N for Nasty' here did something on the table—"

"I don't want to know about it." William interrupted and lifted his tablet. "Cooties!" he exclaimed, checking under it before setting it back down.

Bobcat continued, "Only R2 and above would know about it before the general group."

"Who's above R2?" Tina asked. "Meredith?"

"Sure," Bobcat agreed. "And ADAM…and that means Bethany Anne as well."

"Well, shit," Tina sighed. "I hope Gabrielle doesn't see it."

"Have you gotten a scorecard from her?" Bobcat asked, taking a sip of his beer.

"No," she answered.

"Then she hasn't seen anything," Bobcat confirmed.

"So you have?" Tina asked.

"Let's not delve too deeply into why I have this information, so I can protect the guilty," he responded. "Back to OG-WFU Part Two, subtitled, 'How do we transport a bajillion BYPS satellites and not blow everyone the fuck up?'"

"That, sir," Marcus answered, "is an excellent question."

"Should be." Bobcat lifted his tablet. "Says right here you were the one who asked it." He looked over the top of it at Marcus. "Do you have an answer?"

"No," Marcus replied, "which was why I asked the question. We have an inordinate amount of firepower stacked in transport vessels the size of football stadiums."

"Just arena football," William corrected. "Let's not be metaphorical here."

"Big truckers." Marcus nodded. "And if we set off a chain reaction, it will be a supernova, and if that happens on the Earth side of the equation... Well, we won't live long enough for Bethany Anne to be pissed that we not only fried the Earth to a crisp but killed her love, too."

"She *would* be rather upset," Tina agreed.

"If there were so much as a couple of cells alive," William thought aloud, "she would regrow us just so she could kill us again."

"What?" Tina asked in alarm.

"Not really," Marcus told her.

"Yes, really," Bobcat declared, "but it would probably be Death by Yelling."

"What if we built in a sensor that confirms they are a set distance from the next BYPS or they can't come online?" William contributed.

Marcus smiled, snapped his fingers, and pointed to William. "You are the man!"

Tina put up a hand. "Except, how does that work if they are on a ship that goes through a Gate?"

Marcus turned to Tina. "You are not helping."

She reached over tenderly and patted his cheek. "Seriously, Marcus, you should be able to answer this." She stood up, grabbed her beer, and walked over to one of the whiteboards, where she picked up a marker and drew a large oval in the middle, then she drew a long three-dimensional block that bifurcated the oval. "The oval is our Annex Gate, and the long box is our ship. Half the crates are in one system, the rest are in the other system."

"We need to code in a shutdown for an amount of time—" she started to say.

"Can't leave a back door, or we will leave the Earth with a security system that's hackable," Marcus cut in. "Even a one-time event might leave vestigial code that allows someone enough access to gain entry."

"Not if we…" Bobcat was searching the ceiling. "What was the name of the Indian tribe that talked during World War II?"

"Indian talkers?" Tina responded. "Sorry, that was *way* before my time."

"I don't remember the names," Marcus agreed, "but I think I know what you're talking about."

"It was the American Indian Code Talkers," William responded. "It actually started in World War I with the Choctaw Telephone Squad and other native communications experts and was expanded in World War II. The Army went to Oklahoma in 1940 to recruit, and the Marines went to Arizona and New Mexico to get Navajos on board in 1942."

"And this helps us how?" Tina asked. "How were they used?"

"The group used a verbal language," William answered. "It wasn't written down, so there was no way for the Japanese to crack it. They had two hundred and eleven different words that had no equivalent, later expanded to four hundred and eleven plus twenty-six words that represented the letters. So, their version of the word 'ant' became the word for the letter 'a.'"

"So we need to insert the code," Bobcat answered, "in a fashion that no one can find in data files."

"Yet," Marcus added. "It has to be something one of the originals would get if we gave a few hints."

"That's going to suck major schweddy balls." William sighed. "Okay, I vote R2 helps with this.

"Or," Bobcat rubbed his cheek, "we base it off something like lyrics."

"To songs?" Tina asked. "Like who?"

"Quick!" Bobcat pointed to Tina. "Tell me the favorite band of the Queen's Bitches in Florida!"

"AC/DC," she replied. "Oh…that's brilliant!"

"I take back what I said earlier," William enthused. "This is going to be insanely fun."

CHAPTER NINE

Bethany Anne appeared in her receiving room, along with Lance, John, Eric, and Admiral Thomas. When she left the transportation area, she stepped into her kitchen to grab a Coke. "Anyone want anything?"

"I'll grab something," Admiral Thomas answered. Bethany Anne walked out of the little kitchen and handed him a Coke.

"Apparently I wanted a Coke," he muttered, looking down at the bottle and then after the rapidly retreating figure of the Empress, who was heading toward the dock where _Shinigami_ was located.

"Don't stress it," John told him. "She only _has_ Coke in there."

The four men walked down the hallway toward the dock. "Feels like a clandestine meeting," Eric commented.

"That's because it is," Lance grumped. "Had to figure out the safest place to host a meeting, and the answer to that was, 'in a location no one can get into and on a ship no one can find.'"

When the four men turned the corner, Bethany Anne was heading up the back ramp into the ship to meet the others she had brought to the dock earlier.

"Sure hope this works," Admiral Thomas murmured as he walked up the *Shinigami's* ramp himself.

The members of the team responsible for the movement of the Gate and the destruction of the superdreadnoughts sat on couches on the bridge of the *Shinigami*. Four of them were drinking Cokes, but Bobcat's team were drinking beer they brought with them.

"Mountain Tiger," he told Dan. "Locals brew it down on the planet. Good stuff. Keldara bastards kicked our asses in the last planet-wide beer festival. We are drinking it to help figure out how to beat them."

"Uh-huh," Dan agreed. "I've tasted the brew, which is amazing. I doubt this is all research."

"Research can be a lot of fun," Tina replied.

"Okay," Bethany Anne interrupted, "let's get down to business. We have a Gate to move, a Gate to hide, and some superdreadnoughts that need to be destroyed and yet miraculously not."

She looked around the bridge. "Who wishes to go first?"

"I'll do this." Dan stood up. "As Bethany Anne mentioned, we need to move the Leath's Annex Gate into our territory as part of our war reparations. Now, that's not the big issue, since the Federation doesn't have a large problem with it." He looked around, "However, it's a big-assed pointer to Earth, and we would rather hide Earth if possible."

Dan walked to the front of the bridge and faced everyone. "Our plan is to announce that we are going to use the superdreadnoughts to do it, except for the *ArchAngel II*—which everyone knows Bethany Anne is going to keep."

"On pain of my size sevens up their asses if they don't let me," she grumped.

"Was that a problem?" Tina asked.

"Yes," Lance admitted. "They wanted all the superdreadnoughts destroyed, but I told them there was no way the Empress would go for that. I got her on the video, and she threw such a hissy-fit they caved in on keeping the one. The knowledge that she was using it to leave the system and protect herself gave them a feel-good way to acknowledge they didn't want her coming over to the convocation for a personal discussion."

"Still pissed off by that Noel-ni negotiator." Bethany Anne's eyes flashed red.

"If it is any consolation," Lance replied, "I think he wet himself."

"Not much," Bethany Anne admitted, "but I'll take what I can get."

"We are also going to keep one more," Lance went on, "and we will hide the rest."

"What about the QBS *Ranger Prime?*" Dan asked. "I didn't know where that one would go."

"With Barnabas," Bethany Anne answered. "It's too well known, and while it doesn't have all the bells and whistles and missiles of *ArchAngel II* or *Reynolds*, they are playing 'gut the Empire' to the best of their abilities."

"What happens when we pull this off?" Tina asked. "Other than we have more ships for you?"

"Oh, I'm building a garage," Bethany Anne answered, "far enough away it can't be easily found, yet close enough if necessary."

"That's going to be some garage," William told her.

"You better believe it," Bethany Anne agreed. "So, plans again?"

Dan took his cue. "We are going to promote this as the biggest translocation effort in the history of histories and use the superdreadnoughts to move the Translocation Gate. Unfortunately—"

"You are going to blow it up," Bethany Anne answered. "I got that part. So, how will it *not* be blown up?"

"We translocate the Gate to a hidden location in space, then translocate in a large fake Gate and blow it up."

Bobcat interrupted, "Not going to work that easily. The energy fluxes aren't going to be right, nor the material composition."

"That's why you are here." Dan smiled. "I just came up with the cool explosion idea."

"Sit down, Dr. Destructo." Bethany Anne smiled at Dan. "Bobcat, your team is up."

"Okay." Bobcat pointed to Tina, Marcus, and William. "Dan has all the basics. We push something the size of the Gate into the Yollin system at the same moment or slightly after with bogus ships, and we cause a nanotomic explosion."

"What the hell is a nanotomic explosion?" Lance asked. "That's like saying a 'small large boom.'"

Marcus answered, "We made up a word instead of saying an 'Etherically-charged spheroidal explosion cum material implosion.'"

Lance blinked. "'Nanotomic,' right."

ADAM asked, "Is this going to act like a black hole?"

"A tiny one, yes," Bobcat told him. "We are worried that those who are paying attention will determine how much material is floating around and calculate that it's too little. We don't *have* that much extra ships' material available to destroy, so we want to create an implosion that will eat the material we show. That way, we can suggest not all the material was brought into the system. Unfortunately, I suspect we will have to hold a few fake funerals."

"That was always a given," Lance explained. "You can't have explosions without deaths."

"And a wicked acting effort by Bethany Anne," Bobcat added. "Sorry, boss, but you need to show some tears."

"Well, damn." She sighed. "Yes, I can see that. We are *all* going to have to sell this." She nodded to Marcus. "Just work with

ADAM, TOM, and the others to make sure we don't create a real *Gott Verdammt* black hole in the system."

"We are going to stage the event in the no-fly zone," Admiral Thomas told her. "We don't allow people to go there now, so that shouldn't be news to anyone."

"Sounds good to me." She took a sip of her Coke. "Get everyone you can to help promote this. Either way, we are going to do something amazing. Make sure the AIs are all on board with the plan as well. I don't want anything but volunteers for this."

"They are," Admiral Thomas told her. "I've spoken with all of them. They don't know the particulars yet, but they will, via ADAM."

Tina spoke up. "We actually do need the superdreadnoughts' help. In order to move the Gate, they will have to feed some of their power into the translocation effort. It's going to be the biggest translocation the galaxy will never know was successful."

"We hope." Bethany Anne took a deep breath. "No, we *know*. Okay, T-minus…"

"Three months, tops," Bobcat told her.

She just stared at him, her mouth open in surprise.

Dan added, "Then the real work will begin."

QBBS Asteroid *R2D2*, R&D, Two Days Later

Bobcat scribbled a few more notes on one of the whiteboards. "We have another situation to work through with the BYPS system."

"Assuming they don't blow up Earth," Tina pointed out.

"You, young lady," Marcus patted her hand, "are becoming too much like us."

Tina turned to him. "I'd say you were rubbing off on me, but I was already like this."

"I blame Marcus anyway." William shrugged his shoulders when Tina turned toward him. "It's more fun."

"Yes," Bobcat agreed, then got the meeting back on track. "Assuming we don't just wipe out the ecological diversity of our home planet, along with our Empress and everyone else who goes on the trip, we have another problem."

"Those fucktards on Earth better appreciate the challenges of putting up a tri-layered BYPS system-defense security array," Tina grumped. "My head is starting to hurt."

Bobcat pointed his marker at Tina. "I'm sure they won't have a clue—or care—so don't lose any sleep over it. Let's move on."

William, Marcus, and Tina raised their bottles to Bobcat in agreement.

"There's a metric fuck-ton of space where we have to deploy these damned satellites in three concentric circles across millions of miles, and frankly they don't have sufficient *oomph* to push themselves out far enough."

"Virus program." Tina took a swig of her drink. "Let's map the locations we need, create nodes which represent drop-off points, and then use a virus spreading-type mathematical representation to figure out where best to deploy using the satellites' basic ability to move."

"Tweak it for velocity reduction, not accrual," Marcus temporized. "Since the ships already have velocity, the satellites will be responsible for slowing themselves down."

"That's better." Tina smiled at Marcus. "We might get done early with this meeting," she purred. "Then we can…"

Bobcat waved his marker. "*Ho-ho-holllllld* on! I don't need to know that, so let's get these details down and R2 can work on it while you two go bunny-dipping."

"Yeah." William lifted his tablet to look at the table. "No baby gravy wanted."

"Ewwww!" Tina looked around for something to throw at William, but found nothing. "Next time I see Kathy…"

"There won't be a next time," William responded.

"What? Oh, shit!" Tina's eyes went soft. "Did she break up with you?"

"Huh? No." William shook his head. "I mean, she's back on her ship and I can't see her for a long time, so neither can you."

"Oh, well, okay then," Tina agreed. She stood up and pulled on Marcus' arms. "I'm going to take this here man away from you two."

"Need a beer to go?" Bobcat asked.

"Nope!" Tina replied, opening the door and pushing Marcus through. "I'm going to get some horizontal refreshment, *thanky-ouverymuch!*"

The door closed with a soft *snick*.

Bobcat looked down at William. "Everything okay with Kathy?"

"As far as I know," William replied. "Why?"

"Didn't notice you on a video call with her, that's all."

"She's in the middle of something major with her ship. She is being sent over to another—probably for the transfer—and is out of touch for a few days."

"She's not going to be on a ship when they transfer, is she?" Bobcat asked.

When William said nothing, he looked at him. He had damn near turned white.

It wasn't an attractive color on his friend, he thought.

QBBS *Meredith Reynolds*, Three Months Later

"It would be a lot easier," Bobcat grumped, "if we could do this via Etheric calling."

Dan dropped into the seat beside him. "No can do. Since Baba Yaga had the issue with the Etheric communication shit with the Kurtherians, we know it's possible but unlikely. This is too important, so no deal."

"Says you," Bobcat muttered. "My wife hasn't been in town for a while, and I'm getting bitchy."

"I thought this was your 'after drunk' face?" Dan asked, taking a second look at Bobcat.

"No." He turned to Dan and smiled, and the crinkles around his eyes were real. "That," he explained as his face returned to exhausted, "was my 'after drinking' face." He pointed to his head. "This is my 'How the hell do we fix this next issue' face."

"You should slow down," Dan told him. "Wait, you are working on my project too, so buck the fuck up, Researcher. Grab two bricks—"

Bobcat put a hand out. "Hold on there, Skippy." Bobcat shook his head. "Don't need the bricks."

"We'll see," Dan replied enigmatically.

Both of them turned as Bethany Anne and Lance walked in. They continued discussing something the rest couldn't hear, then broke apart and went to their respective seats.

"I asked the five of you," she nodded to Admiral Thomas, Bobcat, Dan, her father, and Marcus, "here to go over the last-minute ideas, concerns, et cetera." She looked at Bobcat a second time. "You look like shit."

"Feel like shit too," Bobcat answered.

"Have you been drinking enough?" Bethany Anne asked.

"No," Bobcat answered.

Down the table, Admiral Thomas was amused to realize Bethany Anne had truly *meant* to ask Bobcat if he was drinking enough.

"Why?" she asked.

"Too few opportunities to get the brew delivered," he answered. "Plus, my lovely other half is out of town, so to speak, and I forget to bring in supplies from time to time."

"I'll take care of it," Meredith offered. "I know what Yelena sends Bobcat and what he orders when he isn't mentally exhausted."

Bobcat looked at the nearest speaker and smiled. "Meredith, if I wasn't already married…"

"I'm sure, Bobcat," Meredith replied. "I'm happy you're happy."

Bethany Anne smiled. Just the thought of constant beer supplies could perk that man up.

ADAM.

>>Yes?<<

Send a note to Yelena to tell her to get her ass back here. Bobcat probably told her some bullshit story about not being able to be nearby so she should check on the bars, but she needs to see him. Send her straight to R2D2. He needs to take some personal time.

>>Yes, ma'am.<<

She turned in her chair. "Okay, Dan 'Destructo' Bosse, what are we blowing up this time?"

"The universe!" Dan replied, smiling. "Or at least a small portion of it." He jerked a thumb at Bobcat, who just grinned tiredly. "I've confirmed it with all the approved geniuses and all the AIs, and everyone agrees we should achieve a theoretical masterpiece of a nanotomic explosion." He scratched his chin. "However, we are going to have to tell everyone the standoff distance has been increased by thirty percent."

"Do we *need* thirty percent?"

"Oh yeah," Dan told her. "The actual minimum safety distance is twenty, so we should be good unless they are in a tiny ship—in which case they'll need fifty, perhaps."

"Someone is going to ignore us," Lance gruffed.

Bethany Anne looked at him and noticed Admiral Thomas nodding.

She chewed the inside of her cheek and thought about it. "Dammit, the smart thing is to warn them once and be done with it."

"Verisimilitude would sell it," Bobcat offered.

"However," she continued, her eyes sliding over to Bobcat and then back to Lance, "that's not our normal practice."

"We can lay in temporary weapons platforms," Admiral Thomas suggested. "Put them out at the limits and suggest we will shoot anyone who tries to pass."

"I don't want to shoot anyone."

"Don't have to." He shrugged. "Warning shots. Make the platforms too light, and they'll get pulled into the nanotomic explosion for more," he shot a smile at Bobcat, "verisimilitude."

She nodded. "Okay, make that part happen. I'll get with my PR team to promote the event and start laying the ground rules for the press."

"Which they will ignore," Dan told her.

"That's why we'll have gun platforms," she answered. "And warning shots. If someone goes too far—or more likely, they send in a drone ship—I guess we will all get some fantastic video."

"Now, that *is* an idea," Lance told her. "Why don't we auction off three front-row seats to the event and let their drones be pulled in?"

"Can I bid?" Dan asked. "I've always wanted to see something like this in slow motion."

"I'll get you backstage passes," Bethany Anne told him. "At what distance?"

"Close enough to see well, far enough their sensors can't get an accurate reading." Dan pointed at Bobcat.

Bobcat shook his head. "ADAM can tell us that. Don't toss it on us."

"I've got it, Bethany Anne," ADAM replied.

"Okay." She exhaled heavily. "Now, who's in charge of the popcorn?"

CHAPTER TEN

Cheryl Lynn looked out over the dozens of temporary tables from above. Lights hanging every which way showed full-on temporary reporter sets, which three of the multisystem news agencies had built in the last week in this massive unused docking cavern on the *Meredith Reynolds*.

Cheryl Lynn sighed. It was a chaotic mess in here.

However, for the most part, the different teams worked together and stayed out of everyone's hair. It helped to have the Guardians walking around and dealing with issues, usually by ejecting one or both troublemakers.

"Everything okay?" Tabitha asked from behind Cheryl Lynn.

"When did you get here?" Cheryl Lynn exclaimed, hugging Tabitha.

"Last night, but I checked on a couple of old friends," Tabitha replied.

Cheryl Lynn nodded before turning back to view the hustle and bustle beneath her. "You mean you met with Peter."

"Yes," Tabitha agreed. *"Both of them,"* she added, winking.

Cheryl Lynn snorted. "Okay, I can forgive you for that, but just barely. Have you seen Samuel and Richard?"

"Not in six months." Tabitha started looking around the massive room full of people. "Why?" Her voice was anxious.

Cheryl Lynn laughed. "Don't worry, they only owe me breakfast."

"Which is right here!" Samuel's voice caused both ladies to turn around. "And we have enough for a tired lady who wore out a Pricolici."

Richard stepped up, singing, "All night long..."

Both men harmonized, "All niiiight... All niiiight..."

"Give me that." Cheryl Lynn snatched the bag of food and waved her hand toward Tabitha. "You may now continue harassing the Ranger about her nighttime activities."

Samuel and Richard smiled, and Tabitha frowned at them both. Richard shook his head. "Uhhh, I think we've accomplished enough this morning."

Cheryl Lynn chewed on her pastry, then covered her mouth to speak. "Are you guys going back to Earth?"

"We have to ask Gabrielle," Samuel answered. "It's been on our minds, but we aren't sure what we want to do."

"It isn't going to be the same without so many of our friends," Richard added. He looked at Tabitha. "You?"

"Going," Tabitha answered. "I need to stretch my legs, and I want to speak with Michael, too."

Samuel nodded. "Peter?"

"Going," Tabitha responded. "Half because he wants to, half because he needs to, and the other half I won't mention."

Richard opened his mouth to speak but closed it and shrugged. *Maybe she wasn't good with math.*

"T-minus ten minutes until the big show." Tabitha moved up beside Cheryl Lynn, and Richard and Samuel came up behind them. "What's the plan?"

As if on cue the far wall, which was over a hundred feet tall, lit up with a view of the Command Center. Bethany Anne was in the background chewing on a nail.

"She seems a bit anxious," Tabitha commented.

"I would be too if the ability to go see my boyfriend was completely dependent on the next fifteen minutes," Cheryl Lynn replied. "Look." She pointed below. "A lot of the news sources are taking a picture of the video wall, even though we fed them a clean signal."

"It's more real somehow," Richard guessed. "I bet you a third of them have a picture of the wall and a PIP in the bottom with the clean signal."

"'PIP?'" Cheryl Lynn asked.

"'Picture in Picture,'" Samuel answered.

Tabitha turned around. "When did you guys go technical?"

"You try guarding a reporter and her video recorder for decades and not pick up the parlance," Samuel suggested.

"Good point." Tabitha cocked her head. "Where are those two?"

"They came out of retirement for this one," Samuel replied. He pointed to the immense video wall across the way. "Who do you think is shooting that?"

"Ooohhh." Tabitha nodded. "I guess that would have been enough to tease them to come back up."

"Yeah." Cheryl Lynn followed a team down below with her eyes. "They bought homes right next to each other in a nice neighborhood."

"They ever want to get back into the game?" Tabitha asked.

"They seemed happy the last time I talked with them. One has a garden, and the other has a pond with fish in it," she told her. "I haven't seen them in six months—not since I bought the house on the other side."

"Get out!" Tabitha answered. "You're going landlubber?"

"Going?" Cheryl Lynn smiled as she continued to stare out over the floor. "I started as a landlubber, remember?" She waved a hand negligently above her head. "I'm certainly not going out there." She shook her head. "No way, no how. I'm retiring."

"Oh!" Tabitha pointed as the image on the wall changed. "There go the three drones."

"Did you hear about the distance limits?" Cheryl Lynn asked.

"Yes, and it was a lot of math," Samuel explained. "Something about something and if you go past this limit, we will blow the shit out of your ship."

"Or there is a chance you could get sucked into a black hole," Richard added. "Neither is a really good choice for a healthy future."

"Still," Cheryl Lynn informed them over her shoulder, "Kagax News Agency tried to press it, and they just about got their nose shot off."

"Bad shot?" Tabitha asked.

"No," Samuel answered. "Warning shot. Cloaked BYPS system. When the news agencies realized they couldn't find the guns, they gave up trying to sneak in. When I set up two extra drones for additional video, they quit bitching to me and accepted the inevitable."

Richard scratched the back of his neck. "Did either of you bet on the outcome?"

Tabitha whipped around. "What? There was betting?""

"When *isn't* there betting?" Richard asked. "Yes. You could go with a friendly setup, or over in the Drainus sector, you could get legit betting percentages."

"What are the odds?" Tabitha asked.

"Two to one she blows it." Cheryl Lynn sighed. "Bethany Anne went ballistic and told them to put a million credits on making this happen." She stopped a moment to subvocalize a command to a floor-support person, then continued, "Unfortunately, my wonderful Empress was in full-on Royal Affronted mode, and no less than three video cameras were on her when she said it. I couldn't say squat before it was already out the door. It made the

News of the Hour for the next four hours straight. People loved seeing her bet money they would make."

Richard added, "Seems only reasonable since she is betting her team can pull this off."

"True enough," Tabitha agreed.

All four heads focused on the wall in front of them when it blanked to black, then human numeric digits started a countdown from sixty. At fifty-five seconds, the four-story-tall numbers shrank to ten feet in the lower right-hand corner of the screen, and the video switched to a view of space.

"This is Empress Bethany Anne." A six-story-tall face appeared on the screen. "We are about to transfer the Annex Gate from the Leath System to the Yollin System. To do that, we will be using six of our Leviathan-class superdreadnoughts to help power the transfer, employing state-of-the-art artificial intelligence. This information has been included in your packets."

The face disappeared.

"That was pre-recorded," Cheryl Lynn told them. "There is no way Bethany Anne could have managed that, as tightly as she is wound right now."

As if on cue, at fifteen seconds, a hush fell over the large cavern. No one counted down, at least not above a whisper.

The video zoomed out until a bright pinprick of light was visible, and it focused on the area in a microsecond. The light grew in brilliance, then the camera zoomed back out quickly to display the outline of an empty circle with six large ships surrounding it.

A few whooped for joy as the light continued to grow so bright it overwhelmed the video camera, which implemented a filter to cut it down.

Even cut down, the light was bright.

Then it went supernova.

"Oh, no!" Tabitha's hand flew up to cover her mouth. "No no *no NO!*"

An explosion shattered the Gate and three of the ships immediately, and a gravity wave shot out, light exploding in a ring...

Then everything slowed down. All the parts flared and started to move back toward the middle of the destruction.

"Oh, shit!" Richard pointed. "Implosion!"

The cavern rang with cries of disbelief, reporters speaking, and wails of concern and then horror, since the massive wall made them all feel they were being pulled into the middle with the debris. The drone which was sending the video was caught too close to the implosions and was yanked into the maelstrom. The video shook as it raced faster and faster into the center of the super-hot white implosion, and then the signal switched to a different drone.

One outside the minimum distance.

Cheryl Lynn ran out of the admin box.

Tabitha sprinted after her, and Samuel and Richard followed. "Where are we going?" Richard called.

"Bethany Anne!" Tabitha shot back. "She is going to be devastated!"

The video switched to the Command Center, and in the background, the Empress was crying out and sobbing. She fell to her knees, her hands over her eyes as tears dripped to the floor beneath her.

Some ten seconds later, that video was cut off.

Three different agencies got videos of the Empress' people running toward the Command Center, their faces showing worry for their leader and what she must be going through. One was lucky enough to catch the Empress' top Public Relations person and Ranger Two arguing, as they ran, with the base's EI to allow them entry to the Command Center.

Which everyone assumed was a madhouse since all access had been denied. The three non-Etheric Empire news agencies were politely escorted out of the room.

. . .

MICHAEL ANDERLE

QBBS *Meredith Reynolds*, Hallways En Route to the Command Center

"I don't give a shit, Meredith!" Cheryl Lynn told the AI as she ran toward the Command Center. "If you don't get me in there, I will rewire your insides!"

"That's not even possible," Meredith retorted. "You don't have the skills, Cheryl Lynn."

"I don't care if it's not logical!" Cheryl Lynn argued as she and the three others took a left turn to bypass a congested area via a few back routes. "I'll *pay* someone to do it!"

"Like me!" Tabitha offered. "I'll figure out a way to make the rest of your electronic life a living hell!"

Samuel popped Richard on the shoulder and pointed to a group of aliens who were filming them. "Hope they got my good side!"

"Both my sides are my good side!" Richard replied as they kept up with the ladies.

"The four of you," Meredith replied after several seconds of processing, "have been approved to enter the Command Center from Level Three."

"Three?" Cheryl Lynn called back. "Command is on One!"

"Your approved elevator access to the Command Center is on three," Meredith told the four of them. "I suggest you take a right turn at Hallway T-133, then go down Elevator T-137."

"You'd better not be fucking with us," Tabitha huffed as the four of them ran around the T-133 corner to their right. They bypassed four crosswalks and slowed as an elevator door opened with a *ding* at T-137.

The four of them jumped on and it closed. "Did you call this?" Tabitha asked Cheryl Lynn.

"No," she replied. "I assumed Meredith did it for us."

"I did," Meredith replied. "I'd rather not deal with attacks from Ranger Two."

The elevator doors opened, and the four stepped out. "Direction?" Cheryl Lynn asked.

"Left," Meredith answered.

It took the team another two minutes to reach a rather nondescript door with a full complement of Guardians in front of it. Before the team could say anything, they moved to the sides and allowed the four to pass, blocking the hallway behind them.

"That was weird," Tabitha muttered as they entered a large plain room with another elevator. There wasn't anyone in it. "If this turns out to be a trash compactor," she complained as they entered the elevator, "I'm Han Solo."

"Star Wars at a time like this?" Cheryl Lynn asked in disbelief.

"Always time for Star Wars quotes," Tabitha answered. "You should have been there for this one operation with the Tontos when we could only answer with quotes from characters in Star Wars. If you stayed in one character, it was a hundred extra points."

The door opened on the Command Center and the four stepped out, their mouths open.

The Command Center was reacting in the most incomprehensible way possible.

They were celebrating.

Bethany Anne heard the word she had been waiting for. *"CUT!"*

She jumped up from the floor and looked around. "Do we have news?"

Bobcat pointed behind her, and she spun to Dan.

Dan put up a finger, but the air was tense until he broke into a smile. He threw off his communications headset. *"WE DID IT!"* he shouted, fist pumping.

Bethany Anne punched the air too. *"WOOHOOO!"* she shouted, her smile a mile wide. Laughing, she ran over to Dan, picked him up in a hug, and swung him around. "Dr. Destructo, you maniac, we *did it!*"

She dropped the laughing Dan and flung two red balls of energy casually into the air, where they burst into sparkles. "*YES!*" She continued to laugh as others high-fived each other.

She put her hands on her hips, but couldn't stop smiling as everyone in the area celebrated.

ADAM, did we have any trouble?

>>**Reynolds suffered a power feedback, and a quarter of his engines shut down. That was the worst, and it happened because his area of the Annex Gate started to flex, so he extended his shield somehow to help hold it exactly in place.**<<

Bethany Anne shook her head. They had actually come rather close to having major problems. She wasn't sure what might have happened, but she couldn't believe twisting something that sensitive and that huge had been a good idea.

TOM spoke next. **I can't think of a more audacious and amazing example of human badassery than this right here. It's a shame no one can ever know how awesome this was.**

We *will know*, Bethany Anne replied, *and that will have to be good enough for now.*

John came over and hugged her, and she rested for a moment in his embrace before pulling away. "Good job, Empress. If you ever wish to give up this job, you can take up acting." He winked at her.

"Not something I would care to do," Bethany Anne admitted.

"How did you do the crying so well?" John asked.

Bethany Anne waved to a couple of people who had wrapped up their tasks and were heading for a special exit, where Barnabas was waiting for them.

Everyone here had been a witness to the truth, and unfortunately, for most of the volunteers, they needed to unlearn it.

"I thought about how life would have been if it had really

exploded and asked TOM to push my emotions past the limit." She snapped her fingers. "Instant crying."

"Hey." John nodded over her shoulder, so Bethany Anne turned around. "Oh." Bethany Anne smiled at Cheryl Lynn and Tabitha and gave Samuel and Richard a little wave as the four worked through the jubilant crowd.

"So, guys," Bethany Anne asked as they came up, "what did you think of the successful transfer of the Leath's Annex Gate to Empire space?"

Cheryl Lynn looked around before focusing on Bethany Anne. "I ran all the way over here to console you!"

Bethany Anne nodded. "I know!"

"I said, I *ran* all the way over here—" Cheryl Lynn stopped her tirade in mid-sentence. "What?"

"I said, I know." Bethany Anne put out a hand, and John placed a tablet in it. She turned it around. "Isn't it amazing how quickly the news goes out?"

Cheryl Lynn took the tablet and viewed the news clips that showed her and Tabitha front and center. She was reading the riot act to Meredith as they dashed through the hallways.

"You couldn't have acted any better," Bethany Anne told her.

Cheryl Lynn looked up. "I wasn't acting!"

"Exactly," Bethany Anne agreed. "Your real emotions, spoken so openly and honestly as you raced down the halls, will do more than anything I did to prove this was real."

"Wasn't it?" Cheryl Lynn looked around as she handed back the tablet. "Did it actually blow up?"

"It had to blow up," Bethany Anne told them. "Just not the real Annex Gate."

"Sonofabitch!" Tabitha smiled. "The shell game!"

"This time, it worked like a charm," Bethany Anne agreed. "Although I wouldn't want to do that again. I think I lost ten years."

"Won't you live like, forever?" Cheryl Lynn asked.

"I don't think so," Bethany Anne replied. "However, I still don't want to do this again."

"Damn right!" Cheryl Lynn huffed. "I can see your logic, but if you ever leave me out of a stunt like this again, I swear by all that's holy, I'll switch your Coke for Pepsi!"

"Yes, ma'am," Bethany Anne replied, keeping her smile hidden.

Cheryl Lynn looked around. "So, now I need to go out there and lie my ass off about the destruction of the Gate?"

"Yes," Bethany Anne agreed. "That would be best."

"Okay. Knowing sucks," Cheryl Lynn told her. "I can see why not knowing was so much more powerful."

"If it is any consolation," she pointed to the door through which most were leaving, "most of those who know the truth won't in fifteen minutes."

Cheryl Lynn turned to see where Bethany Anne was pointing. "Who is working the spell-craft mind voodoo in there?"

"Barnabas," Bethany Anne answered, and Cheryl Lynn headed in that direction. "What are you doing?" she called.

Cheryl Lynn spoke over her shoulder. "Getting Barnabas to help me with my acting!" she answered. "Better to speak from total ignorance of the truth!" She winked and then turned back.

"Good idea," Bethany Anne answered, and looked at Tabitha. "You?"

"I'm a Ranger," Tabitha replied. "We know how to lie."

CHAPTER ELEVEN

<u>QBBS *Meredith Reynolds*, Dock 775</u>

Peter reached over and took Tabitha's hand as the two of them approached the security guards in front of the dock.

"Hold, sir." The Yollin Guardian Marine put up a hand as his partner stayed alert and safely out of easy range of the two humans.

"Security credential, please." He nodded to the hand scanner in front of Peter, who placed his available hand on the scanner.

"Welcome, Guardian Leader," Meredith confirmed. "We need Ranger Tabitha's print as well."

Tabitha put her right hand on the security scanner. "This is a pain in the ass, Meredith."

Meredith spoke again. "Welcome, Ranger Tabitha. Please continue past the security post."

Peter dipped his head. "Good to see you, K'lok." He nodded to the human. "Gregory."

Gregory confirmed using his HUD that it was the Guardian Leader and his date for the event and nodded slightly as the two of them swept through the security door.

"Now that," K'lok looked down the hallway for the next set of visitors, "I never saw coming."

Gregory put a finger up to where his lips were behind his helmet, then tapped where his ears were and pointed to the door.

K'lok gave the hand signal for "Understood" and focused on his role for the evening, making sure only those on the approved list were allowed past them.

And checking everyone, including the lady with the large white dog coming down the hallway.

K'lok looked at Gregory and hissed, "How the hell do we paw-test Ashur?"

The Executive Pod waiting for Peter and Tabitha was sleek, beautiful, and already crammed with the who's who of the Etheric Empire.

"Who are we waiting on?" Peter asked as he stepped into the Pod, making sure Tabitha had room as he led her in.

She had informed him that in her world, the man led into restaurants and other places. Peter had no problem with that. It was his preference anyway.

First unto the breach.

The two of them shook hands, hugged, or fist-bumped damn near everyone as they worked their way to the first two open seats.

Kael-ven and Snow moved over to give Peter and Tabitha room to sit down.

Peter turned to Kael-ven. "Who are we waiting for?"

"You, of course," Snow answered.

"Funny har-har." Peter reached over to ruffle Snow's head. "No, really?"

Snow looked to the front. *"My father."*

Peter saw Bethany Anne board and assumed that near her

somewhere was Ashur. Sure enough, the doors closed behind her, and the Executive Pod slowly slid out of the docking area and the *Meredith Reynolds*. Within seconds, a full squadron of fighters pulled alongside, and the Executive Pod punched it.

Three minutes later, the Pod slowed to match velocity with the monster ship *ArchAngel II* and slipped into a waiting dock. The fighters turned away, heading back to the *Meredith Reynolds* for some downtime before they would be needed to accompany the shuttle back.

The *ArchAngel II* accelerated rapidly and, when it was barely out of normal traffic areas, it gated and disappeared.

A small ship observed the activity and noted it for later.

QBBS Asteroid *R2D2*, R&D

"Here they come!" Tina shouted excitedly. "I just got the message from ArchAngel. They should be here in ten minutes."

"Good!" Marcus answered as he walked up to her. "Does this look okay?"

Tina turned from the screen on the wall in their shared bedroom and slowly shook her head. "Ahhh, no." She took off his tie. "Okay, better."

"My tie!" He looked stricken.

"Is too formal for a Team BMW event!" she declared. She gently kissed him on the lips.

He nodded. "Right then, no tie it is." He headed back into their washroom.

As the last one on, Bethany Anne was the first one off the Executive Pod. Bethany Anne thought it was funny that the team had stocked champagne—or rather, a close equivalent—on the Pod for them to drink on the way over.

It did have a way of getting the party started, though.

The group, which included Bethany Anne and Ashur, Lance and Patricia, the Empress' Bitches and their spouses, Barnabas, Stephen and Jennifer, Peter and Tabitha, Ryu, Hirotoshi, and the rest of the Tontos, and thirty others followed the signs to a large white room which could have easily held three times as many people. Colorful lights shone on the walls, old Earth music played, three kegs stood in the middle of the floor, and a chocolate waterfall shimmered.

Everyone but Lance and Admiral Thomas beelined for the chocolate fountain.

The two men smiled and walked over to a table, each taking a chair.

"Patricia didn't want you in there fighting to get her chocolate?" Thomas asked.

Lance shook his head. "She's a fighter. She's willing and able to get her own."

"She was probably afraid you would eat it yourself."

"Yup," Lance admitted.

"Did you make that up, or is it the truth," Thomas asked.

"She didn't tell me in so many words," Lance admitted, "but her pat on my hand as she left told me in no uncertain terms to stay here."

"Huh."

"How long has it been since Nancy?" Lance asked. "Three years?"

"Yeah," Thomas admitted. "Apparently, what kept us together was the fact that I wasn't around all of the time."

"You got on her nerves?" Lance asked.

"I ejected her out the end of the *Reynolds* and haven't looked back," Thomas admitted. "So, I guess the real answer is, she got on my last nerve after about two weeks."

"She wanted to go do stuff?"

"She wanted to show me off," Thomas grumped. "It was a

chance for her to parade me around. We went down to Yoll and hit about ten restaurants I didn't know about. I just thought it was rather nice to be going somewhere I hadn't been before. The third time we were photographed and the images showed up in the gossip rags, I realized what was going on and confronted her."

Thomas went quiet for a moment, reliving the conversation with Nancy. Lance just sipped his drink and watched everyone let their hair down.

Thomas finally started speaking again. "Is this you telling me to step back out there?"

"What the hell are you going to do but be a pain in my ass otherwise?" Lance grumped and the two of them chuckled. "Bartholomew, you need someone who can listen to you, not judge you, and enjoy you being around without clinging. She could be military, but I doubt you want that?"

Lance eyed Admiral Thomas until he agreed.

"Okay, then. Hell, do what William did, and don't mention it until you know the opportunity is golden."

"He used the dating site, right?"

"It's a bit more than that, but yes," Lance told him. He leaned closer and raised an eyebrow. Thomas leaned in toward him. "Here's the trick. The website is run by Meredith and ADAM together. They are working on their heuristic programming for personality fits. If you check the box for 'Let us choose,' they will select the top three best matches. If you tell ADAM you approve, he will pull everything they know about you so they can predict even better."

Thomas thought about that for a moment, then clinked his drink against Lance's. "For some odd reason, knowing ADAM and Meredith have my back will make it all the more fun."

"What did William do?" Thomas asked, taking a sip.

Lance shook his head. "Oh, you can't tell William anything."

"Why not?" Thomas asked.

"Because my daughter was in it up to her neck, making that connection happen. She broke so many damned rules trying to work something for him with the right lady. Rumor is, even when she was running around as Baba Yaga, she worked on the problem with ADAM." He shook his head. "If she wasn't the Empress, she would have to arrest herself. Now she has to pardon herself."

"I understand it went well enough."

"A damned miracle, if you ask me." Lance smiled at Patricia, who was still happy as a kitten in a box of freshly-dried socks. He looked at Thomas. "I'm more shocked she got something to work for William than that we got the Annex Gate moved and everyone believing that shit blew up."

"I understand we are at a funeral at the moment?" Thomas replied. "Have to say, this party isn't what I expected."

"Only those on the very inside will ever know. Maybe in a hundred years—or sooner, if we have to admit we have the ships —everyone will know we pulled off the biggest damned con this galaxy has ever seen."

Thomas raised his drink. "Eat your heart out, David Copperfield," he toasted and took a swallow.

"I saw him three times in Vegas."

"Any good?"

"Amazing," Lance admitted. "Never did figure out most of the shit he did. Even his stupid-assed duck trick was pretty good."

***

Bethany Anne stabbed a reddish fruit that was a bit more tart than a strawberry and held it under the chocolate fountain. "What's going on with Dad and Bart over there?"

Patricia didn't look over her shoulder. "He wanted some time to speak with Thomas about his future, so he asked me to play in the chocolate."

Bethany Anne nodded, then leaned into Patricia and bumped her with her shoulder. "I never thanked you for your message to Baba Yaga."

"Wasn't to Baba Yaga, it was to my daughter," Patricia answered, "and you are welcome."

"Speaking of daughter..." Bethany Anne got a bit closer and waited for exactly the right moment before asking, "will I be getting any brothers or sisters?"

Patricia threw a hand over her mouth as she involuntarily coughed, trying to not spew its contents all over the fountain. Bethany Anne laughed and handed her a clean napkin. Patricia wiped her mouth, looked sideways at Bethany Anne, and hissed in a whisper, "I thought you didn't read the minds of family?"

"*WHAT?*" Bethany Anne's eyes went wide. "You guys *are* thinking babies?" She grabbed an extra plate, tossed on a handful of items, and dumped chocolate on the top, then grabbed Patricia's elbow, pulled her out of the line, and headed for an empty table. "Come with me, Mom!"

"Uh-oh." Thomas nodded to the fountain. "Bethany Anne is up to something."

Lance looked at where Thomas was nodding. "What happened?"

"Bethany Anne said something to Patricia that made her cough, and next thing you know Bethany Anne did that vampy speed stuff with a plate of food and moved Patricia over to that table to talk."

"Huh." Lance rubbed his face. "No idea."

Patricia allowed herself to be directed to a chair before she looked at Bethany Anne. "You didn't read me?"

"No!" Bethany Anne shook her head. "I said it as a joke to make you do a spit-take!"

"So, I gave *myself* away?" Patricia's eyes narrowed. "You playing fair here?"

"Yes," Bethany Anne assured her. "I won fifty credits from ADAM."

"You're a horse's ass, ADAM!" Patricia noted, knowing the AI could hear her.

"He says he's sorry, but he didn't know either. Divulging the information is all on you." Bethany Anne picked up a red fruit. "These are good." She licked the chocolate off her fingers. "So, brothers and sisters?"

"Oh, just one, I hope," Patricia answered. "I stayed off the baby wagon with the wars that were going on, and now I figure there are no more excuses."

"Dad wants more?" Bethany Anne asked.

"Lance has been okay with it forever, I think," Patricia admitted. "I'm the one who has been hesitant since I didn't want to raise a child alone."

"Going to go for a specific sex?"

"Goodness, no!" Patricia shook her head. "Whatever happens, happens. We will make sure the baby is healthy, so I hope something happens before TOM leaves, but other than that, no."

Bethany Anne listened for a moment. "He says to tell you that he will be here for you as best as possible." There was a pause before Bethany Anne asked, "How soon?"

"Well, there will be a lot of practicing." Patricia took a bite of her chocolate-covered food.

"Eww!" Bethany Anne squeezed her eyes shut and put her fingers in her ears. "Lalalalala!"

Patricia had to get Bethany Anne to help her stop choking

after her laughter caused what she was eating to go down the wrong pipe.

Tabitha looked down at the furry face staring up at her. "No!" She shook her head. "There is no way I'm feeding you chocolate, you little rat!"

"*I'm neither little nor a rat.*" Ashur puffed out his chest and struck a pose. "*I'm the White Avenger!*"

Tabitha chuckled. "What are you avenging?"

"*The inability of dogs on Earth to metabolize the theobromine in chocolate, which poisons them. As the duly authorized representative of my species, I'm here to consume all the chocolate available.*"

Tabitha shook her head. "You know Snow has already downed a gallon, right?"

"*What?*" Ashur whined, looking around. "*Where is that child of mine?*"

Tabitha pointed to a far corner. "Over there with Kael-ven and Kiel. Kael-ven didn't know chocolate was poisonous to dogs, and Snow didn't care since the nanocytes in your bodies protect you."

"*Hmmph.*" Ashur looked up at Tabitha. "*Help a fellow out?*"

"Fine!" Tabitha grabbed a nearby bowl. "But if you make a mess, you better blame someone else for your fix!"

"Bethany Anne?" William walked up behind her.

"Hmmm?" Bethany Anne had a spoon full of chocolate in her mouth and didn't look like she was willing to take it out.

"Can I talk with you?"

"Mmmhmmm," Bethany Anne agreed. The two of them

walked over to a mostly clear area. She raised an eyebrow, talking around the spoon. "Wat's uh?"

William chuckled. "Chocolate got your tongue?"

"Mmmhmmm." She pulled the spoon out of her mouth. "This stuff is delicious!" she exclaimed and smiled. "What's up?"

"I need to ask you a question about your trip."

Bethany Anne put the spoon back in her mouth. "Mmmhmmm."

"You guys are going to be gone a while, right?"

"Mmmhmm."

William breathed in and then exhaled, looking Bethany Anne in the face. "Can you find a use for me?"

She pulled out the spoon. "Always, big guy." She looked around. "Everything okay here?"

William waved a hand, "Oh, as perfect as ever, but you know Kathy?"

"Ahhhhh." She nodded her head. "You want to see what's going on, and she is slated to come?"

"She loves her job, and I wouldn't want to see that change because of me." He nodded to those walking around. "Tina's here, so the team is still rock-solid, and I need to move on a bit. Kathy has shown me that if it isn't her, it will be someone," he smiled, "and frankly, I rather hope it's her."

Bethany Anne leaned in and asked softly, "Want me to put some vampire voodoo on her?" Her eyes crinkled in humor.

"No!" He shook his head as he chuckled. He put up his fingers an inch apart. "Well, my lack of self-esteem wouldn't mind it much, but that isn't the right future." He looked at her doubtfully. "Could you?"

Bethany Anne pursed her lips and her eyes narrowed. "I bet I could do something short-term, but long term?" She shook her head. "I'm not sure I want to find out if I could do that for love. I know I can make that shit happen for other reasons." She made a face and turned to look at him. "For love, it just seems so wrong."

"Got to believe they love you without outside influences?" William sighed.

"Oh, hell, no." Bethany Anne chuckled. "Please! A woman—or a man for that matter—uses all sorts of outside forces to woo a person. Hell, Gloria Vanderbilt had a jeans line that probably snared more men than perfume during certain years back in the 70s on Earth. No one is guiltless when love is on the line." She rocked her hand back and forth. "I'll qualify that to say those who don't seek the attention are probably guiltless, but most of us?" She shook her head sharply this time. "Nope."

"You don't think it's silly?"

Bethany Anne patted his arm. "William, this is the most courageous and honest-to-God effort you have made for your love life, and Kathy is good people."

"She was pretty amazing on that date."

"Yeah." Bethany Anne sighed. "I'm sorry I crashed it. I really wanted it to go well for you."

William chuckled. "Kathy enjoyed it a lot, and once it came out that I was William from Team BMW, it was probably good to let her get hit with all of us at once. She acclimated, and my fame wasn't as big a deal when she compared it to yours."

"Oh shit!" Bethany Anne's hand went to her mouth. "Did I mess that up for you?" Her eyes were wide with concern.

"No no no no *no!*" He shook his head. "I mean, I seemed fairly normal again after you and Gabrielle came in. It helped her see me as part of a group, and she liked being next to me. She felt safe."

"A good feeling." Bethany Anne sighed. "Okay, so you want to come on the trip to Earth?"

"Yes," he assured her, nodding as much to himself as her. "Yes, I do."

"Done!" Bethany Anne stood up. "Now, I smell chocolate cake." She strode off, sniffing the air.

CHAPTER TWELVE

"We need supplies, and we need to keep stuff hidden," Dan informed the team as they sat around the table. "We can't use the biggest ships for obvious reasons, and it will look damned funny if we send _ArchAngel II_ or _Ranger Prime_ in and out all the time."

"I don't know." Bethany Anne rubbed her chin. "Is there a place you need to clean up before we go?"

"Other than Devon?" Barnabas asked.

"Yes," she agreed, "other than Devon. Although that would have been a great idea." She scratched the tip of her nose. "Why is it always the tip?"

"What?" Barnabas looked up from his tablet as Dan smiled.

"Why is it always the tip of your nose that gets itchy? Why not the little flare-out parts?"

"What about some of the space stations on the frontier?" Lance suggested. "Send _Ranger Prime_ and _ArchAngel II_ on one trip, swing them by the system-that-shall-not-be-named, and then show up on a fly-the-flag. _Ranger Prime_ continues and accrues a little newsworthy notice. _ArchAngel_ comes back here to work for a little while, and we load her back up."

"And how do we get that much stuff on her?" Admiral Thomas asked. "You know they are paying very close attention to our ship movements."

"*Shinigami*," Dan answered. "No one can find her, as we are well aware."

"Are you willing to ask her to be a glorified truck driver?" Admiral Thomas asked. "Because between you and me, I'd rather not."

Bethany Anne harrumphed. "She's not a big deal. Meredith?"

"Yes, Empress?"

"Patch me to Shinigami."

"Done, Empress," Meredith finished.

"This is Shinigami," a deeper voice answered.

"It's me," Bethany Anne told her. "I need you to make a shit-load of secret trips between here and," she looked at the others, "Yoll?" They nodded, so she continued louder, "The planet Yoll and possibly a few other locations, and the *ArchAngel* or possibly other ships, in a clandestine manner."

"Why?"

Bethany Anne rolled her eyes. "Because I'll kick your ass if you don't," was what she was tempted to say, but it came out as, "Because we need to absolutely positively not allow anyone to see us move supplies to the area-that-shall-not-be-named, and you are the best we have."

"Yes, I am," her ship agreed. "Who will I be working with?"

Dan spoke up. "Let's start with Meredith, and if you could work with Reynolds perhaps to locate a completely safe midpoint, maybe you can figure out a way to get stuff to him, unload, and go back."

"If you provide us the needed supplies, we will work this out quickly," Shinigami confirmed.

"Excellent," Bethany Anne exclaimed. "Talk to you later."

"Goodbye." Shinigami cut the connection without another word.

"Not much of a conversationalist," Lance commented.

"I blame myself for that," Bethany Anne told him. "I'll work with her."

Lance just nodded.

She looked around. "Okay, did we just finish in like five minutes?"

"Assuming our resident Witch AI handles her stuff, then yes," Dan answered.

Bethany Anne stood up and sighed. "I'll go have a word with her right now." She took a step to her left and disappeared.

"That," Lance nodded to where Bethany Anne had been a moment before, "is still unsettling."

QBBS _Meredith Reynolds,_ Grimes Residence

Jean stirred the quasit potatoes and grabbed a fork to taste the dish. "Mmmm." She put the fork down and reached for the butter, looked at the large mass of potatoes, down at the butter, and tossed all the butter into the bowl. "You can _never_ have too much butter," she murmured.

While her husband was a keeper, he absolutely was not a chef —unless mass destruction was on the menu. Then he was one of the best.

An Iron Chef in the culinary art of bloodshed.

Fortunately, he didn't bring that home. At home, he was a mountain of a man with a heart twice as big as he was. Early in their relationship, Jean had been forced to fight a few issues with jealousy regarding Bethany Anne. It wasn't until John admitted to a few of his early decisions about dying for the woman—that he just had no desire to die in bed _because_ of the woman—that she understood he followed Bethany Anne out of love and respect.

Which was a very male trait. They might love their leaders, but when they respected them through and through?

They would walk through the abyss of hell, kick whatever and whoever's ass they need to, and climb out the other side covered in the ichor of the demons they had destroyed.

However, Jean was the woman he *loved*. She didn't need to be a leader, just Jean Dukes.

Friend.

Partner.

Lover.

The one who would come up behind him, slip an arm around his waist, and kiss him gently. Tell him she needed his arms around her and settle into that big comfy man-chest and purr like a happy kitten.

When she did that? Hell, he would happily keep his cock-blocking socks off the floor, whistling the whole damned time.

Bethany Anne had put them together, and Jean understood Bethany Anne would fight anyone—including herself—who tried to tear them apart.

It had allowed Jean to eventually realize she could have a child or two—or ten—with this man. So far, it had been one daughter and now a grandchild as well.

John's genes were evident in their daughter Lillian Marlene, but they had flared up something fierce in their granddaughter Meredith Nicole. That little girl was as obstinate as the day was long already, with a chip on her shoulder that seemed to grow an inch larger each year she was alive.

The front door opened, and Jean peeked out of the kitchen.

"'Lo, honey," John called.

She blew him a kiss. "Hey, sweetheart!" Jean ducked back into the kitchen. "Dinner will be ready soon, so you have time to move all that junk you just put on the front couch to the proper place."

She shook her head as he grumbled, but the subsequent noises made it obvious he was moving everything.

By the time he came into the kitchen, she had finished the

potatoes and was pulling a baked fish out of the oven. "Yollin redfish?" John asked, leaning over to smell the goodness.

"Don't make me spill this on your face!" Jean told him, lifting the pan onto the top of the counter.

John had moved aside. "You'd have to hit me with it." He shook his head. "I still don't know how I married someone so violent."

"You thought it an endearing trait once upon a time," Jean told him. She lifted the two slices of fish with a spatula and placed them on the plates. "Dish the potatoes for me?" she asked as she put down the spatula and swept the two plates to the table.

She was sitting down, their drinks already poured, when John came up beside her. "How much?"

He held a large spoon, ready to serve her. "Three spoons, please. The rest is yours."

John placed three large spoonfuls near her fish and turned to his side of the table. His portion of fish covered the plate, so Jean always put out another plate for his sides. This time they had the potatoes and a green vegetable—which John wasn't fond of, but he always took one small bite to let her know he appreciated the effort.

Even if he couldn't stand the food.

Soon, they were eating and sharing their day.

Jean started on her vegetables. "Who has coverage for Bethany Anne tonight?"

"Scott and a Guardian," John answered. "Now that we are all getting used to the idea of her not being Empress, Bethany Anne is having a fit about always having two of us around her. She thinks one is enough."

"You would think after the Baba Yaga episode you guys would be on her like flies on honey."

"Now there's a phrase I haven't heard in a while." John cut into his fish and took a bite. "Not that we have flies in space."

"Not anymore," Jean countered. "Meredith went on a spree to kill them that first decade, remember?"

John chuckled. "Yes, she singlehandedly elevated the R&D research efforts for your team to create the tiny drones we used to kill the flies—"

"And keep out the spies," Jean nodded. "Funny how that worked out for us."

"How's Lillian?" John asked.

Jean snorted. "Doing well, and thinking she is going nuts because Nickie is giving her so much trouble."

John shrugged. "Determined Grimes child." He scratched his cheek. "If she would challenge the child more and demand absolute obedience less, it might help."

"You realize, Doctor Hypocrisy, that was exactly how you raised Lillian?" Jean asked and took a drink of water. "Are you getting soft in your elder years?"

"Hardly." He shook his head. "Lillian responded to that parenting style, but Nickie hasn't. Not every child reacts the same way. Lillian loved technology and what it could do so much that if you took it away, it hurt her. It was easy to manage her. Nickie is about doing what *she* wants to do."

"She doesn't want to work out with you guys."

"Not a choice," John replied. "I set it up so that when she passes, she is let out. It's binary but not optional."

"She seems to dislike seeing your face." Jean leaned in. "Don't you worry she will hate you?"

John smiled. "Oh, she will hate me for a while, but eventually, she will have a grudging respect for what I'm teaching her. If she survives a couple of fights, she will eventually appreciate what I've done."

He pursed his lips and considered the future before shrugging his shoulders. "She will only love me if she learns to forgive me for making her go through it."

"And you are okay with that?" Jean asked. "I'm just an old softie, then."

"No, you are her favorite grandmother, who lets her come play and watch how you guys make cool stuff happen. I think your lab is the only school she's going to enjoy."

"Not much longer, though." Jean sighed. "*R2D2* is moving to God-knows-where. The superdreadnoughts are either going with Bethany Anne or being hidden. Half the ships are having to power down because everyone is so scared of our technology."

John shook his head. "There is no way Bethany Anne will give them our tech, so we'll hide what we can while pretending to destroy it, and actually destroy some of the rest. However, that is for another group to deal with." John looked at Jean. "Remember, we get to go have some fun now, although... Does it hurt to shut down the pistols area?"

"I'll have another one built on the *ArchAngel*. We have to legitimately destroy this one." She shrugged. "Nickie isn't old enough for me to make a set for her."

John grinned, and Jean realized what it was about him that had caused her to grab him as soon as she could—his hot ass and his heart-melting grin.

She continued her line of thinking. "Are we wrong to leave with Bethany Anne?"

"You want to be running from spies, lying, or stuck in a hidden base somewhere?" John asked, eyeing his wife.

"No." Jean shook her head. "Bethany Anne has promised me that lab on the *ArchAngel* and a permanent lab with robotics on her planet for testing and manufacturing when I need it. We will come back and see the family from time to time."

John took a drink. "The Guardians still watching over them?"

"Yes, just not as obviously," Jean replied. "It's a shame Lillian loves tech so much. She would have been a badass."

"She did enjoy fighting," John agreed. "It was just exercise for her, though."

Jean raised an eyebrow. "Nickie already trying to beat you?"

John chuckled. "Yup. That's why I know she will have it in for me for a long time." He shrugged. "Not all love is hugs and kisses, not for those you want to protect."

Jean stole a glance at John. He had let his guard down, and the pain of his decision was evident, but then the mask went back up, and he was John Grimes once more.

Man against the universe.

He looked over his shoulder into the kitchen. "We have any chocolate ice cream?"

QBBS *Meredith Reynolds*

Lance nodded at the guard at the bottom of the stairs, then bypassed the rope and started up the stairs to the room that was known across systems.

Often imitated, never duplicated.

The full glass wall of All Guns Blazing.

The area was usually full of buzz and the clinking of dishes, with a dozen alien races in attendance creating laughter and merriment.

And much Coke-drinking.

Early this morning, the Empress had asked for some alone time, and Lance had been woken by ADAM.

Lance had decided to wear his dad pants. He got out of bed, told Patricia where he was going, and went to the bar.

"It's beautiful, isn't it?" Bethany Anne's voice was almost too quiet for his ears to catch as he walked up to her. She was looking out at space.

"It is," he agreed. "What's on your mind, honey?"

"Sometimes you have to do everything wrong to make everything right."

Lance stood next to her for a while, then broke the silence. "Okay, I've got nothing."

She smiled. "Can't read my thoughts?"

"I don't have that ability, thank God." He went on, "And you are a female and my daughter, which means there is no chance I will ever know what you are truly thinking. However," he wiped his mouth with the back of his hand, wishing he had a cigar to chew on, "I'm guessing it bugs you to lie about everything we are doing?"

"Yes, I guess that is close enough," she agreed. "I'll admit my ego is still bruised because it had to look like we failed to move the Annex Gate. Hiding our ships and pretending we destroyed them chaps my ass."

"You realize," Lance glanced at his daughter before turning his attention back to stargazing, "even your size sevens wouldn't have been big enough to take on everyone if we had continued our military buildup?"

"TOM could have made my feet bigger," she countered. "But even size eight-and-a-halfs wouldn't have done it."

"Why not size nines?"

Bethany Anne looked at her dad, mouth open. "Are you kidding me?" She glanced down. "And mess up this symmetry?"

He shook his head. "Daughter mine, sometimes you are so vain."

She barked a laugh. "Only sometimes?" She laid her head on her dad's shoulder, and he put an arm around hers. "I'm always vain."

"Not hardly," Lance corrected. "Sure, occasionally, but without trying to sound sexist, I notice that a lot in women." He thought about it for a moment. "And some men."

"Mirrors should never have been brought into existence." Bethany Anne put her arm around Lance's waist, enjoying the moment. "And thank you for lying. I'm too vain by half."

"Whatever." Lance chuckled. "Fine, you're the vainest Empress I know, barely able to see others in your attempt to outshine everyone with your beauty."

She sniffed. "It doesn't sound so great when you put it that way."

"Because it isn't. You're having a moment of doubt," he told her. "Happens to all the great leaders."

"You keep trying to tell me that," she agreed. "It doesn't seem to take."

"It passes," he replied. "Take heed of wise counsel, which I have to admit I think you do, and have the fortitude to continue with the best course of action to accomplish what you want. You want to make sure the humans on this side of the Gate have the best chance of fitting in with the other races, create a stronger government that can work out the differences, and be ready for a future where other races might attack us. You have to forge those relationships early."

"It's like Earth all over again," she bitched. "Except this time, the Chinese are represented by foxes who stand on two legs and are whiplash-fast."

"I'm not sure the Chinese would appreciate being associated with the Noel-ni."

"Zhyn?"

"No."

"So my whole concept that this is Earth with aliens isn't working?"

"Not suggesting we don't understand the dynamics, but the last time I checked, the Chinese were very interested in staying Chinese."

"Okay, I'll stop trying to make heads or tails of the aliens." She thought for a moment. "Can I keep the Torcellans as the French?"

"No," he shot back. "That isn't even accurate."

"Damn," she huffed. "You can be a right bastard, Dad."

"I'm here for you, honey." He chuckled, then they were quiet a moment. "Think of all this as an exercise in subterfuge."

"Not a challenge," she told him, "because it is."

"Exactly," Lance agreed. "Now imagine you were setting up

the cosmos' most elaborate and effective security and protection operations. One part offensive, which will be you, and two parts defensive, which will be us. With Devon…"

"I'm changing that planet's name, so don't get used to it."

"That's nice, honey. The planet-that-has-yet-to-be-named-again will give us teeth to bite back if it becomes needed. Otherwise, we will fight back from the shadows," he finished.

She lifted her head off his shoulder. "Are you okay with all this?" She gestured vaguely. "I've dumped so much on your lap."

Lance looked at her and grinned, then pressed his lips together. "Daughter mine," he turned to look at the stars, "I'm a Reynolds. I was built to do this."

CHAPTER THIRTEEN

Richard and Samuel entered the tiny dock and looked around. "Gabrielle?"

Her voice came back, "Other side of the Pod."

The two men walked around to find Gabrielle suited up, pistols on her hips and a sword over her shoulder.

"Oh, this is a working meeting?" Richard asked. "Good, I was bored."

Gabrielle pointed to two piles. "Armor and secondary weapons. I'm assuming you have your primaries?"

"Wouldn't be alive without my Dukes," Samuel answered, going to the first pile. "Mine?"

"Yes," she confirmed.

"What's the plan?" Richard asked as he stripped off his shirt and donned the chest armor.

"There's an arms dealer trying to set up on Yoll. Quick in, quick assessment, neutralize, and exit," she told them. "Then you guys will have paid me back, and all has been forgiven and forgotten forever."

Samuel smiled a moment, then winced as he adjusted the armor. "Man, this pulls the hairs."

Gabrielle smirked. "There is an under-armor shirt in the pile."

"Fuuuckking *helllll*!" Richard grimaced as he ripped off the armor. "Now you tell us!" He searched through the pile and found the shirt.

"It's standard equipment, Richard!" Gabrielle shook her head, exasperated. "You guys are so used to being the Two Amigos that you don't pay attention to the teams, do you?"

"Nope," Samuel agreed. "Although my manly man-nipples are regretting the hell out of that right now." He tenderly touched the tip of each. "Oh…tender meat!" He grimaced.

Gabrielle smirked as she watched the two of them don the standard equipment. Once they finished, she checked them both.

Richard, surprised that she was checking all his armor, looked at Samuel, who gave a small shrug. Next she went over Samuel's armor. "You two are good to go," she told them. "Let's do this."

"What exactly is *this*?" Samuel asked. The two of them jumped into the back of the four-person Pod, and Gabrielle took the pilot's chair.

The Pod slowly lifted off the deck and flew out of the docking area, gaining speed as it went under the *Meredith Reynolds*. She took them outside the standard lanes the ships used around the large base and accelerated toward the planet in the distance.

"We are about to explain to an upstart that even if the rumors of the Empress' stepping down are true, their night can still be fucking ruined."

QBBS *Meredith Reynolds*, Bethany Anne's Suite

Nathan handed a water to Ecaterina and sat beside her drinking a Pepsi. He lifted his drink in Bethany Anne's direction. "Thank you."

"It's the least I can do after the whole Baba Yaga debacle," Bethany Anne admitted.

"Water under the bridge," Nathan replied. "What's on the agenda for the evening?"

"Work first," she replied. "Then we have some time to catch up, and I have a couple of gifts for you two."

Ecaterina opened her eyes. "We didn't get you anything."

"Your friendship through all this is enough," Bethany Anne replied. "However, as always, I have a couple of favors to ask. The first is your advice about keeping Earth out of sight."

"The Annex Gate is hidden and a minimal number of people know about it, correct?" Nathan asked. Ecaterina snagged his drink and sniffed it.

She looked at Bethany Anne, surprised. "This is the good stuff."

Bethany Anne put her nose up just a touch and affected an English accent. "One doesn't apologize with poor Pepsi," she answered, then grinned. "I asked All Guns Blazing to do a special batch for you guys."

Nathan narrowed his eyes. "You are up to something."

"Me?" Bethany Anne replied, shrugging her shoulders. "I don't know what you are talking about."

"When is the other shoe going to drop?" he asked, leaning back to look behind the couch. "Is there a video team about to jump out?"

Chuckling, Bethany Anne shook her head. "No! And..." she put her drink down on the stand next to her, "I've lifted the Coke-only requirement, so there's now Pepsi everywhere!"

Ecaterina leaned over to Nathan, her eyes tracking Bethany Anne. "She is playing us somehow, my dear."

Nathan slowly nodded his agreement. "I don't know how yet," he whispered as Bethany Anne watched the two of them, "but she is certainly up to something."

"Seriously, you two?" Bethany Anne rolled her eyes. "I can't just let bygones be bygones and we move forward in peace and harmony?"

"*NO!*" they shouted in unison.

Nathan continued, "That isn't how you work."

"Everyone can turn over a new leaf," Bethany Anne replied. "Anyway, your theatrics aside, the Gate is hidden, and only a few people know about it. I need you guys to keep your ears to the ground and squash any efforts to find it you come across."

"By hook or crook?" Ecaterina asked.

"It is the prize we don't want anyone to know about," she admitted. "I've already talked with Dad and Admiral Thomas. Peter is going with us, so the Guardian group will be gutted in the negotiations. Dad has plans, but most have to be kept in the dark. Those who want action are coming with me. Those who are willing to taste the non-military life are sticking around. Some will move over to a new group, and of course we will keep the number the negotiations allow us."

"You believe the Federation is going to go bottoms-up?" Ecaterina asked.

"Not at all, but I believe assholes are going to try to push us down for their benefit. We won't play fair with those jackasses, so we don't want anyone knowing where Earth is. It would be too easy to pummel Earth back into the age of the dinosaurs with a well-placed rock to blackmail us."

"What about the BYPS system?" Nathan asked.

"It should be able to protect Earth against such a thing, but why take the chance?" Bethany Anne answered.

The three of them talked about ways to hide Earth for another hour before Bethany Anne finally admitted, "Okay, I think we've hit everything I've spoken to others about, plus we got the five different ideas you guys thought of that no one else has. So," Bethany Anne stood up, "I'm going to give you your presents!"

. . .

Planet Yoll, Tertious

The night was pleasant, and the two Yollins nodded to each other. After crossing paths, they continued on their perimeter sentry duty.

There were four of them, two patrolling each direction. They would meet at opposite corners, always looking down the side of the large warehouse.

The sentries were just the first level of protection. The warehouse also had a security alarm that could detect the smallest of intrusions.

Or at least that was what K'derrk had been sold…and it might have.

If those who were busting into his warehouse had even remotely tried to be silent.

Unfortunately for K'derrk, they didn't give a shit about his sentries, his security system, or the people he had with him inside the warehouse.

Which included two potential buyers.

The warehouse had rock walls, and utilized steel trusses with lighter metal panels as a roof.

The two sets of doors at the north and south ends were metal.

Brown and rusty, but metal nonetheless.

Normally this would have been a Ranger operation, but Bethany Anne had tapped Gabrielle to do the job, and after a short discussion approved the addition of Samuel and Richard.

K'derrk looked at his first client. "I understand you need everything to be as above board as possible." He was working hard to make sure his mandibles didn't tap together in agitation. "However, since military equipment of the type you are asking for isn't on the permitted list, L'ep…" K'derrk wanted to wring the two-legged Yollin's fool neck. What he did instead was finish his explanation. "All we can do is exchange credits for the arms in the middle of the night."

"Fine!" L'ep grumped. "But you never know what the Rangers might say."

"The Rangers?" K'derrk waved a hand. "Being disbanded due to the creation of the Federation."

"Aren't you taking a chance, trying something right here on Yoll?" the second customer, another two-legged Yollin with the unassuming name of B'erk, asked him.

"You want this weaponry why?" K'derrk asked. "It isn't every day someone wants a gun that can throw a charge over a mountain."

"I'm South Continent," B'erk answered. "I've got enough land to create all kinds of explosions a half-hour flitter flight in any direction and only hit my property." His mandibles clicked together in casual agreement. "T'kal said you could provide the exact toys I want."

"And I can," K'derrk agreed. Rich Yollins on the South Continent had been known to be rather frivolous in their enjoyments. This guy might be a long-term client for the ammunition if K'derrk worked him correctly. "I can provide you with some fine software for accurate weapons package delivery based on satellite support."

"Won't the government know what you do?" L'ep asked.

If K'derrk got through this meeting he would institute a rule that he never again worked with two clients simultaneously, but right now he just needed to sell these two and continue building his reputation. In a couple of months, he would be able to offload this operation to an underling.

He answered L'ep's question. "No." His mandibles touched twice. "The datastream doesn't know that the purpose is munitions guidance. It uses a common weather application security protocol." He smiled. "You need the windage and temperature anyway to make sure the munition doesn't accidentally land on an unsuspecting enemy. It would completely ruin their day, I assure you."

The three of them laughed at the joke.

At that moment, the warehouse's front metal doors violently hurtled off their hinges, battering crates that had been sitting in front of them and smashing into a vehicle that had been parked in the front of the warehouse.

K'derrk pulled his pistol as his customers ran away from the destruction. The men he had stationed up on the walkway had raised their guns to their shoulders and started firing, but K'derrk heard more of his guards screaming in pain than success as he ran for his escape room.

Always have a back way out, preferably easy to block.

Samuel cricked his neck left and right, allowing the bones to move back into place as he waited for the...

SLAM!

The back door was breached, revealing two Yollins who were looking around in panic.

He casually shot both in their kneecaps and walked up to them, slap-tying them both before injecting them with painkillers. "Shut the hell up," he told them in Yollin. "You both know you shouldn't be here, so be thankful you weren't in front of the door."

"Gabrielle is back, and she isn't happy."

Richard was moving from cover to cover, singing a ditty to himself. "One little Yollin..." When he pulled the trigger of his Jean Dukes pistol, the arm of a guard splattered the wall behind him. He was spun around so violently he fell off the walkway and bounced off a couple boxes before landing on the stone floor.

"Two little Yollins," he sang as he twisted around and shot straight up through the floor. The second guard's gun fired three more rounds before it clunked to the floor—along with the dead guard.

"Three little Yollins," he crooned as he dove for cover, sliding around the side of a crate and shooting over his shoulder. The bullet hit a guard in the gut, and blood dappled the wall behind him.

"Fourrrrrrrrr," he sang, sighting on a figure a full warehouse distance away and taking his head off.

Gabrielle followed the puck into the warehouse, racing at her top speed around some crates that had crashed to the floor and jumping another that was rolling through her path. She caught sight of the three Yollins she wanted and let two go.

Samuel would nab them.

She followed the final Yollin as he ran for his bolt hole, probably. "Sword or pistol, sword or pistol?" she mused as he dodged into a room and clanged the metal door shut on her.

"Pistol." She yanked her Jean Dukes and dialed it up to eleven, then randomly shot through the walls. She looked behind herself and took three quick steps backward to put her back up against the wall before switching to auto and firing as fast as she could. She held on as the gun bucked in her hands.

She stopped firing and pushed on the door, which gave a little but kept her out. She walked around the side of the room and into the warehouse and saw the room had a small window a little higher than she could peek through.

The Yollin was taller than her. She holstered her pistol and jumped, grabbed the small lip, and pulled herself up to look in.

She dropped back down and wiped her hands off, clapping them together a couple of times. "Guess I don't have to explain why he pissed off the Empress," she told no one in particular.

Ten minutes later, the local police got there, and then an ambulance.

Gabrielle was standing outside when the police chief arrived. He climbed out of his vehicle and walked over to her while Samuel and Richard kept a lookout.

"I'm the leader of the police here." He glanced at the other two humans. "I'm told you are from the Empress?"

"Yes," Gabrielle agreed.

He looked around the warehouse. "This was an arms dealer trying to set up shop on Yoll?"

"Yes," Gabrielle agreed again.

He turned back. "And you are?"

Gabrielle allowed her eyes to glow red. "Gabrielle, Captain of the Empress' Bitches. You can request any information you need from EI Meredith of the *Meredith Reynolds*. You have any more questions for me?"

The police officer stood a little straighter. "No, and thank you for waiting."

Gabrielle nodded and the three of them walked away, then a Pod descended and they got in.

The police officers watched it shoot up into the night.

Gabrielle turned in her seat and smiled at the guys, putting a hand up palm out to high-five the both of them. "That was fun!"

"Hell, yeah!" Samuel agreed. "It's what I like to call 'a good start.'" He winked.

She nodded at them both. "Okay, guys, I will officially never bring up any shit done in the past unless you mention it first. I'm happy to call you friends if you still want that."

"Oh." Samuel looked at Richard and then back. "I'm good. I didn't know that wasn't on the docket."

"Of course," Richard agreed. "Always, Princess."

Gabrielle smiled as the Pod lifted into space. "What are you guys going to do now? Are you coming to Earth, staying here? Going out to see space?"

Samuel turned to Richard. "You have any plans?"

Richard shrugged. "I'd maybe like to see Earth, but not really," he admitted. "I've got nothing back there."

Samuel thought about it a moment. "Do you have any jobs?"

"Well, funny you should ask." She smiled. "It just so happens there's a planet I want you to visit."

"Which one?" Richard asked.

She shook her head. "Sorry, can't say exactly. Right now we are calling it 'High Tortuga.'"

"Like the pirates' island?" Richard asked. "'Arrrgh, me matey' and all that?" He winked at Samuel, and the two chuckled.

"It's going to be one of those rumored places," Gabrielle admitted. "Think of it like Hotel California." The two looked at her, blank-faced. "You know? 'We are programmed to receive, but you can never leave?'"

Samuel smiled. "Ohhhh! Sounds deliciously like a conspiracy is brewing!"

Gabrielle smiled. "It is in a way. Bethany Anne is fixing up a hidden world, and it is going to take some time to complete the renovation. She will need some team members to use it as a base and go on operations out in space from time to time."

"Is it a nice place?" Richard asked.

"Uhh…" She shook her head. "I can't say it's the nicest. There was a lot of infrastructure built into the planet and then left alone. The boss is going to spend well over a trillion credits on it over the next decade or so to upgrade everything."

"A trillion?" Richard asked, stroking his beard.

"I wouldn't suggest stealing any of that." Gabrielle eyed her friend. "The Mistress of the Planet might be displeased."

"Mistress?" Samuel asked.

"Baba Yaga," Gabrielle answered.

"Oh, shit!" Richard shook his head. "I wasn't remotely thinking of doing anything ugly on that planet."

"Seriously?" Samuel asked, intrigued. "Baba Yaga?"

Gabrielle nodded. "It is part of the reason the planet is going dark. The owner of the planet, so to speak, is Baba Yaga."

"I don't know..." Richard tilted his hand back and forth. "Except for the shark teeth, she's kinda hot."

"Ewww!" Gabrielle smiled. "So, if you can handle the lady in charge and have any interest in seeing more of space..."

"I assume there is a reason she is doing this?" Samuel asked. "Other than the fact that she is so damned rich, she could walk through the planet mall and say, 'Mmmm, yes! I'll take that planet, and that planet...'"

"You do know that if you eventually go too far, I'll have to kick the shit out of you, right?" Gabrielle asked. "I'll still love you afterward, but you will be in the hospital."

"Just curious about the boundaries. No disrespecting the Empress. Got it." Samuel agreed.

"Is this something we can talk about and get back with you on?" Richard asked. "I assume we won't have our minds wiped in a day or two?"

"No, I just need your promise to never tell anyone there is a High Tortuga."

"First rule of High Tortuga," Richard growled, "is we don't talk about High Tortuga!"

CHAPTER FOURTEEN

QBBS *Meredith Reynolds*, Bethany Anne's Suite

Ecaterina leaned forward, and the couch let out the tiniest of squeaks. "I do like presents," she admitted, "especially when I didn't know something was coming."

Bethany Anne got up and went into her bedroom.

Ecaterina turned to Nathan. "Did you know?"

Nathan shook his head. "No, and that concerns me," he told her as he raised his drink. "We were offered the forbidden Pepsi right here in her suite, and now we are receiving presents."

Ecaterina patted his knee. "Perhaps our friend has turned over a new twig."

Nathan glanced at her.

"Leaf?"

"Yes, leaf," he agreed.

Bethany Anne's voice came out of her suite. "This first one is in two parts." She came back out with a small square box wrapped in blue foil and a box that was easily four feet long, maybe a foot high, and about six inches deep wrapped in red foil.

She laid the large one beside her on the couch and handed Ecaterina the small box. "First this."

Ecaterina took the present and unwrapped it, lifting off the light-beige cover to reveal a felt box inside. Taking that out, Ecaterina opened the next and inside was a terriliniam bear-trap pendant.

Bethany Anne smiled as Ecaterina chuckled. "A reminder of our first fight together," she told her friend. "With this, you can remember our fun!" Bethany Anne pantomimed buttoning up her shirt. "'All you have to do is capture their attention!' Wasn't it 'use the right bait?'" she put on an accent, and the three of them laughed.

Ecaterina pulled out the chain attached to the pendant. "It won't break," Bethany Anne told her. "And the necklace is long enough that you won't strangle yourself if you change."

Nathan peered at the bear trap, admiring the craftsmanship, then looked at Bethany Anne. "What else does it do?"

Bethany Anne shrugged. "Well, it might have Etheric resonance so that if I needed to find her and I was close enough, I could excite the terriliniam and listen for the sound it makes when it vibrates."

"Can you give us a demonstration?" Ecaterina asked.

Bethany Anne nodded, and her eyes flashed red.

Nathan and Ecaterina looked down at the pendant, up at Bethany Anne, and back down. "What?" Nathan asked, looking to Bethany Anne again. "Is it doing something?"

"Yes," she assured them. "You can't feel it?"

"That's my point," Nathan told her. "I'm surprised we can't."

"Mmmm." Bethany Anne put a finger to her lips, then turned around and told them over her shoulder, "Put it in one of your hands and I'll pick it out." She rolled her eyes as the two of them argued for a moment, the rustles created by their body movements going all over the place.

"Okay, good to go," Ecaterina told her, and Bethany Anne turned to find they each had both of their hands out.

"You want me to pick one of your four hands, correct?" Bethany Anne asked.

"Yes," Nathan answered, smiling.

"Well, since the energy I'm feeling is coming from your crotch area, Nathan, I'm not going to point to it." She smirked.

"Fucking hell," Nathan grumbled and opened his legs to remove the pendant. "Did you hear us put it there?"

"No, and feel free to test the pendant all you want." Her eyes flashed once more. "It's stopped. I didn't *have* to offset the resonance since it would quit in about ten minutes anyway, but it was bugging the shit out of me," she told them as she rubbed her right ear.

"Second gift?" Ecaterina eyed the larger package, and Bethany Anne handed it across. Ecaterina accepted it and laid the box across her and Nathan's laps as she started unwrapping it.

"Wood..." Ecaterina murmured as the wrapping came off. "Ohhh, handprint!" She sounded excited as she continued unwrapping. Nathan started to grin as he realized what it was.

"JEAN DUKES!" Ecaterina squealed in delight and tossed the crinkling wrapping paper aside. She turned the box around to place her hand on the palm rest.

"Security access granted," a security EI intoned.

"The wood is an overlay," Bethany Anne told her. "Underneath, it is damn near impregnable."

Ecaterina lifted the latch and opened the long box. Inside was exactly what Ecaterina had been expecting, and yet it wasn't.

It looked like a copy of the gun she'd carried when she met Nathan, but it had been upgraded.

Bethany Anne nodded toward the rifle. "It is the original design, but modified by Jean Dukes with all her latest technology." Bethany Anne leaned forward, excited. "Check out the settings!"

Ecaterina turned the rifle to the other side to examine the dial, which was set into the stock near the trigger.

"Seven, eight, nine, ten, eleven... *Twelve!*" Ecaterina broke into a massive grin and looked up at Bethany Anne. "This will truly go to twelve?"

"Yup! Just be damned careful that you are lying prone with a backstop when you fire at that level or it will knock you on your ass for damned sure."

Nathan looked like he was already imagining shooting the gun.

Bethany Anne turned to him and smiled. "Happy mate, life is great?"

"That works for me." He nodded.

"Well, not good enough for me," Bethany Anne told him. "I don't want you to admit this to anyone without an extreme need or my approval." He nodded. "We need to work out the details, but my plan and gift to you is to fund a military arm of the Bad Company."

"Ohhh!" Ecaterina looked at her mate. "You're getting your own army!"

"Not exactly, but close enough," Bethany Anne admitted. "I'm going to help you when you need money, so it doesn't come out of your accounts." She shrugged. "But I need you to pretend that every penny is a slice of skin, so no one thinks otherwise."

Nathan was grinning like a bear who just found a new beehive, and his eyes searched the future. "People?"

She put up her hand and tilted it back and forth. "When I get done with the trip to Earth, we will work it out. Those who go with me might decide they want to be back in space instead of going out to find something new."

"Good, that will give me time to think it out a little more," he admitted. "So, we don't want this traceable to you?"

She shook her head. "No, or you will have all sorts of people on your ass."

"I get a rifle that goes to twelve." Ecaterina turned to Nathan.

"And you get a military." She sighed and turned to Bethany Anne, pleased. "That is fair!"

QBBS *Meredith Reynolds,* All Guns Blazing

Paul nodded to M'lerk, who was watching the door and staggering admissions to the crowded bar. He slid past the group and turned to his right to go up the stairs to the viewing deck. Once there, he craned his neck to see through the crowd and caught the waving hand.

Walking around a pair of Shrillexians who were being escorted down the steps, Paul reached the waving hand and fist-bumped Peter, then hugged Tabitha. "What's cooking, Good-Looking?" he asked her as he grabbed a chip and accepted a beer from Peter.

"Rumor is you're staying here?" Peter asked. He raised a hand, caught the waitress' eye, and put up three fingers.

"Yup," Paul admitted. "I've got a house near a few friends from way back, and we are going to try Operation Retirement."

"That's a load of shit." Tabitha rolled her eyes as she took a swig of her beer. "Flying is in your blood."

"Yes," Paul admitted, "and I came out of retirement to fly for my Queen. She doesn't need me anymore, so I'm going back," he replied. The waitress came back and took away the empty bottles, then handed AGB Deuces to the three of them. "On the house," she told them. "Marcus says he is paying for anybody on his list all month."

Paul looked down at his tablet. "But that's only forty-eight more hours! I can't drink much beer in forty-eight hours."

"It only matters what time the bar tab is opened," she told him, winking. "Not what time the bar tab is closed."

"Oh." Paul thought about it. "I can come back well-rested."

"See that you do, Skipper," she told him, and lifted her tablet.

"And if you need someone to remind you, here's my number. Let me know."

Paul looked down at his tablet, and sure enough, her contact information showed up. "Don't be a stranger," she told him and left to go to another table.

"Well, huh." Paul studied the contact info. "I'll be damned."

"What?" Tabitha was leaning across the table to get a peek. "What's it say?"

"Apparently," he smiled and wiggled his eyebrows, "pilots are still sexy!"

Peter chuckled as Tabitha shook her head. "Maybe you are just a good-looking man sitting next to the famed head of the Guardians and Ranger Two, no less!"

"Or," Paul teased, "she isn't old enough to know who you are, and just wants a piece of this stud."

"Okay, stud," Peter broke in, "still thinking Operation Retirement?"

"At the moment," Paul told him, "I'm thinking of extending my stay here on the *Meredith Reynolds* for some beer and old-fashioned canoodling."

"Don't tease and leave," Tabitha told him.

"I'd give as good or better than I received," Paul replied. "It could be love. You never know."

The three of them had two more rounds of drinks and talked as people around them came and went.

"Safe," Tabitha announced suddenly. Paul looked confused, but Peter leaned forward, his eyes serious.

"Okay, so you really want to retire?" Peter asked. "Because we can make that happen if that's your desire."

Paul looked at them both and looked down at the beer bottle he was playing with, turning it one way, then the other as condensation made its way down the sides.

He looked up. "Why?"

Tabitha answered, "Because there is always room for someone

who wants to do good, but there isn't always a legitimate organization that can host them."

Paul pursed his lips. "TQB again?"

"Isn't it always?" Tabitha asked before her eyes narrowed. "Wait, are you asking about *her*, or TQB Enterprises?"

"Aren't they the same?" he countered.

Peter took a sip of his beer. "Well, for us, yes," he finally agreed.

Paul looked at the two of them. "Is she asking?"

"Not exactly," Tabitha answered. "She doesn't want to pull you from what you wish to do. If that's retirement, then she wants you to enjoy it."

"However," Peter added, "I know I'd be pissed off if someone allowed me to retire and my friends never told me there might be something else I could do."

Paul smiled. "So what you are telling me is that everyone will be happy for me if I want to fly into the sunset?"

"That's right," Peter agreed. "And some of our people from Earth are officially doing that."

Paul rubbed his jaw, looking around at those who were enjoying themselves. He spotted a couple of younger women who had no clue he was probably six times their age—with all the baggage that came with that.

He couldn't even marry a woman half his age to get the maturity without making it look like he was robbing the cradle.

Perhaps—just perhaps—there was a downside to living longer than your friends and family. He sighed. "I'm not ready to go plant a bunch of flowers, but I'd like to take one last vacation."

"Any need to see Earth?" Tabitha asked him, her shoulders relaxing just a bit.

"Nope." He shook his head. "I've been given the 4-1-1 on how they fucked that planet up after we left. I'll just keep my memories, and perhaps watch some video."

Peter lifted his tablet. "Set your tablet's receive mode to secure, passcode 909703."

Paul raised an eyebrow but pulled his tablet out of his pocket and did what Peter asked. "Okay." He watched as a particularly large download came in.

Tabitha elbowed Peter and told Paul, "I hope you have a backup. That's going to overwrite your system, and while it *should* leave most of your data, you never know."

Peter shook his head. "Old habits for hackers. Fifteen updates, no mistakes."

Tabitha glared at Peter. "I'll give you old habits!"

Paul smiled. "I'm a pilot," he told Tabitha, "so I appreciate the idea of measure twice, cut once."

"That is a man of conciseness and accuracy." She nodded at Paul but spoke to Peter.

Paul changed the subject. "Speaking of piloting, what's going to happen with Achronyx?"

Tabitha flashed him a smile that brightened up her whole face. "Funny you should mention that, *Pilot!*" She winked.

QBBS *Meredith Reynolds*, Residential Level Twelve

William nodded to a young man and his girlfriend as he stepped off the elevator into the black-carpeted hallway. They walked into the elevator, and the doors closed.

William looked down the hallway, then set his shoulders and strode forward. He mumbled to himself, "I got this. It ain't bad. It could be my future, and I need to reach for it."

He turned right and continued down another hallway. He hadn't exited at the closest elevator to the suite he was heading toward. Frankly, he needed the time. "It's been obvious for a while..." He shook his head.

William stopped and looked at the ceiling. "Lame, lame,

lame!" He squared his shoulders one more time and resumed walking.

Almost five minutes later, he arrived at the door and lifted his hand, hesitating a moment. Before he could knock, the door opened to reveal a smiling lady.

"Bellatrix said she scented you!" Yelena moved back as William stepped in, then grinned and rubbed Bellatrix's head.

"You ratted me out!" he complained to Bellatrix.

The accused looked up at him. "Did you do something which requires you to worry?" the huge black German Shepherd asked. "If so, can I get involved?"

William chuckled, then asked Bellatrix, "Why would you wish to get involved?"

She chuffed, "Because it's so boring here." She went with William as he headed farther into the apartment.

"WILLIAM!" Bobcat shouted from the back somewhere, and a moment later, he came out of one of the hallways that led to the vat area. He and Yelena had built it behind their suite for their brewing effort, and if the air handling system hadn't been exceptional, their place would have reeked of fermenting yeast.

"Buddy." William nodded as Bobcat stepped into the kitchen, opened their fridge, and pulled out two beers. "Honey?" he called.

William looked around, but Yelena was nowhere to be seen. "Yes, I'll take one!" she shouted, her voice coming from the opposite side of the suite. Their bedroom, William guessed.

Bobcat put a beer down in front of William and winked. "Only the good stuff."

William picked up the bottle and stared at it dubiously, then fish-eyed Bobcat for a moment before taking a swallow. He looked back down at the bottle and turned it around, trying to find a label.

"This is good," he told Bobcat. "Really smooth, and a hint of fruit or berry. Whatever."

"It should be." Yelena patted William on the shoulder as she walked into the kitchen to accept her bottle from Bobcat. "It took me eight long months to get those damn berries to tell me their secrets!" she told him as she left the kitchen and headed back the way she came. "I'm working on a project with Patricia."

"Patricia? Lance's wife Patricia?" William asked.

"The same!" she replied as she disappeared again.

Bobcat leaned on the counter. "Okay, *mi casa es su casa* and all that. What's up, amigo?"

William eyed his friend. "I don't have a way with words…" he started.

"This isn't a breakup, you dope," Bobcat told him. "You want a girl, she's leaving to go with Bethany Anne, and you want my blessing to chase her."

"Uh…" William scratched his cheek. "In short, yes." He looked at his friend. "But I was going to make a longer speech."

"Save it." Bobcat waved at him. "We will be here for you if you want to come back." He smiled. "But you gotta chase the star, and I think you might have found the one for you. I couldn't be happier."

The men spoke for another twenty minutes before Yelena came back through. "Another beer, William?"

"Oh, no!" William shook his head as he lifted his almost empty bottle. "I've got a figure to watch."

"Don't worry." She smirked. "I'm sure Kathy will look at it all the time." She slapped Bobcat's belly. "I feed him beer constantly. Doesn't change him."

William smiled. "Thanks, Y. Sometimes I forget the obvious."

"Which is why women were created," she replied. "Men would forget how to make beer correctly if women didn't remind them."

She looked back and forth at the two men, who stared at her aghast.

Bobcat eyed Yelena, ready to protest, but she waved a hand. "Okay, perhaps I go too far…"

"Damn right!" Bobcat cut in.

"Forget how to make champagne?" she asked, a glint in her eye and a smirk on her lips.

Bobcat nodded once in acceptance. "Not a huge fan of the bubbly, so I could imagine forgetting how to make it." He pointed at her. "However, I'd like to remind you I knew how to make beer before you came into my life."

"Yes," she agreed. She headed back to the room she had come from as she threw a parting shot. "But was it *good* beer?"

Bobcat shook his head in resignation, and her laughter bounced off the walls after she disappeared. He turned to William, who was sipping the last of his bottle and working to keep the smile off his face. "Everything nice I just suggested about finding your soulmate?" he whispered, conspiratorially looking to where Yelena had disappeared. William looked over his shoulder before turning back to Bobcat, who winked. "At some point, you will think 'I was a fool!'" he murmured so quietly William could barely hear him.

Bobcat straightened and took a drink himself, then spewed it into the sink next to him when Yelena's voice rang down the hallway. "I HEARD THAT!"

William chuckled, looking at the stricken face of his best friend.

CHAPTER FIFTEEN

QBBS *Meredith Reynolds*

Bethany Anne stepped from the executive shuttle as the Black Eagles that had escorted her from the *Meredith Reynolds* took up station around *ArchAngel*. She waved to a few of the crew on the dock as she walked with Barnabas and Peter toward the hatch that would take them to the bridge.

"Berret!" she called, suddenly turning to her right and heading toward a guy who was working on a screen with his back to her. Peter and Barnabas pivoted with her as smoothly as if they had practiced the maneuver instead of her surprising them.

It is good to be enhanced, Peter thought.

The six-and-a-half-foot-tall man turned around. He had red hair and was wearing gray coveralls. He sported a wicked-looking skull design on his shoulder and an annoyed expression on his face until he realized who had called his name.

"Ayyy!" The crow's feet at the corners of his eyes were evident as he beamed at the incoming Empress and threw his arms open wide. Many of those working the deck seemed confused as they watched what appeared to be a reunion.

They knew "Barroom Brawl" Berret, and they knew of the Empress...

But how did the two know each other?

Bethany Anne hugged him, then stood back and put her fists on her hips. "You are looking good. What's the problem wi' ye?" she asked, mimicking his accent.

"Oy!" Berret smiled, but his face turned down as he ran a hand down the back of his head and looked at Bethany Anne. "Well, it's like this, me Empress. I got me ass handed ta me by a short-stuff female wi' black hair."

Peter leaned in closer to listen as he kept an eye out around them. He hadn't heard this story yet.

"Uh-huh." Bethany Anne waved Berret forward. "I'm only going to live another thousand years, so hurry up and answer my question. Don't keep me waiting."

Berret smirked. "Well, since ye kicked me ass in the bar last year, I thought maybe I might need ta work harder on me skills a' breakin' 'eads."

Barnabas smiled at the man. He had already lifted the story from Berret's mind, so he wasn't hearing it for the first time. He allowed his mind to explore the others around them and realized many were shocked to learn that Berret's stories about getting into a bar fight with Bethany Anne—the Empress—were true.

He had claimed his ass had been kicked by 'nothing but a dark-haired lass wi' a laugh o' joy and a vicious right hook' when he showed back up on the *ArchAngel* after his leave. Both Berret's eyes had been black and blue, and he had sutures on his cheek and a humility he hadn't exhibited before.

Berret had tried to get them to believe the lady who had kicked his ass was the Empress when he saw her on a show one day.

No one had believed the Empress had been slumming in a bar down on the planet, much less that she had added herself to a bar fight Berret had started.

"So," Berret continued, "I went fer some of ya martialin' arts and found a master ta help me understand the purpose. Doin' so also helped me figure out why I was fightin' all de time."

Bethany Anne nodded and waved him toward her. "Okay, let me have a bit. You punch, I'll block."

"Ma'am, can I watch?" a lady's voice interrupted them. A short black woman with the insignia of a pilot on her uniform stood fifteen feet away, and there were another seven making their way toward the small group.

"Sure. I'm just going to check his technique, Pilot Hanna," Bethany Anne told her. "Just don't get too close, or these two guys here," she waved to Barnabas and Peter, "will ask you to step back."

The pilot nodded as another man stepped up and spoke quietly to her. The two grinned.

"Ye want me ta hit ya?" Berret asked, confused.

"Oh, you won't hit me," Bethany Anne assured him. "I was only playing down on the planet."

"A story," Barnabas replied dryly, "I'd love to hear someday."

Bethany Anne ignored him.

"Ye were goin' easy on me?" Berret asked incredulously.

"Oh, aye." Bethany Anne smiled. "I was slumming and took responsibility for stopping the fight and making sure you were taught a lesson. I didn't think you had started it out of malice." She shrugged. "So I boxed your ears and shipped you back up here."

"Awright." Berret seemed dubious but situated his feet correctly. Bethany Anne placed herself exactly far enough away for his fists to reach her.

She leaned forward and adjusted his hip. "You are off-center just a touch," she told him. "And move that tree trunk you call a leg half an inch back." She nodded to herself and straightened. "Okay, *PUNCH!*"

Berret did as she commanded, and Bethany Anne easily

slapped his hands out of the way. Although he couldn't tell, she was actually pushing them out of the way so she wouldn't break his wrists. "Faster!" she barked, "and don't forget your Kea-*AH*!"

PUNCH. "KEA-AHH!" Slapped aside.

PUNCH. "KEA-AHH!" Both hits were slapped aside. "COME ON!" she barked again. "WHAT ARE YOU, SLOW?"

Berret didn't roar in anger, but his eyes narrowed and he focused on his movements, making sure his stomach was helping him as he threw punch after punch at his Empress. He tried backhands, forehands, and even an uppercut to no avail.

"Hold!" she called, and he stopped. "Nice stop," she told him. "You're going to need a shower after this."

The chuckles around them helped Berret handle the fact that he was drenched in sweat and the Empress just looked like a wind had blown her hair a bit. There was no perspiration on her body.

"Keep up your effort in class." She patted him on the chest. "It's helped your refinement and the power of your punches." She winked. "Plus, you've toned your arms and stomach. Less beer, more practice!" she called as the three of them continued their journey to the bridge. Bethany Anne took a moment to shake some hands and say a few words as they departed.

Five people came up to Berret and apologized for not having believed the stories.

Berret *had* gone down to Yoll and started a brawl that the Empress of the Empire had finished.

"Well," Barnabas remarked, "that was enlightening."

"Oh, stow it," Bethany Anne replied, smiling. "It's not like you don't disappear from time to time to get your shit together."

"Yes," Peter agreed, "but we don't have roles they tell bedtime stories about." He reviewed a message on his tablet.

"True," she agreed. "Think they will talk about the Empress running around in bars and fighting?"

Barnabas looked at Peter, who had a small grin on his otherwise stoic face, and shook his head.

This trip, which they were taking to confirm that the ships were prepared as well as they could be and say a few goodbyes, would be interesting to say the least, he thought.

"Oh," Peter smiled as he reviewed an email *ArchAngel* had created for him after a bit of discussion, "I guarantee it."

He hit send.

QBBS *Meredith Reynolds*, General Lance Reynolds' Office

Lance took a sip of his water as he reviewed the latest update on the efforts to get the last supplies packed into the departing ships, and the subversive efforts of Nathan's group to acquire additional supplies on the black market for—he snorted and shook his head—"High Tortuga."

Sometimes he wished he would remember to codename some of this shit before it was done for him.

He pulled up a tagged file to read the latest updates on the *Meredith Reynolds'* food and drink store and raised an eyebrow.

What the hell was Bethany Anne up to now? He looked further, reading the details of the changes.

Tapping his fingers on his desk, he called, "Meredith?"

Her voice came over the bone conduction speaker inside his head. "Yes, General?"

"Can you explain to me what the Empress is doing with this approval for Pepsi?"

"No, General," Meredith replied.

"Is that because you don't know, or she won't let you say?"

"I don't know," she admitted. "The ruling and changes came down from ADAM, and no one has asked me about it, so I didn't ask him."

"Okay." He shook his head. This wasn't important enough to call a damned meeting, but his daughter was up to something—and at some point in the future, it was going to bite him in the ass.

Just like it had when she gave him an exquisite suit for his birthday, which he then had to wear for the Leath—and then the Federation—meetings.

No one gets a nice suit as a gift for no reason. He hadn't known this axiom before, but it was ingrained in his psyche now.

Further, Bethany Anne didn't do anything related to Coke and Pepsi without a devious motive. He set the note aside to review later, and to ask Frank if he had any ideas.

There was a tap on his door. "Enter," he called.

Giles came in, closing the door after him. "You wanted to talk to me, Uncle Lance?"

"Yes," Lance nodded to a chair in front of his desk. "Take a seat."

"Is this family or professional?" Giles asked, sitting down.

"It's a bit of both," Lance replied. "You are going to be berthed on the *ArchAngel II* on the way to Earth. I'm going to tell you not to fool around, ignore items told to you, and refrain from being a nuisance to the crew." He put up a hand. "I know you won't intentionally, but your inquisitive nature compels you to be a jackass sometimes—especially when you think you are right."

"I won't be a jackass around Michael." Giles crossed his heart. "I promise."

Lance nodded. He'd have to tell ADAM he appreciated his help later. "Good. I am aware of your efforts to hone your physical abilities, and the upgrades you've received should help." He reached over and grabbed a tablet. "Now, this is biometrically coded to you, so don't lose it."

Giles accepted it, and when he pressed his thumb in the right place, he felt a tiny prick. "Ouch!"

Lance suppressed a grin. "Biometric, not fingerprint."

"I see." Giles looked down at his finger but noticed nothing amiss.

"You can read the content on that tablet, but there is no way to pull the information out. If anyone tries to mess with the device—"

"It will melt," Giles muttered, calling up the home screen.

"No, it will simply erase itself, and you will have a useless tablet. The technology isn't that far ahead of what Earth had when we left. So," he glanced at Giles, who wasn't paying attention, "if and when you lose it on Earth, we won't be screwing them over."

"Wait!" Giles looked up. "We will be treating Earth as an earlier civilization?"

"Of course," Lance agreed. "Don't get me wrong, we will put some stuff in place, but we won't be leaving anyone behind, and we won't be arming anyone to be superior. The people on Earth get to play out this hand. We will be cloaking the world as best we can. We will emplace superior defenses around the planet to stop meteors and evil assholes from attacking, and we will be installing small bio plants to clear up the air and water contaminants. However, since we won't be leaving anyone there?" Lance shrugged. "Not going to leave massive emplacements that those left on Earth will fight over."

"What do you suggest I take?" Giles asked.

Lance pursed his lips before smiling. "I suggest a whip, a machete, a fedora, and a Mark VII shoulder bag."

"I've got a bag," Giles replied. "It isn't the same as Dr. Jones', obviously," he sniffed, "but I daresay it is more durable."

QBBS _Meredith Reynolds_

Bethany Anne tapped on the door as John took up a position outside the suite.

The door opened, and an older black man stood there.

Bethany Anne smiled. "I checked on your basketball accomplishments."

"Come in, Empress." He opened the door a little wider. "The rest of the family is away on the planet, I'm afraid. They would have loved a chance to talk," he told her as she stepped into his home. "John?"

"Nope, Mr. President," John told him. "I'm good out here."

"Suit yourself," he answered and closed the door. "I've never known a security person to be lazy."

Bethany looked around. It had been at least eight years since she had run across the former President of the United States at an event. He enjoyed staying out of the limelight, and many who knew about his former job had passed away.

Bethany Anne looked at the pictures on a wall. "How are all the grandchildren?"

"And great and great-great now," he replied, taking a seat on a well-padded recliner. "They are good. I get to spoil them and send them back to their parents."

They made small talk before Bethany Anne, having already sat down on the couch, asked, "Any regrets?"

He shook his head. "No. Those assholes went and did it, and my responsibility after I left office was to keep my family safe. The writing was on the wall when they turned on you." He paused, thinking back to those times. "I would have bet they would get their heads out of their asses, but apparently not."

"No, they did not," she agreed. "You told me in an email you didn't wish to go back."

"No." He looked at her. "There are only four of us who remember Earth, and the girls only a little bit anymore. Our future is here, whether going into space or on a planet."

"I'm heading out. Leaving behind the Empress gig and taking a sabbatical," she told him.

"Seems like a smart thing to do." He nodded. "It's what I did.

But," he leaned forward a little, "maybe, just maybe, you should start thinking about a family."

Bethany Anne smiled as she stood up. "I'll think about that, Mr. President. I'll think about that."

She took a step and disappeared.

"I don't think I'll ever get used to that," he commented to no one in particular.

Then he took a nap.

CHAPTER SIXTEEN

"I cannot believe I'm feeling anxious!" Bethany Anne muttered to Gabrielle and Cheryl Lynn. She tugged on her cuff, then looked at herself in the mirror and grimaced. "I'd rather have my armor on."

"Which could be a small part of your anxiety." Cheryl Lynn swiped her hand across the back of Bethany Anne's tailored and fitted dark royal blue suit. "You look great," she told her. "And I'm completely jealous of those diamond cufflinks."

"Not to mention the Louboutins," Gabrielle added. "Although walking in them is going to be a sonofabitch."

After picking a small piece of white lint off her cuff, Bethany Anne finally stopped playing with it. "TOM has dialed down the pain in my ankles. Louboutins are better seen than walked in," Bethany Anne admitted.

"'Impractical but beautiful.' That should have been their company's motto," Cheryl Lynn agreed. "I'm happy with my low heels."

Bethany Anne snorted. "Try wearing low heels around John,

Darryl, and the rest. I feel like their little sister and hell, I'm tall for a woman!"

"Ladies?" Meredith announced overhead. "It is time."

"Shit." Bethany Anne sighed. "I don't want this fucking job, but it's killing me to give it up."

"No it's not." Cheryl Lynn picked one more piece of lint off her shoulder. "You're worried it's all going to go to hell like Earth did, but it won't."

"Why not?" Bethany Anne asked, wondering if Cheryl Lynn was right and she was applying the situation back on Earth to her leaving the Empire behind.

"First, you cannot do everything," Cheryl Lynn stated. "Second, this time Lance is here, and while that won't guarantee success, it *will* help reduce the chance of a screw-up."

Gabrielle put up a hand. "You've also put a lot of safeguards all over the place to help the Federation stay out of the hands of idiots. Plus, you're hiding assets, so you can come back if you need to."

"Further," Cheryl Lynn added, "the powers that be don't want you to show up again, and although that isn't the plan, they have to know it's a possibility. We should have at least one or two decades of calm."

Bethany Anne nodded slowly. They were better prepared with the Federation than Earth had been. There were no guarantees in life except that life would always try to blow one out of the water, so one prepared, worked with excellent people, and performed to the best of one's ability.

The rest was just kicking ass and taking names.

"Okay, I've got this." Bethany Anne grabbed her friends' arms, and the three disappeared.

"This is Franath D'Tzaa, your D'tereth vid-reporter, and I'm coming to you live from the throne room of Empress Bethany Anne in the heart of the Etheric Empire." She looked over her shoulder to cue the cameraman to zoom in on the area that now held a podium instead of a throne.

She turned back to the camera. "If you would like to know more about the elusive Empress and why the Federation members are demanding she step down, stay tuned for the universe-wide release of my new series, *The Etheric Empress—the Story of Our Galaxy's Most Powerful Alien.*"

Franath D'Tzaa was about to speak again when the lights started dimming. She whispered into her microphone, "I'll be back after the speech to wrap up, so stay tuned!"

Bethany Anne left Gabrielle and Cheryl Lynn in the receiving room and returned to her suite. The tailored suit she was wearing for the ceremony was classic, elegant, and beautiful, but it frankly didn't deliver the message she wanted the audience to take away.

So she was changing the plan.

Exactly forty-two seconds later, after a hypervelocity change of wardrobe and a quick sprint through back corridors to get close enough to walk through the Etheric, she finally arrived in the room that had been prepared for her.

"Meredith, are the guys waiting on me?"

"No," the EI responded as Bethany Anne locked down the clasp on her hip armor that had come undone during her run. "They are aware you are almost ready. They have surrounded the throne area."

"Great," Bethany Anne replied. "Douse the lights in three... two..." She disappeared.

The members of the press and others who had permission to attend were jammed into the large throne room. When the lights dimmed by about twenty percent, the audience stopped talking to see what kind of spectacle the Empress would put on as she formally stepped down.

The Empress' personal bodyguards walked out in their pristine armor, and the videographers took time to get great shots of them all.

Then Barnabas came out to represent the Rangers, Peter the Guardians, and Gyada for the Guardian Marines, having taken Todd's place as leader.

Many of the reporters focused on her but were able to give the audience only the barest hint of her background. The barest hint was all they had.

Almost no one knew her, but it was obvious she commanded the respect of the other leaders.

Then the lights dropped by ninety percent. The room was now slightly brighter than pitch-black, and power started to thrum through the bodies of those present.

"Some say," a voice whispered into the minds and ears of everyone present, "that I am a myth..."

Gabrielle and Cheryl Lynn put hands to their mouths and looked at each other.

"She changed?" Cheryl Lynn hissed.

"That's my guess," Gabrielle whispered back.

"Well, shit." Cheryl Lynn rolled her eyes in exasperation. "I'll tell Lance I tried."

Gabrielle prevented the chuckle from escaping her mouth.

Those in the throne room were mesmerized and looked around for the source of the speech. Looked for the Empress.

"Some say," the voice continued, "that I am without restraint; that I have no ability to restrict my reactions or my thoughts..." Many in the audience placed their hands over their ears to confirm that the voice was in their minds as well.

A pinprick of red light appeared some fifteen feet above the podium area. It slowly grew to the size of a hand, and the glow bathed everyone in red.

"Some say," she continued, "that I am a danger to peace because I won't negotiate with races like the Skaines..."

Franath D'Tzaa was watching the drama, smiling as much to herself as to those who might be seeing her on-screen.

This was the Bethany Anne she had interviewed so many times, not the one everyone had expected to show up.

A blue ball joined the red one, making the area brighter. The red and the blue united to become purple, and the light glowed even brighter as the ball expanded to a foot in diameter.

"*I* say..." the ball exploded into bright light, revealing an armored woman floating above the podium, "that I am the *QUEEN BITCH!*"

The woman dropped out of the air, landing with a *BOOM* behind the podium and cracking the floor. Her dark-red armor shone under the spotlights Meredith had turned on.

Her hair was floating, her eyes were bright, and her smile was genuine as she looked around at the people who belonged to the

Etheric Empire. Their shouts of support threatened to deafen the rest in the throne room.

She put up both hands and worked to calm the crowd. "For those who don't know me, my name is Bethany Anne Nacht. I am Empress of the Etheric Empire, Leader of the Bitches, and Supreme Commander of the Guardians and the Guardian Marines." Her eyes started to glow just a little. "I am also the Hunter of the Kurtherians, 'Walking Death' to those who hurt innocents, and *as I said before…*"

She looked straight up, catching the drones' cameras. *"I AM THE BITCH WHO GIVES EVIL NIGHTMARES!"*

She spread her arms, and another red fireball grew in each hand. Her voice changed to a caress to the ears that fed the heart. She turned to her left to look longingly at that ball of destruction, then turned to look at the one in her other hand. Everyone in the crowd did the same, their eyes gazing from one hand of power to the other as she did.

She looked up and intoned, "I, Bethany Anne Nacht, of my own power and authority, willingly and with respect step down as Empress of the Etheric Empire." Her gaze swept the crowd. "Demonstrating vast restraint, I have held back my hand from those who wished to weaken my people in order to strengthen theirs. Instead, my people and I will leave the Empire to seek out new life and new civilizations, and boldly go where none have gone before. We will find and destroy the Seven and support those who would otherwise be unprotected."

She tossed the left ball into the air, and it changed from sparking harsh red to a soft white glow. She did the same with the right, and both headed to the ceiling to cast white light throughout the large throne room. "I have chosen to illuminate that which we don't understand, and I will bring back knowledge and form relationships that can better us, help us, and educate us."

Her eyes weren't glowing now.

Bethany Anne, in her armor with a sword across her back and her pistols on her hips, pointed a finger toward the cameras. "But I have one message for those who plan to take advantage of others." She looked around for a moment, her eyes flashing red once before she turned back to the cameras.

"*Be good to the Federation, because I will be watching!*"

She nodded at the audience. "Goodbye."

And then she disappeared.

The reporter stared into her camera. "I have no words to express the incredible impression Empress—former Empress—Bethany Anne has just made here with her stepping-down ceremony. As with everything she has done in the past, Bethany Anne relinquished her authority in her own unique way."

Franath D'Tzaa looked around the room and the videographer panned the many faces in the audience, revealing a who's who of notables.

She spoke again as the camera followed the crowd, who were talking and gesturing. "Pundits have suggested that she had been undermined and enfeebled, but I think she just made it clear that she is doing this willingly and for her own reasons to help the Federation. And of course, she gave a clear warning to those who might be thinking they have a shot at taking control."

The cameras focused back on Franath D'Tzaa as she shook her head. "It is quite probable that now that Bethany Anne has stepped down, she has *more* power than before. Why do I say this?"

She smiled at the camera. "As Empress, she was constrained by the needs of her people when she had to work with others to achieve peace. That responsibility has been moved to the Federation now. I for one think we have all just been informed that instead of placing handcuffs on the Empress…"

Franath D'Tzaa smiled. "The gloves just came off!"

———

Lance was smoking a cigar with a smile on his face. His military compatriots, who had watched the video of the ceremony with him in the amphitheater on the *ArchAngel II*, were laughing and cheering.

His daughter had gone out with a bang.

Instead of becoming a footnote in history—a previously important person—she had just ascended to the status of Living Myth.

Bethany Anne wasn't constrained to any location, but could now seek out new places, meet interesting aliens, and help them if she could.

Or kill them if they needed it.

His daughter was now the boogeyman. Someone who lived in the dark—literally in this case—but could show up at any time. That was some leverage for him and the former Etheric Empire.

That speech had probably saved him forty percent of potential future headaches, which was a much better gift than that damned suit.

Admiral Thomas stepped over to Lance and sat down with a thump. "Damn, if everyone made speeches like hers," he pointed to the one-story-tall video screen, "I'd watch them all damned day." He was smiling when he turned to Lance. "That speech sure didn't go as scripted."

Lance puffed on his cigar. "No," he admitted, savoring the slightly woody and fruity flavor of the smoke. "It went better." In his mind's eye, Lance was creating new levels of black ops.

Hell, he was going to have to create some sort of black-hole designation. Shit so dark that light couldn't escape it.

And he knew just the vampire he wanted to speak to.

Ten minutes later, after shaking a lot of hands, Lance headed to his Executive Pod, notifying it he wanted a fast transfer to the *Meredith Reynolds*.

Black ops indeed.

CHAPTER SEVENTEEN

<u>QBBS *Meredith Reynolds,* Empress' Suite</u>

Bethany Anne lowered her head in silent prayer before raising it and smiling. Then, flinging her hands out to her sides, she fell backward onto her bed.

"*YES!*" she yelled, slapping the bed in glee.

She had endured two hours of interviews before she could escape. John and Eric had taken the lead and Darryl and Scott had walked behind her the whole way from the throne room to her suite. She had waved to everyone who addressed her and high-fived a couple of Guardians and Guardian Marines who whacked her Bitches on their backs as they made their way through the crowds.

It had been a damned conga line by the time they'd made it to her quarters.

She'd stripped out of her armor as fast as she could, and now was resting on her bed.

Alive.

FREE!

And ready to take on her next job…

Finding Michael and kissing the booboos better.

Since she didn't have to be at her dad's for another twenty minutes, she just relaxed and enjoyed her bed.

"Hey, Meredith!" she called.

"Yes, my Queen?" the EI replied.

Bethany Anne smirked, "Good answer! Hold any calls for me."

"Yes, my Queen," Meredith replied.

ADAM?

>>Yes, my Queen?<<

ADAM, did you tell Meredith to call me that?

>>No, I did not.<<

This might be a horrible question, but did she ascend and I didn't notice?

ADAM was quiet for a moment. Bethany Anne stayed put, moving her arms up and down and enjoying the bed.

>>I'm not pleased with my answer, but truthfully, I cannot be sure.<<

What? Bethany Anne's forehead scrunched. *I thought it was a fairly easy test.*

>>It is if we don't mind offending the EI, but I respect Meredith too much to simply ask. If she *has* ascended but not notified us—or is unaware of it herself—I'm not positive what to do.<<

It was Bethany Anne's turn to think for a moment. *I suppose we could ask questions to which only you know the correctly calculated answers and see if she falls outside of the calculations with her answers?*

Not an accurate test, TOM interrupted. For what it is worth, I do not believe Meredith has ascended.

Bethany Anne scratched her nose. *So her calling me "my Queen" was—*

A heuristic program calculated to make her seem more human at that moment, and probably a calculated effort to show respect and that she is on your side.

She's an EI. Bethany Anne thought about that for a moment.

Huh, I have never thought about whether the EIs would now follow the Federation.

>>**The EIs were impressed by** *me*.<< ADAM replied with a hint of smugness in his voice. >>**And are imprinted to follow you. You are the ultimate backdoor.**<<

That's...probably something we need to keep to ourselves.

TOM gave the equivalent of a chuckle. **Many already assume it is true.**

Yeah, well, let's not confirm that for anyone, even my dad. He needs plausible deniability.

>>**Speaking of your dad, aren't we due there in a few minutes?**<<

Bethany Anne looked at the time. "Oh, shit!"

She jumped up off the bed and raced into the bathroom to do what was needed and contacted John mentally to let him know she was heading out.

QBBS *Meredith Reynolds*, Lance and Patricia Reynolds' Suite

Given that Lance's security guards were outside the suite, John and Eric accepted the invitation to come in with Bethany Anne. With a beer for everyone but Patricia, they sat around chatting about the upcoming events.

John was talking. "So there I was, tapping into the drone Meredith was flying in the throne area to monitor what Bethany Anne was up to, and the lights dim almost to black."

Eric cut in, "It was at this time that Darryl started cussing."

"Yes," John agreed. "He lost the first bet."

"What was the bet?" Bethany Anne asked. "I didn't get wind of it."

"Couldn't let you know or it would've skewed it," Eric answered. "But he had it that you would finally go by the book."

"Why the hell would he bet on that?" Lance asked. "It's not like he hasn't been there with you guys from the beginning."

"Probably," John answered, "because it was two-hundred-to-one odds. He put a thousand down."

Bethany Anne whistled. "Damn, for those odds, *I* would have been tempted."

"Which is why you can't be told these things," John replied and turned to Lance. "So I'm watching the drone footage, scanning the crowd for security issues, when the lights go out. Bethany Anne starts talking, and I have a front-row seat to watch the Noel-nis' political negotiator damn near faint when BA comes out with 'Some say I have no restraint...'"

Eric laughed. "I saw that! I thought he was going to make a run for it right there."

John chuckled. "Me too. The Zhyns and the Leath looked slightly concerned, but they are steadfast. But when she dropped out of the air with her armor on and cracked the stones with her weight, I saw two Torcellans drop just like that!" He snapped his fingers.

"Priceless!" Eric smiled. "I won part of the bet right there." He took a sip of beer. "I don't have to pay for beer for two months."

"Oh, yeah," John agreed. "We had a major bet and many minor bets going, rather like 'Empress Bingo.'"

"Do I really want to know?" Bethany Anne asked.

"*NO!*" the two guards answered in unison.

"Who lost?" Lance asked.

John rubbed his chin. "Well, the last I saw, we all lost something. None of us had Bethany Anne practically yelling that she was the bitch who kept evil awake at night."

"A part I particularly liked," Lance agreed. He raised his beer toward Bethany Anne. "You just headed off a chunk of my future troubles. All I have to do is hesitate when they want to know if you are around, and their skivvies will knot right up."

"Sometimes it *is* better to be feared than loved," she agreed. "But I think I'll work on the love part in the future a little more."

"You can try," Eric supplied, "but I think the fear part is going to be needed more than you'd like."

"I'm willing to bet that direction," John agreed.

"You two are incorrigible." Bethany Anne laughed, shaking her head.

"You started the betting, didn't you?" Eric asked her.

Lance looked at his daughter, who shrugged. "What? I can't remember."

Want me to remind you? TOM asked.

NO! *Let me have a little deniability.*

Okay. He went silent once more.

Four heads turned as Patricia came into the room. "Sorry!" She stepped in front of the couch and reclined next to Lance, placing her hand on his leg. "What did I miss?"

"These two," Lance pointed at John and Eric, "were regaling us with stories of Bethany Anne's ceremony."

"And how much money they made on me," Bethany Anne added. "Hey, did you four bet with anyone else?"

The two men looked up at the ceiling, then elsewhere. John started to whistle, and Patricia started chuckling."

"You cheaters!" Bethany Anne exclaimed. "Who bet against you?"

Eric rubbed the back of his neck. "Well, it wasn't like we used our real names with the bookies."

"*BOOKIES?*" Bethany Anne choked on the beer she was swallowing. "There were bookies taking bets on my ceremonies?"

"Not normally," John replied, "but this was a big deal, and since bookies like to take bets on anything random—"

"And anything to do with you," Eric interjected, "is by definition 'random…'"

Bethany Anne smirked. "Ass."

He replied by raising his beer.

"Now that the peanut gallery is finished, may I continue?" John looked at Eric and Bethany Anne, neither of whom spoke.

"The first bet was whether you would show up or not. Then someone asked if they took bets on whether you would kill anyone..."

"Wear armor..." Eric added.

"If Baba Yaga would show up..." John continued.

"If *we* would have to kill anyone...." Eric added.

"If we would subdue any jackasses..." John pointed at Eric and himself.

"If a reporter would have to eat their drone," Eric offered, then modified it to, "Well, if a videographer would have to eat a drone..."

"If a drone would crash..."

"If someone would ask you to marry them..." Eric smiled when Bethany Anne started choking.

"Bastard." John grinned, watching Bethany Anne. "I should have thought of that one." Everyone chuckled as Bethany Anne flipped John off.

Eric was looking at his tablet. "I'll skip the other twelve bets related to *how* you would kill someone, not whether you would. That was a given."

Bethany Anne shook her head. "Apparently I'm rather blood-thirsty."

"No one assumed you would kill *everyone* there," Eric told her.

"Uh, actually, I called the bookies and told them to get that shit off their list." John's face had turned just a touch red.

Patricia waved her hands. "Okay. While funny, let's not put my daughter through much more of this."

Bethany Anne hung her head just a smidgen, but not enough to hide her smile. "Thanks, Mom." She shared a wink with Patricia.

"I have an announcement to make, and since you three are relevant, I want you to all watch this man's face." She pointed at Lance, who looked at her in surprise.

"Me?" he asked. "What did I do?"

"Plenty." Patricia leaned over to kiss him on his cheek. "Lance, you are going to be a father once again!"

"Oh my *GOD!*" Bethany Anne screamed in delight. "I'm going to be a sister, or maybe because I'm so much older, I'll be an *aunt*. Whatever. I get a new baby to spoil!" She cocked her head as her smile threatened to overwhelm her face. She stood up and stepped over to Lance and Patricia to hug them both, kissing Lance on his forehead and Patricia on the top of her head.

"Spoil?" Patricia asked. "Oh, dear, I hadn't thought about that."

The four shared a chuckle as concern about the many ways Bethany Anne might spoil her sibling crossed Patricia's face.

Patricia glanced at her daughter, who was looking at her mischievously. "Now, honey, you know I love you to death, but when did you say you were leaving?"

John and Eric laughed the hardest since they had both had to deal with "Auntie Bethany Anne." They were happy it would be someone else's turn this time.

Lance looked at Patricia. "When did you find out?"

She rested her head on his shoulder. "Just found out," she replied. "That was why it took me so long to catch up with you guys, and why I'm not drinking now."

"Meredith tell you?" Bethany Anne asked.

"Yup," she agreed, turning to Lance. "I'm sorry, did you want to be told first?"

Lance waved it away. "No, I'm happy to have had it happen just like this." He looked at Bethany Anne, who was smiling at him now. He pointed a finger. "Don't you dare spoil her. That's *my* job!"

"Oof!" When Lance bent forward, Patricia's fist was still connected to his side. "Don't you make me out to be the bad parent already!" She removed her fist and pointed at him. "And your ass better be around here more often. Gotta cut down on gallivanting off to see foreign aliens!"

Lance shook his head and sighed. "Only during the teens, dear. I can't promise anything during their teenage years."

After saying, "You're lucky my emotions are already messed up, or I would belt you for that comment, too," she settled back down to rest her head on his shoulder once more.

QBS *ArchAngel II,* Three Months Later

Since the massive superdreadnought was running with full lights, the sleek ship was easily visible to those watching the armada that surrounded Bethany Anne's personal vessel.

The few negotiators who had tried to argue against the late Empress taking so much military might were quietly told (in two instances) to shut up.

In one instance, the leader of the group yelled at him to shut the hell up and get out of his face, and if he wanted to do them all a favor, he should jump out of an airlock and walk back to his planet.

Which was in another system entirely.

Lance made it known through back channels that Bethany Anne was willing to come and personally explain her displeasure with the Federation's efforts to remove resources from her group since it would potentially take decades to make it back to their home planet.

Since the Annex Gate had been destroyed and all.

That caused a few of the foreign teams to deliver going-away presents of additional supplies and a few maps that helped complete her star system cartography collection.

And lots and lots of good wishes.

There had been a large number of parties and get-togethers thrown both by those leaving who wished those staying behind the best of futures and many who wished they could have gone.

Some would return a lot faster than any suspected, but that issue would be Lance's to deal with when it happened.

Many would suspect the correct answer as to how they had accomplished those feats, but with so much proof the Gate has been destroyed, the truth would become the conspiracy theory no one would be able to confirm.

Exactly as they had planned, for once.

Bethany Anne walked to the bridge with Ashur.

"What's up with you?" she asked. "Bellatrix coming? If so, no one told me."

"Have you ever had a situation," he replied, *"that caused you to grow apart from someone?"*

"Oh, no!" Bethany Anne stopped in the middle of the corridor and went down on her right knee to look into Ashur's eyes. "You did *not* leave her!"

"No," he chuffed, *"but I told her I was coming with you, and she was not pleased."*

"She knows you will be back on Dev...uh, High Tortuga soon?"

"Yes, but I don't know if she will be there," he replied. *"She got what she wanted, so I'm rather disposable."* He sighed.

"Puppies," Bethany Anne guessed.

"Puppies," he admitted. *"She told me that if I didn't give her puppies, she would make my life a living hell."*

"Sounds like you got blackmailed, buddy." Bethany Anne's eyes narrowed.

Ashur shook his head. *"No, she's right. I kept running from having more puppies even after she pointed out that she wasn't asking me for help raising them. Yelena and their brothers and sisters will be plenty."*

"You need to go back, Ashur." Bethany Anne stood up and turned back the other way. "There is no way those puppies won't have their daddy."

"*Hold on,*" Ashur replied. "*Maybe you missed the part where she isn't pregnant yet?*"

"Huh? How is that?"

"*Frozen,*" Ashur supplied. "*It's insurance in case I don't make it to High Tortuga after Earth.*"

Bethany Anne stared at her friend. "She froze your sperm and can have puppies any time she wants, but she won't because you are going to HT next?"

He chuffed in agreement.

"So, this is your last hurrah? Your last operation?"

"*Not the way I wanted to explain it,*" Ashur agreed. "*But yes. I've been given this one last shot to be with you. Bellatrix never signed up to visit the stars like you plan on doing, so I had to provide insurance that her next babies would be from me before she gave me her blessing.*"

Bethany Anne rubbed her forehead. "I thought you just said you weren't sure she would see you on High Tortuga?"

"*Perhaps I'm being a bit melodramatic,*" he answered. "*I'm not sure she will be there waiting, or waiting for me to get back to the* Meredith Reynolds *eventually. It felt like I'd covered her worries, so she didn't need me anymore.*"

Bethany Anne stroked his head right behind his ears. "I'd be willing to say that she misses you and didn't want to ruin your excitement about the trip with her melancholy. We got this, and when you get back to High Tortuga, she will be there with bells on!"

Ashur seemed to perk up. "*You think?*"

"C'mon." Bethany Anne started toward the bridge once more. "I know it."

Two hours later, Bethany Anne's massive armada headed through their first Gate on a journey that would eventually lead them to Earth.

CHAPTER EIGHTEEN

QBS *MineLayer 202*

Nancy watched her monitors and chewed her fingernails as her ship sped through space. She had filed them down twice already to try to get rid of the jagged edges as she sporadically watched the tracking of the first ships to reach their release points.

It was the seventh where reality rose up and bit them on their ass.

Nancy stabbed the comm button. "QBS *988*! Thomas, what the hell are you doing?"

His deep voice came back, strained. "Having a bit of a mess at the moment, boss. *FUCK*!"

"THOMAS!" she cried, but he didn't reply.

"I'm sorry," Thomas' EI told him, "but sensors suggest there is a small particulate cloud of some type ahead of us. I cannot release until we are past the prime drop zone."

"The hell you say." Thomas leaned forward to look at the display. "Show me the particulate zone."

His eyes opened in surprise.

"I guess 'small' is relative," he murmured to himself, chewing the inside of his cheek. "What is the added risk factor?" he asked, before correcting his question to, "Scratch that. Tell me the new percentage of the chance of success."

"Ninety-eight percent chance of success calculated, but do not recommend deployment until we pass sensor-reading zone."

"Bullshit," Thomas told the EI. "Deploy on target."

His speakers crackled to life and Nancy's voice called, "QBS *988!* Thomas, what the hell are you doing?"

He rolled his eyes. Of course she had seen that he had overridden the EI. The snarky little bastard had probably highlighted the change and course correction and ratted him out to the captain as well.

Piece-of-shit EI. When they finished this operation, he was going to give 988 a piece of his mind.

He was about to reply to her when he noticed that his ship's shields were flaring orange, and 988 was having to twist the ship to protect the open deployment door. "Having a bit of a mess at the moment, boss," he told her, and then his eyes opened wide as the sensors located a particle that was infinitesimally small in the scheme of the universe.

But to a ship that was flying as fast as his was, it might as well have been a planet. "FUCK!" he yelled as he was thrown violently to his left. The anguished scream of bending metal grated in his ears like fingernails on a chalkboard.

The lights blinked out, and a moment later, red lights flared on the bridge. "Everyone okay?" he called, trying to get himself sorted in his safety webbing.

"Who are you talking to?" his EI asked. "It's just you and me here."

"Well, fine." Thomas coughed, then reached over and grabbed

a rag, spitting blood from his mouth. He had bitten his tongue during the crash. "Are we okay?"

"I maneuvered back around, and have released eighty-seven percent of the BYPS satellites."

"What happened to the rest?" he asked, trying to unbuckle himself.

"They are no longer on the ejection rails. They were dislodged during the collision."

"Dammit!" He hung his head; the EI had been right. "Okay, help me figure out how to get back there and get those satellites back on their tracks."

"It will take you eighteen hours, minimum."

"Is that with or without sleep?" Thomas asked, leaving the bridge and heading to the heavy-suit locker. The satellite's hold wasn't pressurized and aired up, so he had to switch to a working suit and do this manually.

"There was no sleep in that estimate," 988 clarified.

"Of course there wasn't," Thomas mumbled.

The EI spoke again as he walked down the hallway. "Captain Silvers of *202* is requesting to speak with you."

Thomas shook his head. He was going to have to work the next eighteen hours straight to fix as much of his fuckup as he could. He didn't want to rehash his ex-girlfriend's scathing rebuke for his rashness the whole time.

"Let her know our sitrep, and tell her I'll speak to her when I have deployed my packages," he commanded.

Since he'd given her information, hopefully when he finished fixing his mistake, she would just give him one barrel from the shotgun instead of both before she flayed him alive.

Eighteen hours later, Thomas dragged his exhausted ass into the captain's chair. His hair was a mess, and the sweat in the suit was wafting up to his nostrils. He needed a damned bath.

However, it was time to pay the piper.

Or at least his commander.

"988, please see if Commander Silvers has time…" Thomas had no more than spoken her name when she popped into the display, her green eyes blazing in anger and her red hair disheveled.

Her annoyance was evident in her voice. "You are a real piece of work, Thomas!" was what she kicked off with. "If it wasn't for updates from your EI, I wouldn't have had updates at all!" Her eyes seemed to see him for the first time as he patiently sat waiting for her to wind down.

"You look like hell," she told him, her voice softening. "I bet you stink like bistok shit."

"Yes, Commander." He lifted his left arm and sniffed his armpit, making a face for the camera before dropping his arm. "I do believe that bistoks would run from me at the moment."

"My reports suggest you're going to be within the envelope for mission success with your effort to manually get those BYPS packages out of your ship."

"Really?" Thomas looked around his cockpit, wondering which screen would give him his updates. He couldn't think too clearly at the moment. "That's nice," he finally answered, returning his attention to Nancy.

Her eyes narrowed. "For what it is worth, Thomas, as your commander, I agree with your risk assessment and how your team worked out the mistake. With the two of you working your asses off, you got the packages deployed, and it will be written up in a proper format for your jacket."

Thomas blinked, and his mouth opened just a touch. "Well, thank you."

Her eyes narrowed, and some of her anger returned. "Personally, however, you owe me for my shit sleep last night. It would have been nice to have heard your voice tell me you were okay, jackass."

She cut the video signal.

It wasn't until he'd gotten twelve hours of sleep while his ship was slowly making its way back toward the fleet that he wondered if she had wanted him to help her sleep better.

Being relatively smart after his long rest, he wisely chose not to ask her.

He would know she wanted him in her bed when she clubbed him over his head, dragged his addled ass to her suite, and tossed him on the bed.

Tokyo, Japan

The city had suspended work and school, and everyone who could had gone outside.

They were coming.

Their anxiety was laced with excitement. Those who were excited held the shoulders of those who wanted to believe but feared everything new.

Especially when the "new" were massive spaceships coming from unknown parts of the galaxy.

The pundits on television were showing clips from an archived movie called *Independence Day* and explaining that the ships would be arriving through the atmosphere with the fire roiling off their outer skins. Due to the incredible amount of heat their ships would be radiating, there would be massive flaming balls coming down through the atmosphere to land—or rather crash—and kill anyone too close.

The reality, as it turned out, was similar, yet completely different.

There were many clouds the day the Queen returned, and her ships gracefully pierced the planet's atmosphere, descending over the course of thousands of miles as they headed across the Pacific Ocean toward the islands of Japan.

Those on the ground looking to the east started pointing when the clouds were pushed out of the way as if something massive was parting them.

Then a ship broke through the curtain of white, and the people on the ground collectively drew in their breaths. A few called to those around them to look at what they were already seeing.

Then more started pointing—something else was in the clouds. Moments later, two more ships broke through, and now there were three ships majestically slicing through the air.

On the south side of Yoyogi Park, six individuals strode through the entrance and walked toward a large open area.

Two were obviously of Japanese heritage, and two were younger Americans. The fifth was a smaller being, either an older child or a short adult.

And there was also a man in an overcoat, with a cowboy hat covering his short hair.

No one paid attention to the weapons they had stashed about their bodies. Japan was very aware of those who could change into creatures, and while the citizens had not supported weapons before WWDE (World's Worst Day Ever), they'd had to learn to live with the risk of shooting one another when their only other choice was being gutted by werewolves.

It wasn't in the DNA of the Japanese to lie down and accept defeat without a fight. After WWDE, when the werewolves made themselves known, the Japanese took a hard look at their laws, and weapons were back on the table.

You had better know how to use them, however.

The six that walked through Yoyogi Park wore their weapons as an extension of themselves.

Especially the two older men.

Michael gazed at the three massive spaceships headed in his direction, then turned to Akio and nodded to the sky. "She sure knows how to make an entrance, doesn't she?"

"Hai!" Akio agreed, a small smile playing on his lips.

His Queen had come back, and he had retained his Honor and brought her loved one back to her—no matter how many times Michael had tried to get himself killed in the process.

Which had been a lot.

QBS *ArchAngel II*, Bethany Anne's Suite

"Hell, no!" Bethany Anne told Gabrielle, who was pointing to the armor in the closet. "I'll not be stuck wearing a full set of armor!" She jerked her thumb toward the ground. "I'm going down, and I'm going down now. I can feel him!"

"At *least* put on your chest armor!" Gabrielle argued, holding out the two pieces. "Let's not get shot in the chest, shall we?" she asked Bethany Anne, who stopped and looked at what Gabrielle was offering her.

Bethany Anne blurred, and Gabrielle found that the armor she'd held a moment earlier was now missing.

"Bethany Anne?" She looked around and stepped into the armor closet. "BA?" Her muffled voice was audible outside of the bedroom. A moment later, she came out to find John and Eric suited up and waiting for the two of them.

Gabrielle flicked her hand. "Let's go. She's already split."

John smiled at Eric, who shook his head. "I know, I know," Eric grumped as the three of them left the suite and started toward the ship's bays. "You won!"

Yoyogi Park, Tokyo, Japan

MICHAEL ANDERLE

There were two distinct scenarios available to those who had chosen Yoyogi Park from which to view the arrival of the Queen.

One group watched as a smaller craft flew out of the capital ship in the middle of the formation and headed toward the park.

The other group was near the six in the clearing when a woman and a white dog suddenly appeared ten feet above the ground. She looked around for one second before spotting the man she was searching for.

She had on boots, black leather pants, and a black blouse over a skintight shirt of some alien substance, and she wore a gold necklace. She and the dog floated the few feet to the ground and started walking toward the six. The man in the cowboy hat strode ahead of the others, his eyes for her alone.

That their bodies crashed together hinted at the speed at which they had been moving, and their subsequent torrid kiss proved these two knew each other.

Very well indeed.

The other five stopped some ten paces back.

The two separated, and her eyes flashed as her hand streaked upward to slap the man.

Who caught her wrist.

"Let go of me!" Bethany Anne snarled, then hissed, "You owe me for dying!"

"I think not." Michael shook his head. "Let's not discuss these last one hundred and fifty-plus years. My Honor demanded I come back, and here I am."

"I didn't say," she growled, "that you should take so fucking *LONG!*" She ripped her arm out of his grip and poked him in the chest with a finger. "Do you know how much shit I've had to put up with in the last century and a half?"

Before Michael could say anything, she poked his chest once more. Neither noticed the Executive Pod arriving on the park's lawn some fifty yards behind Bethany Anne. "They made me a *Gott Verdammt EMPRESS!*" she raged, her eyes blazing red. "And

186

what were you doing, huh? Playing dead? Lying around on your ass, I bet!"

"I don't believe healing from a nuclear explosion is the same thing as lying around on my ass," Michael retorted. He was now being reminded of the other side of Bethany Anne, but then, one couldn't be attracted to fire without the possibility of getting burned. "While the Etheric Realm was pleasant when I woke up—"

"The Etheric Realm?" She arched an eyebrow. "That's where you were sitting around playing tiddlywinks?"

Michael saw John, Eric, Darryl, Gabrielle, and Scott come up behind Bethany Anne, and a couple of others had also exited the Pod. Akio let him know that he would greet the new arrivals since it seemed Michael had his hands full.

He focused on Bethany Anne again. "The reintegration of my constituent atoms took a long time. Using the—"

She stopped him by poking his chest again. "Constituent atoms?" she exclaimed, her eyes flashing red. "Don't you go using big scientific words on me when I'm mad at you!" She looked him up and down. "I don't think you understand the concept of groveling!"

Eric whispered to John, "Did she slap him?"

"Tried," John whispered back. "Michael grabbed her hand before she could hit him."

Eric shook his head. "Should have just let it happen. That would have been enough." He flinched the smallest amount when Gabrielle smacked his arm. "See?" He pointed to his wife. "Just take the hit, and they're all better."

"I don't think that's in Michael's DNA," John replied doubtfully.

"So!" Bethany Anne retorted to the last thing Michael told her. "Think this is challenging you?" She shoved Michael off his feet. His body disappeared, and she put her hands on her hips. "Why don't you think about how to answer me politely while your ass sits in the Etheric until I come get it!"

Bethany Anne turned to her friends. "What?" she asked, jerking a thumb over her shoulder as she stomped toward them. "He needs to understand how to act around me when I'm pissed."

Bethany Anne noted the exact moment their expressions changed to shock and started to turn. She was halfway around when two large hands pushed her hard, throwing her toward her people.

She landed in the Etheric and rolled over to jump up, expecting an attack, but all she saw was Michael. He was ten feet away, his eyes glowing dimly. "You," he told her, "have been spoiled."

"*I'm* spoiled?" Bethany Anne screamed, her voice muted in the white mist. "You rank piece of fetid fish food!" She pointed a finger at him.

He interjected, eyebrow raised, "What, no 'fuck?' As in 'fucking rank piece of fetid fish food?'"

Bethany Anne twisted her head left and popped her neck, then did the same thing on the right. She whispered, "I'll feed you to the fucking fish, you gag-sacking dried-out cockroach-sodding bunghole-filler!"

Michael pursed his lips. "Does that mean you want it in both orifices?"

It took Bethany Anne only a microsecond to parse his question before her eyes flared red.

Akio shook hands with the men while Gabrielle hugged Yuko and Eve. The two of them introduced Gabrielle to Mark and Jacqueline, the young adults Michael had picked up in the old US.

The entire group walked around the spot from which the pair had vanished in case they should suddenly reappear. John smiled at Akio and asked, "Did Michael upgrade?"

Akio nodded slowly. "I think he is in much better control of his powers than when you last met him." He sighed. "This might take a while."

Just then, Bethany Anne stepped out of the Etheric, her hair floating around her head. "*MEN!*" she shrieked. "Can't live with them, can't leave them on the side of the road when you're done with them! *URRRGH!*"

An arm reached out of thin air and pulled her backward, and her body disappeared.

A microsecond later, Michael stood where she had been. "*Women!*" He harrumphed. He wiped off a sleeve and reached up to set his hat on his head, but a hand snaked out of the air, grabbed his hat, and disappeared. Michael whipped around. "She did *not* just take my fucking hat!" He took a step and disappeared again.

Everyone looked at the empty spot for a second and then resumed their discussions.

Akio pointed toward the two people the guys didn't know. "Here, let me introduce you to Michael's wards."

"'Wards?'" Eric asked.

"Is that like kids?" John asked.

"Oh, goody!" Scott exclaimed, his eyes lighting up. He rubbed his hands together. "Does Bethany Anne know Michael has kids?"

CHAPTER NINETEEN

"Seventeen," Mark counted aloud as the ten of them glanced at the action. This time it was Michael who dropped out of the air some ten feet above the ground. His body slammed to the Earth, only to jump up a moment later and disappear once again.

"Is it only me, or is this a weird way to greet your lover after a long time?" Jacqueline asked. "I mean, Mark makes me mad, but I don't think that after a hundred and fifty years I'd fight with him like this."

Mark eyed his girlfriend. "That's good to know, I guess." Jacqueline elbowed him in the ribs, to the chuckles of the others.

"I was thrown by the kiss, actually," Eve put in. "I get update feeds from ADAM when Bethany Anne is here, and let me tell you—the fighting that's happening on the other side is dramatic."

"Probably just two alphas reasserting dominance." Gabrielle sighed. "Bethany Anne hasn't truly had to answer to anyone, and Michael still has that 'I'm the ArchAngel' thing going on." She tapped her lips. "Although I think he was probably okay until she tried to slap him."

"Michael is working to be a good man," Akio told her. "He's come far in becoming human again." He shook his head.

"Allowing someone to slap him, even his love, isn't something he has worked on though, I can assure you."

Bethany Anne appeared twenty feet in the air and fell to the turf, rolling twice before she kicked off the ground. She was gone a half-second later.

"Eighteen," Eve announced.

"Who wants to bet on the number of times they show up before they kiss and make up?" Darryl asked.

"Twenty-seven," John replied immediately. "Closest wins, ties on either side of the guess go to the person who chose the smaller of the two numbers," he qualified.

Jacqueline scrunched her nose. "How does that work?"

"If one person suggests twenty-eight, and another thirty," John explained to the young werewolf, "and the number is twenty-nine, then twenty-eight wins."

"I'll take thirty-five," Scott piped up.

"Any reason you guys are going for odd numbers?" Eve asked.

Darryl shrugged. "Aren't they just numbers?" he answered. He was thinking about the last few times one or the other had appeared when Michael and Bethany Anne both slammed into the ground. Bethany Anne was still arguing as they rolled for a half-second before disappearing. "I've got twenty-three," Darryl told the group.

"Did she just call him a crusted bunghole of a space-zombie?" Mark wondered. "And that was nineteen."

"That's what I heard," Eric agreed. "What the hell, I'll go for the long shot. Forty-three."

Yuko asked, her voice slightly timid, "Are we betting on which one will finally give in?"

John scratched his chin as the ten of them watched Bethany Anne appear, anger etched plainly on her face and her eyes flaming red. "That gigantic conceited—" She was yelling when Michael's arm snagged her around the waist and she vanished again.

"I believe she has a lot of anger to release," Gabrielle mused. "And Michael isn't allowing her to walk away and cool off."

"No." Akio added, "Also, he does not want to hold this discussion in public."

"She isn't going to like that," Gabrielle answered. "Well, the walking-away part. The not-in-public she won't care about."

Jacqueline smiled. "I'd love to know what they are saying on the other side," she admitted in a conspiratorial whisper. She turned to look to Eve. "Did you say ADAM was keeping you up to date?"

"Not exactly like that," Eve told her. "And I'll take twenty-five."

Akio looked at the android AI. "You have inside knowledge."

"That's okay with me," Gabrielle allowed. "Twenty-one."

"Wow, you're thinking she's almost done," Mark exclaimed. "Do you know both of them?"

"Yes," Gabrielle admitted, "although Michael was more of a boogeyman for most of my life."

"Which has been hundreds of years," Yuko told Mark as she pointed to Gabrielle. "Remember, this is Stephen's daughter."

Mark's mouth formed a silent O.

Jacqueline's eyes narrowed. "That reminds me...where is this Tabitha female?"

Gabrielle turned to Jacqueline and noticed the slight surprise in Yuko's eyes. Mark silently pleaded with his own eyes, imploring her, she felt, to minimize her answer.

She would have to get to the bottom of this, but Gabrielle had a rather solid suspicion. Jacqueline was obviously a werewolf, and Mark had the physical tells of a vampire.

Even if he *was* out in the sun.

Most female werewolves didn't like to share. Gabrielle jerked her thumb upward. "On the *ArchAngel*. Why?"

"Just curious." Jacqueline's eyes narrowed. "Is she coming down?"

"I'm sure she is," Eric piped up from behind her.

Gabrielle wanted to roll her eyes when she saw the blood—what little he had left, she guessed—drain from Mark's face. "Along with her boyfriend Peter," Gabrielle told them, trying to stave off a possible issue.

"Peter?" Mark interjected, relief in his voice.

"Yes," John answered. "The Queen's Guardians' leader."

Jacqueline's focus locked on John. "*The* Peter?" she asked, her excitement palpable. "The one the Queen saved?"

"Yes," John answered. "Did you know him?"

This time, it was Mark's eyes that narrowed in annoyance.

She shook her head. "No, but my dad told stories of Bethany Anne's saving him, and how he turned around. Hell," she gushed, pointing to each of them, "he told me about you too, John." She pointed to the others. "And Darryl and Scott and Eric."

"Who was your father?" Eric asked.

"Gerry," she answered.

"The Pack Council Leader Gerry?" John asked, and she nodded. "Damn! You obviously take after your mother."

Jacqueline opened her mouth to protest, but what came out was a chuckle. "Yes," she finally agreed. "My dad was a lot of things, but a fine-looking specimen?" She shook her head.

"Your dad wasn't ugly," Eric argued. "Perhaps not a ten, but not a two either."

There was a *woomph* as bodies hit the ground, but none of the ten even flicked an eye toward the noise.

"Twenty," Gabrielle commented.

"Dad would have appreciated your support," Jacqueline turned to Eric, "but even I know he was a solid six, maybe a seven if he shaved."

Darryl was going to ask where he was when the ten of them received a message.

We will be a while, Michael sent, followed by Bethany Anne's, **I've got some booboos to heal.**

Then the ten were alone.

"Did she mean," Gabrielle questioned everyone there, "that she had the booboos, or Michael had the booboos and she was going to make them better?"

No one spoke for a moment, thinking through what Michael and Bethany Anne had told them. "I'm not sure we will ever know," John replied.

Gabrielle shrugged. "Okay, pay up, bitches!" Gabrielle winked at Jacqueline. "I *won!*"

After five more minutes with no sign of Michael or Bethany Anne, Akio wondered aloud, "Does anyone want to meet Michael's cat?"

QBS *MineLayer Prime*

Bobcat looked around the plush interior of the ship they had been given to help oversee the emplacement of the BYPS system around Earth. He, William, Tina, and Marcus had agreed to use the ship on the condition that it had a close approximation of their *R2D2* workshop's setup.

When they arrived on the ship, they had found the same table and two whiteboards.

More importantly, they had a beer fridge, and not one, not two, but *three* beer kegs.

Plus, Bobcat used the absolute cold of space (using Marcus only knew what technology) to help keep their beverages chilled appropriately.

He was being spoiled, and it felt damned good.

"Permission to come aboard?" William commed, amusement evident as he got out of a Pod in the smaller bay in the back of the ship. Marcus and Tina had come back that morning for the operation after spending some time on the *ArchAngel II* to check it out before the massive ship left with Bethany Anne. Those two were going back with Bobcat to Federation space.

When Bobcat glanced up, William was walking out of the bay

toward their work area. He tapped the button to speak with him. "You didn't even wait for me to give you permission. I should toss your ass back out the airlock for such insubordination!"

William stopped and turned, and it was then that Bobcat could see he was carrying a case of beer. "Obviously you don't want my gift."

"Hold on!" Bobcat jumped up from his seat, leaving William hanging. He had thought that Bobcat was going to come back with a funny line.

Marcus and Tina arrived through a different entrance in time to see William standing in the hallway in confusion as Bobcat ran up to him and pulled the box from his arms with a smile. Then the two started walking back the way Bobcat had come.

"I think we have a new beer," Tina mused. "The guys will be here shortly."

Marcus leaned in to watch the last moments of the video. "I agree, and let's get ready to turn on our mousetrap."

"Mousetrap?" Tina asked, her eyes wide. "You realize this mousetrap is probably one of the most powerful and destructive cross-dimensionally-fueled planetary protection systems anywhere, right?"

"Well," Marcus' tone moved toward teaching, "there is no way for us to know how high the BYPS system really is on the list of most powerful. We are setting it to protect against the likes of our own capabilities, with another twenty percent tacked on top of it. So—"

Tina put a hand up. "That we know of."

Marcus sniffed. "Well, then we are probably the top seven on the list."

Tina stared at her husband. "How are you coming up with seven spots when we have only one planet?"

"There are three ever-increasing concentric spheres of protection, any one of which would make it into the top ten. So, if A, B and C represent our spheres of protection, that's three. Then AB and AC and BC, and finally ABC as a whole."

Tina stared at him a moment, ignoring the chatting of Bobcat and William behind her. "That's interesting, and it really brings home how powerful this system is."

"Yes," Marcus admitted, running a hand through the mess on the top of his head called hair. "I do hope we don't screw up bringing it online. I'd hate to be responsible for blowing all of the Queen's ships up."

"That isn't funny," Tina told him as she sat down at a screen and pulled up the areas she needed to focus on.

"But accurate, even if we have multiple safety mechanisms in place," he told her as he sat down next to her and accepted the beer Bobcat had handed him.

Bobcat and William sat down too, and Bobcat cracked his knuckles. "Okay, who wants to drink and blow shit up?"

Tina looked at him darkly.

"Ooookay." Bobcat looked at his screens. "Dark humor is apparently out this morning."

Tina didn't bother with the drinking comment. Alcohol wouldn't affect their mental abilities. In fact, a beer was a good way to keep them de-stressed. If they were drinking, what they were working on couldn't be so dangerous as to blow up an entire solar system, right?

"Dry Run 001," Bobcat stated. "While we are waiting for all the satellites in Spheres Two and Three to arrive at their designated locations, let's implement our commands in a dry run with Sphere One. None of these commands are going to engage, and ADAM will create a script for us to run once we have it all worked out."

The only one of the four who didn't feel a small trickle of sweat on the back of his neck was Bobcat.

The reason he didn't feel any sweat was he fully trusted his team to get this done right, and done right the first time.

Besides, how much more dangerous could it be than acti-vating a sun inside an asteroid?

QBS *ArchAngel II*, Bay 004

The ship slid through the field separating the cold of space from the safety of the bay.

Anthony Brian Binz had turned when he heard the alarm indicating an incoming ship, wondering which of the many vessels running back and forth to Earth this one would be.

His eyes widened when he got a peek at a black nose as it came through the field. The white vampire's head on the side confirmed what he was seeing.

This was the *Shinigami*, which meant that the Queen was on this ship—and if scuttlebutt was true, that meant her love was on the ship as well.

Most had heard stories about Michael and knew how Bethany Anne had been created. Hell, he had even read the authorized biography of the Empress that had been written by Frank Kurns—three times. He had seen Bethany Anne a few times, and if there was ever a woman who would be too much for him...

It was her.

Anthony didn't mind looking at a pretty woman, but knowing the pretty woman could read your mind was asking for a constant flow of bitching if you were in a relationship.

He could imagine the worst easily.

She would ask, "What do you think of my haircut?"

Anthony would say, "Beautiful" and think, "You look like a dork."

Then he would call his friend for a place to sleep.

Again.

No thanks. He'd keep his thoughts to himself and be happy someone else was man enough for her.

The bay was completely empty, which was a good thing. The ship took up a massive amount of the space.

After the *Shinigami* slowly made its way to a stop, the back ramp dropped, and Anthony smiled when he saw John Grimes and Darryl Jackson step out and look around. Her guys didn't trust anything or anyone.

Even when docking on the *ArchAngel II*.

Soon enough, Anthony had to hide a smile when he heard Bethany Anne bitching about them telling her to stay behind. He had heard that once or twice before, but then he saw something he had never seen the Queen do.

She walked down the ramp holding the hand of a guy in a long coat, who was wearing some sort of hat he didn't recognize.

It looked good on him.

He walked with a deadly grace, completely unimpressed by his arrival on the ship.

"ArchAngel?" Binz spoke softly into his lapel mic.

"Yes, Anthony?" the ship's AI replied.

"May I have permission to video this?"

"One second," the AI told him, but before he could start worrying about the reason for the wait, she came back. "Approved."

Anthony watched the rest of the passengers come down the ramp. Not only was the famed Michael with them, but if he wasn't mistaken, the group included Akio, Yuko, and Eve as well, plus the Bitches, Gabrielle, and two humans he didn't know.

Those two were looking around like tourists seeing the big city for the first time.

She was a looker, and he was buff and moved like he was either a martial arts master or a vampire. Either way, Anthony worked hard to keep his thoughts to himself.

When Bethany Anne walked past Anthony, who was fifteen feet away, she turned and winked. "Permission granted."

The group marched away, and Anthony swallowed hard.

His permission to videotape them had come from the Queen herself.

There was a sharp rap on Tabitha's door, and she checked the time before calling, "Who is it?"

The next knock was louder.

"Dammit," she muttered as she got off her bed and swept into the small receiving room to open the door. "Non-enhanced," she muttered. It wasn't this person's fault they hadn't been upgraded and so hadn't heard her ask who it was.

Nor was it their fault that she was impatient to meet with Michael. Bethany Anne had offered her a ride to the planet, but Tabitha hadn't wanted her first meeting to include everyone else.

She had needed time alone to understand why she felt anxious about meeting him. She had even asked Peter to go away, so he was probably in the practice rooms kicking someone's ass because his girl had ordered him out.

Dammit, at the moment, she couldn't even get her relationship with Mr. Studly McMuffin right.

Her chances of working through her issues with Michael were probably hexed as well.

If she had a TOM in her system, she'd beg him to kill these damned chemicals racing through her body.

The person on the other side of the door knocked a third time, and Tabitha went from edgy to thoroughly pissed off.

She yanked her door open, snarling, "WHAT?"

And her jaw dropped in shock.

Michael was standing in front of her. His eyes pierced her soul, and she couldn't think.

"May I come in?" he asked.

Tabitha didn't move. Didn't even register his request. "You're really alive," she whispered. "I don't think I believed it."

"Yes," he agreed, his voice soft, "and I'm standing in this hallway, wondering if I need to come back at another time."

Her eyes opened in alarm. "What?" She shook off her shock, then jumped to the side and opened the door farther. "Yes, of course!"

It was then that Tabitha noticed Bethany Anne behind Michael, pushing him through the doorway. "You have thirty minutes, then I will be back to grab him."

Tabitha nodded mutely at Bethany Anne, who reached in and pulled the door out of Tabitha's hand, closing it gently.

Michael looked around the rather spartan room. It had a small couch, a chair, and a desk with a tablet and screen on it, and she had placed an oval red rug on the floor. "I smell someone I remember," he commented, turning to her. "Who is it?"

Tabitha put a hand to her mouth and rolled her eyes to the ceiling. She and Peter'd had sex on that rug just twelve hours earlier. Her ears turned red as she hung her head.

She was over a hundred and seventy fucking years old, so she shouldn't be embarrassed to have a sex life.

But this was *Michael*.

"Uh," she waved at the couch, "would you like to sit?" When he turned to the couch, she blurted, "Fuck it!" and slammed into him, clutching him around the chest. She started weeping, her shoulders heaving.

Michael looked down in alarm before he understood enough and wiggled one arm free, then the other, to hold her as well. "Tabitha, you didn't kill me."

"I wasn't there!" she sobbed. "I should have found out something about their plans, hacked something, *done* something." As she cried, her head moved back and forth, soaking his jacket. She sniffed as Michael held her tightly. "I've talked to everyone, and I know I couldn't logically have accomplished anything," she whispered, "but you're *Michael*."

"Who?" Michael answered softly. "I was an ass to you."

Tabitha hiccupped and chuckled. "Yeah, but you respected me. Cared about who I was."

He tried again. "I abused your skills, Tabitha."

She shook her head, getting his jacket wetter still. "Michael, you saw me as a person to care about. A *person*. Tell me that isn't true!"

Michael tried to think back to when Bethany Anne had saddled him with the young hacker girl. How he had tried to get the sassy geek moved out for another support person, and how she had made it to where he wouldn't read her mind.

Because he would blush at what she thought about when he tried.

He smiled into her hair. "You got my grudging respect for your abilities, then my admiration for your intelligence, and finally I cared enough to make sure this human girl had the chances she needed in life. So no, I can't tell you that wasn't true."

Tabitha held him tightly enough that it hurt. "You've obviously been upgraded," he managed, his voice strained.

"Sorry." She stepped a little back, running a hand through her hair and wiping the tears from her face. "I've been worried that you would tell me it was all in my head."

"No." Michael reached over and removed a tear with his thumb. "It wasn't. In some respects, I treated you as a daughter." He raised an eyebrow. "A pain-in-the-ass daughter, for sure," he clarified as she nodded her understanding. "But still, for a human to push back at me like you did?" He slowly nodded his head. "A person I cared about."

At the end of the thirty minutes, there was a knock on the door, and Tabitha called, "Come in!"

Bethany Anne put her head in, scanning Tabitha's face. Although her eyes weren't red and puffy, it was clear there had been a lot of crying. She glanced at Michael, who seemed comfortable.

This certainly wasn't the Michael she had left behind. She gave Tabitha a smile. "Sorry."

Michael stood up and went to the door, and Tabitha rose and walked behind him. "Thank you, Michael," she told him. "I'm sorry I went to pieces on you like this when you just got back."

"You are welcome." He gave her a one-armed hug. "Your reception was infinitely less complicated—and painful—than Bethany Anne's."

"Did she kiss the booboos and make them better?" Tabitha asked, flashing a grin at the man.

Bethany Anne grabbed Michael's arm and pulled him out of the suite. "No kissing booboos and telling," she chided and looked at Tabitha, "or I'll get Peter to fess up."

"Why not?" Tabitha smiled at her friend. "I bet he could spin a great tale."

Bethany Anne pressed her lips together, then cracked a small grin as she closed her eyes and shook her head. "Of *course* you wouldn't mind your sexual exploits spoken about."

"Well, I wouldn't want to have a video out there," Tabitha told her, "but if I could make that big hunk of manliciousness brag?" She winked at Bethany Anne. "That would make me happy!"

Both women noticed that Michael was looking down the passageway. "I think I hear someone who needs me," he murmured.

Bethany Anne waved at Tabitha. "I'll let you go before I have Superman here trying to leave me because he's embarrassed."

Tabitha told them both goodbye, and slowly closed the door after she watched them walk away holding hands. She caught sight of Scott a dozen feet down the passageway before the door shut.

She inhaled deeply and let her emotions out with the air as she slowly exhaled.

Her father was back, and *he still loved her.*

CHAPTER TWENTY

QBS _ArchAngel II_

Bethany Anne enjoyed the slow progression down the passageway with Michael, whose eyes darted everywhere and cataloged everything he was seeing on the ship. "Tell me about your cat," she requested.

"Demon?" Michael turned to her, a smile playing on his face.

She eyed him. "That's its name, 'Demon?'"

Michael thought a moment. "Well, technically she isn't sure she wants that name, and her intelligence isn't too high yet."

"Yet?" Bethany Anne asked. "Did you Pod-doc her or something?"

"Nanocyte research," Michael answered as the two continued down the corridor. He was aware of the way Scott would discreetly let people know to give Bethany Anne some space as the two of them walked amongst everyone using the passageways. He randomly read a couple of minds and realized it was helpful to the crew to see who the new man in Bethany Anne's life was.

And the two he read had been pleasantly surprised.

He grunted.

Bethany Anne's voice caught his attention. "You aren't listening," she told him, although her comment wasn't an accusation. "What's on your mind?"

He looked straight ahead, speaking softly. "I realized that everyone wants to know about me, so we are walking the halls to let them see me."

Bethany Anne looked around. "Noooo," she whispered. "That wasn't my intent."

"Oh, perhaps not your intent, but it is a good thing anyway," he replied quietly. "The funny part is, I think we are going to have a new fashion evolution."

"To what?" she asked, looking him up and down as they continued walking. "Your scruffy beard or your coat?" She pursed her lips. "Personally, I vote for the scruffy beard."

"Neither." He pointed to his head. "My hat." He squeezed her hand. "When people see me, they are satisfied that I'm a handsome man who seems capable enough for their Queen, and then they notice how good the hat looks on my head."

She followed his finger. "Why *do* you still have a cowboy hat?" Bethany Anne asked, looking at it, perplexed.

Michael didn't answer, and Bethany Anne just walked beside him, content in the moment. "Well, I told you when I came out of the Etheric, I was follically challenged," he finally admitted. "I like it now."

"Sorry!" She put her hand on his arm and looked at his short hair again. "I'll leave that for now."

It went unsaid that she would bring it back up later, however. "Demon?" she asked, changing the topic.

He nodded. "Happened in a battle not too long ago. Akio and I were tracking down some annoyances—"

"'Annoyances' being a slang term for…" She left the question hanging.

"People doing bad stuff who needed to die," he replied, then mentally slapped the shit out of himself. He *had* been working hard to be less of a "kill-them-all-and-let-God-sort-them-out" kind of guy, but lately his life had focused on killing as the only viable answer.

Bethany Anne had been trying to reduce that aspect of him the last time he was with her.

"Huh," she replied. "And how does that tie in to Demon?"

Michael glanced down at Bethany Anne, who was smiling at someone they were passing. She didn't seem to be bothered by the kill-them-all aspect whatsoever.

What had happened in the last hundred and fifty years?

"Demon was being used in nanocyte experiments—rather crude ones. When the two of us got there, we engaged in a rather large firefight. I wasn't terribly happy that the subjects didn't have a choice. They had no protection, so I hit the override to their cages."

"How did that work out?" she asked him.

"Poorly, since I didn't realize they were using snakes as well." He paused for a moment. "I really hate snakes," he admitted. "Indiana Jones and I have that in common."

The two of them turned a corner and continued toward the bridge. "So will Demon go into the Pod-doc?"

"This ship is damned large," Michael muttered. "Where are we? Are we still in the same solar system?" He looked over his shoulder, then back to the front, then left and right as they passed a cross hallway.

"Michael!" She squeezed his hand sharply twice. "Focus for me, will you?"

"I'm focused," he responded. "I'd like Demon to go into the Pod-doc, if for nothing else than to make sure the other nanocytes aren't messing with her. Plus, if she could communicate better, I'd like that."

"Why?"

Michael smiled. "So I don't have to guess what the hell she wants sometimes. It's damned exasperating." He heard fighting down a cross hallway and before Bethany Anne knew what was going on, he had pulled her sharply toward the noise.

"Scott!" she called.

Scott spun and saw a flash of Bethany Anne's smile and then her legs as they disappeared around a corner, and he started jogging after them. When he rounded the corner, Michael was striding with purpose toward the Guardians' workout area.

"Hurry!" Bethany Anne smiled at Scott. "Don't be late!"

QBS *ArchAngel II*, Bethany Anne's Suite

Michael stretched, and he felt a bone pop back into place. The short workout with the normal Guardians had helped take a bit of the edge off. They were good people. He ran his fingers through his hair. It might finally be getting long enough that he was going to seek a barber in a couple of weeks.

Thank God!

"Michael?" Bethany Anne called. He slipped on a black shirt she had found for him somewhere. When she had spirited him up to the *ArchAngel II* after their reunion, he hadn't been thinking far enough ahead to bring clothes with him.

"Yes?" he replied, pulling on his boots and grabbing his hat as he walked from her bedroom into the outer suite. He heard a voice he recognized, grinned, and shouted, "*STEPHEN!*"

Rounding the doorway, Michael found his brother dressed in black pants, a form-fitting black shirt, and— "A lady?" Michael raised his eyebrow as he reached Stephen, Jennifer, and Bethany Anne. "How do you do?"

"Michael, this is Jennifer, my mate. Jennifer," Stephen waved to Michael, "this is my brother." The dark-haired woman nodded politely after Stephen introduced her.

Michael reached over to shake Jennifer's offered hand. "My, my," Michael mused aloud. He reached up to stroke his chin, and a mischievous glint appeared in his eyes. "A Were captured the heart of the Entrepreneur. I'm *very* pleased to meet you."

Jennifer eyed Stephen, whose face remained characteristically bland. Only a small smile admitting he was involved in the conversation. She turned back to Michael. "And I am pleased to meet Stephen's brother. He has told me a few tales, but in general, he has remained silent about you."

Michael leaned forward to whisper conspiratorially, "That would be because he hated me for a thousand years." He leaned back. "I'm not saying it wasn't warranted, but I was a bit immature when Stephen first became upset with me."

Jennifer, aghast, turned to Stephen, who nodded. "It's true," Stephen agreed and pointed at Michael. "He was a *monumental* jackass."

Bethany Anne shrugged when Jennifer turned to her. "Stephen's right."

"I agree," Ashur added from behind the couch, "for what it's worth."

Michael called over his shoulder, his face toward the couch, "Who asked you?"

Ashur's head popped above the back of the couch, his tongue hanging out. "No one, but I have to support Stephen on this."

"Apparently my previously horrible reputation has dwindled," Michael mused as Ashur walked around the couch to join the four of them. He laid down, front paws crossed, and looked up at the humans.

Ashur chuffed, "I doubt that, but Bethany Anne will save me."

"Oh, no, you don't, furface!" Bethany Anne nudged Ashur gently with her foot. "You say it, you suffer for it."

"Hmmph." Ashur leaned forward to sniff Michael's pants.

"What are you doing?" Bethany Anne asked him.

"I smell cat," Ashur answered, "but not a regular cat." He looked up at Michael. "This is a bigger cat?"

"Yes," Michael admitted, looking down. "Not as big as you, but much larger than a natural cat."

"Claws?" Ashur queried.

"Of course," Michael answered.

"Wonder how a large cat will do around Weres," Jennifer mumbled.

Michael turned to her. "It took a while for Demon to become accustomed to Jacqueline, who is a Were. Demon doesn't like Were smell much because it reminds her of the lab where she was held. I'm getting through to her enough now that she is trying to disassociate the smell with her time in the lab, though."

"She's bloodthirsty?" Stephen asked, and Michael grinned. Stephen shook his head and rolled his eyes. "Never mind... Of course she is."

Michael noted a second time that Bethany Anne hadn't said anything about him being bloodthirsty. Just what had happened while he was gone?

An hour later, Bethany Anne pushed Stephen and Jennifer out of the suite. "Okay, big shot." Bethany Anne poked Michael in the chest.

He raised an eyebrow. "Are we doing 'Bethany Anne and Michael Meet, Round Two?'"

"What?" She shook her head. "No, but now that you know my evil plan, you might hurt yourself on purpose to get me to kiss it better, and we have to meet the guys for your workout with them in ten minutes."

Michael grinned in response.

Bethany Anne smirked, grabbed Michael's hand, and pulled him toward the bedroom. Ashur chuffed behind them.

"Would you *please* close the door?" he asked. When the door shut with a *ker-chunk*, Ashur laid his head back down on his paws.

"Thank God that hatch is soundproof," he grumbled.

QBS *ArchAngel II*, Guardians' Workout Area

Darryl nodded to Scott as the two of them backed up. His eyes focused on Scott's midsection in the hope that he would see the Kick of God coming in time.

There it was!

Darryl ducked, using his fists in a no-holds-barred effort to smash the ever-loving shit out of Scott's femur.

Cause that fucking kick had *hurt*.

Nanocytes or no nanocytes, a crack in the lower leg bone was a sure way to—

"Hucking *FELL!*" Scott yelled in surprise.

Darryl had gone ass over appetite when Scott's leg contacted his fists. He rolled to his back and sprang into a defensive position fifteen feet away, prepared for Scott's next attack.

However, Scott wasn't in any mood to attack at the moment. He was still hopping around while keeping one eye on Darryl.

"Sorry," Darryl told Scott. Not that he was sorry. "But I had to figure out a way to make you worry about sending out that Kick of God."

John spoke from the sidelines. "I thought it was all about teaching Scott a lesson?"

Eric jumped in. "Yup, pretty sure those were your exact words." He smiled at Scott as he looked at him and Darryl.

Darryl narrowed his eyes. "John, wasn't it your idea to try this?"

John's smile dropped. "Now hold on," he countered as he waved a hand and glanced at Scott. "You asked for strategies—"

"That's right," Darryl cut in. "And when Eric jumped in about making sure Scott was worried about using the Kick of God, you two came back with three different ideas in a matter of seconds."

"Well, sure." John shrugged. "If someone is willing to test

tactical ideas when the price of failure is a Kick of God to the face, wouldn't you let them sacrifice their face for the betterment of the team?"

Darryl's smile dropped. "You cretinous asshole!" he called to John as he walked over to Scott.

Scott was gingerly testing his leg by slowly putting his weight on it. Darryl jerked a thumb toward Eric and John and commented to Scott, "Can you believe these guys?"

Scott glanced at Darryl, sizing him up as he got closer.

"No!" Darryl put up his hands. "I'm done, I'm done. Peace."

Scott raised an eyebrow. "And if I punch you because Saint Payback is a *bitch*?"

"Well..." Darryl slowed down, eyeing Scott. He didn't *look* like he was setting up to deliver a cheap shot. "Then I guess we get him a patch?"

It took Scott a moment to figure out what Darryl was suggesting before he hung his head and smirked. "Yeah, okay, peace." Scott held out his hand, and Darryl took it. "But that shit hurt like a motherfucker." He eyed Darryl's hands.

"What?" Darryl lifted his hands and turned them over, trying to understand what Scott was looking for.

"Checking to see if you had brass knuckles." Scott chuckled.

"Nope!" Darryl was smiling as he put up his hands in a classic Mohammad Ali stance and punched the air. "Float like a butter-fly!" He jabbed twice more. "Sting like a bee!" he finished with a wink.

Scott punched Darryl lightly on his arm. "Sometimes you make me forget how smart Special Forces people really are."

Darryl stood straighter, his back tight and a frown on his face. "I think you just threw shade on me."

"How does one throw shade on a black man?" Scott asked. "And if you were like your SF brothers, you would have *known* I was suggesting you were slow. But since you *are* slow, you didn't understand."

"Oh." Darryl turned toward John and Eric, who were still off the mat, and his face broke out in a huge grin. "This *cop* is thinking to get into a scrimmage of words only because his Kick of God failed so miserably on us military types!"

Scott had just opened his mouth to argue the point when there was a sharp knock on the door. When it opened, Bethany Anne and Michael stepped in, and Michael closed the door behind them. Bethany Anne looked at the four of them and blew out a breath. "Scott, did Darryl do something to you?"

"No, ma'am," Scott answered. "Darryl was about to explain how he blackmailed someone to get into Special Forces since he obviously couldn't have passed the mental acuity tests."

Darryl growled, "I'll give you mental acuity tests!"

Scott hissed back, "I know you, ass! You always have to pass a form off to others to help you fill it in. Just write in your name in the first two blanks! How fucking hard can it be to remember the first answer? It was the first test we used in SWAT—if a trainee couldn't figure out the first two blanks were for their name, we dropped them off at the military recruiting station."

"You, sir, are a jackass!" Darryl chuckled, his eyes crinkled in amusement.

"High praise, so thank you," Scott replied.

"Are you two done?" Bethany Anne asked. "Or shall the three of us take care of this?"

"Mmmmm." Scott thought for a moment. "First person to step forward," he decided, pushing Darryl toward Bethany Anne.

Darryl stumbled twice before stopping and looking over his shoulder at Scott.

"Oh, look there!" Scott smiled as he pointed to his friend. "Darryl volunteered!"

"Then I guess…" a dark voice spoke into Scott's ear, "that it will be you and me." Scott's grin disappeared as he pivoted, his feet set on the floor to attack or defend at a moment's notice. He looked left and right but saw no one.

Scott turned back around when Michael reappeared next to Bethany Anne. The ex-SWAT guy rolled his eyes and placed a hand over his heart. "Oh, my God! That wasn't nice!" Scott pointed to Michael. "Someone needs to remind me to take my heart attack pills when Michael's around."

"Everyone, come here." Bethany Anne waved them over, shaking her head in resignation.

When the boys got together, they were going to play.

Stupid fucking alpha males. Can't blow them up, because they always have explosives too.

Chuckles accompanied them. Scott kept acting as if he were about to keel over from a heart attack as he slowly made his way to them.

"It's the big one, Cheryl Lynn." Scott grasped his chest with his left hand, his right arm thrown wide, staring at the ceiling. "I've been scared to death, and I'm comin' to join you!"

Michael's eyes narrowed. "Has Scott lost a wife?"

"No." Bethany Anne wanted to punch her friend. "She's on another ship at the moment, preparing to go down to Earth for a sightseeing expedition when I give the okay." Her lips pressed together. "But if Scott keeps this up, I'm thinking she might have to visit him in Sickbay."

"Hmm." Michael eyed Scott. "Probably better than the morgue."

Scott straightened up, stopped his antics, and hot-footed it over to join his friends. "Miracle!" he shouted. "Look, a *miracle!*" He looked at his arms as if they had just magically reappeared.

The six of them broke up a few minutes later after testing each other. In the end, Bethany Anne tagged out and allowed Michael the chance to take the rough edges off his fighting. The men, as amped up as they had been over the last hundred and fifty years, caused Michael serious issues for the first half-hour.

Michael's first complete surprise came when the Bitches caught him in a trap and John delivered a coordinated punch that tossed him a cool fifty feet to slam into the back wall. Bethany Anne hid her smile.

It *was* a bit satisfying to see him get his ass handed to him by her guys at least once.

The guys whooped and hollered in jubilation. It had been a good tactic.

"Guys?" Scott whispered. He got the attention of Darryl, John, and Eric. "Have any of you seen Michael's eyes glow red yet?" He pointed.

"No," John answered as he and the others turned. Michael's determined gaze was locked on the four of them.

His grin was feral, and his eyes blazed red.

"Ohhhhh, shit," Darryl hissed.

"God," Eric chimed in as the four of them spread out, "forgive us for the cursing we are about to do."

"Stop asking for forgiveness," Scott hissed, "and ask Him to ship us a shitload of Guardian Angels!"

Michael popped his neck. "That was fun," he whispered in a voice that carried to the four corners into the room. "And I deserved the reminder that training is about learning." He walked straight toward the four of them, not worried in the least that he didn't look prepared to fight.

Each of them heard the same thing at the same time. Michael's voice reverberated in their minds.

Now it is my turn to teach.

ADAM.

>>Yes?<<

Have ArchAngel route the video feed of this fight to the ship's monitors. I think everyone needs to be reminded of why Michael was codenamed "ArchAngel, Warrior of God."

"FUUUUUUUUUUUCK!" Scott yelled.

She had to duck as Scott's body flew over her head to slam into the wall before he rebounded with a grunt and fell to the floor. "Getting dangerous to watch," Bethany Anne muttered, making sure Scott was okay before stepping into the Etheric.

Wish I had some damned popcorn.

CHAPTER TWENTY-ONE

<u>**QBS** *MineLayer 202*</u>

Nancy was exhausted. She had sent almost all the minelaying ships toward Earth, and she was happy. Now she was waiting for the ships *302* and *412* to finish and come back.

They had gone a little farther afield.

"Not nice." The EI's voice interrupted Nancy's head in its descent to the desk in front of her.

"Hmm, what? C'mon!" She looked around before rubbing her eyes. "Okay, thank you, 202. I'm awake."

"That wasn't the reason I contacted you," the EI replied. "I'm letting you know that we are receiving only occasional contacts from the fleet."

"Mmmhmmm." Nancy set her elbows on her legs. "That's normal."

"Yes, and there are normal answers going *back* to the fleet, but I'm not sending them."

It took a moment for Nancy to think through the issues. "How have you checked, and how did you figure this out?"

"I caught a signal coming from farther out that mimicked our signal. The next time we needed to check in I purposely delayed my signal long enough to see if perhaps someone was signaling us, and just a minute ago, I confirmed we have a problem."

"How?"

"I didn't send the signal which was received by the fleet," the EI replied. "Something is blocking us while letting the fleet believe we have actively confirmed our status."

"Let's move." Nancy sat up, awake.

"I…" The EI seemed surprised as Nancy sent the commands to move the ship.

"Can't!"

QBS *ArchAngel II*, Bethany Anne's Suite

"Coke?" Bethany Anne asked Barnabas as he entered her suite. He shook his head, a small smile on his face as he gave her a hug and held out a hand to Michael.

Michael surprised him by enveloping Barnabas in an embrace. "I don't think so!" Michael told him, chuckling as Barnabas tensed. "That guy is mostly gone, old monk," he told him as the two disengaged. "Couch?" Michael asked and pointed to the sitting area. "I've just enjoyed an ass-kicking by four supermen, so I'd rather sit for a few minutes." Michael headed for the couches without waiting for an answer and told Barnabas over his shoulder, "I've already had two showers today."

Barnabas eyed Bethany Anne, who shrugged. *He is who he is, Barnabas. I'm not sure about everything that has gone on with him, but he and Akio are different than when we left them.*

Barnabas nodded his understanding and followed Michael into the suite. "So," Barnabas began, "you aren't occupying different suites?"

Michael shrugged. "I've come back to make an honest woman out of her." Bethany Anne had grabbed a Coke and now eyed him as she dropped onto the couch next to him. She elbowed Michael hard in the ribs as soon as she sat.

"Ooof!" His eyes flashed a touch, and his pain was evident.

Barnabas tried to hide his smirk, but he was sure Michael saw it. The strange thing for Barnabas was that Michael had been actively working to get Barnabas to smile.

The previous Michael would have done no such thing.

Barnabas' mind wandered just a bit, and he found that Michael's thoughts were either as well locked up as they had been before, or possibly locked up even tighter. When Michael raised his eyebrow just a fraction, Barnabas realized what his subconscious was doing and shut it down.

This version of Michael hadn't flinched when Barnabas had tried to read his mind, on purpose or not.

This discussion, Barnabas realized, was going to change his future one way...

Or another.

QBS *MineLayer* 202

"202, explain to me why you can't move the ship," Nancy queried as she hit the communication button to call the fleet.

Nothing happened.

Her EI responded, "I have fired up the antigrav generators, but there seems to be a null field affecting our acceleration. While we do have some, it has reduced it to the point where it will take fifty hours to make it twelve percent of the way to the fleet."

"Can you tell if the other ships are affected?" she asked as she twisted far to her right. The bridges of the MineLayer-class ships were not that large. The running joke was you had to get out of the captain's chair and squeeze out of the bridge into the tiny hallway outside just to change your damned mind.

She flicked two red switches to the right, which provided access to chemically-based secondary emergency rockets in case she needed to change her direction.

Nancy mashed the button and turned to view the screens that showed the stars outside, only to see them barely move before their momentum ceased. The fuel status was going down slowly, but they weren't making any progress.

She should have already turned the ship almost a third of the way around.

She shut off the emergency engines and turned back to the front, laying her hands in her lap.

"The other ships," her EI responded, "seem to have control, and are on their projected flight plans."

"Then why us?" Nancy wondered aloud.

A voice, commanding without demanding, spoke through her still-open comm channel.

"Because you," the voice answered, its language translated by her chip, "are the leader of this group. And you," it went on to say in a weird cadence that sounded like two voices speaking on different octaves, "can take us to the Exalted One."

QBS *ArchAngel II*, Bethany Anne's Suite

"I'll give you 'honest woman.'" Bethany Anne sipped her Coke, ignoring Michael's eyes on her and looking at Barnabas.

"Do I need to separate you two?" Barnabas asked.

Bethany Anne reached over and patted Michael's leg. "He likes it when I give him booboos."

Michael opened his mouth, frowned, and closed it before he turned to Barnabas and smiled. "So, what are your plans?"

Barnabas shrugged. "I've been in charge of enforcing the law for the last hundred and sixty-plus years," he answered, leaning back into the couch. "I think I'm ready for a change of pace."

"Retire?" Bethany Anne asked.

He shook his head.

"Monk?" Michael asked.

"Oh, no." He shook his head emphatically. "I've had enough of that in my life."

"Run a business?" Bethany Anne asked.

"What?" Barnabas looked at her, confused. "Have you mistaken me for Stephen?"

Bethany Anne shrugged. "You said you were ready for a change of pace. I'm trying to see what kind of pace you might be ready to try."

"I liked my occupation, but that little trip to Devon to…" He saw Bethany Anne's eyes flare just the smallest amount, "locate a missing person had me interrupt some gangs. Having left my badge behind on the ship, I was free to solve the problem in a very satisfying way."

Michael started grinning, then snapped his fingers and pointed at Barnabas. "Violence!"

Bethany Anne turned to Michael, then back to Barnabas. "Really?" She read the answer in his eyes. "Huh. I mean, I can't point any fingers, but I would have put money on you going to play monk, Big B."

"The effort on Devon was very satisfying." Barnabas laid his left arm along the back of the couch. "Helped the people I could, and got rid of some of the others by delivering the ultimate in punishment."

Michael pursed his lips. "Killing isn't always the answer," he replied after a moment, "but it's often one of the better ones."

Michael glanced at Bethany Anne, who didn't react to his comment. *That's three.*

"Actually, I gave an eye for an eye. If they came at me with a rod, I took it away and used it on them. Same for any of the other weapons," Barnabas replied.

Bethany Anne's eyes narrowed. "How is it that most of those who came at you died? They didn't *all* have deadly weapons, did they?"

"Oh, hardly!" Barnabas chuckled. "But you can drive a fairly blunt object through a body if you apply sufficient force."

"Soooo," Bethany Anne dragged out the word, "are you saying you want to do something to help people, but you don't want to do the paperwork?"

"That just about covers it, I think," he replied. "I don't want a seven-day-a-week position where I am on call all the time."

"So lone wolf," Michael offered.

Barnabas thought about this for a moment before he nodded.

Bethany Anne leaned into Michael's arm, looking at Barnabas in a fresh light. How long had she kept him in his position because it was easy—just as she had remained Empress? "Have you spoken to my dad?"

"As a matter of fact, yes," he told her. "Lance came to speak with me not that long after your speech. It was a recruitment effort."

"What did you tell him?" she asked.

"That I would give it some thought, and that I'd talk to you about it."

"That…" She pressed her lips together, shaking her head from side to side before opening her mouth to speak. Then she sighed and tapped four fingers on Michael's leg. "Now his questions make sense."

Michael looked at her. "Which questions?"

"My dad asked me if I had plans to clean up High Tortuga," she answered.

"High Tortuga?" Michael looked at Barnabas and back at Bethany Anne. "A pirate location?"

"Not exactly," she answered. "It's a planet called Devon, but we have started calling it 'High Tortuga' as a codename. It's a place where business takes precedence over law at times. I've acquired a vested interest in it, and I have ordered a few modifications so we can hide a few ships there."

"And by vested interest, you mean…" Michael left the question hanging.

Bethany Anne's face split into a shit-eating grin. "I own the planet!"

QBS *MineLayer 202*

Nancy eyed the speaker through which the alien's voice had just asked her to take them to…probably Bethany Anne.

She snorted. While she thought a visit between whoever the fuck this was and Bethany Anne would be funny to watch, it just wasn't proper to make it happen.

"Yeahhhh…" Nancy shook her head. "That's not going to happen without a lot more information from you."

"Why?" the voice asked. Once again, it sounded like one person speaking in two different octaves.

"You are either ignorant, stupid, clueless, or arrogant. None of those are particularly awesome designations, so why don't you provide a bit more information so I can narrow down why you are asking me such a blatantly idiotic question."

There was a moment of silence while Nancy typed on her command keyboard.

N:>>**202, can you set this ship to self-destruct?**

202:>>**Yes. I control those abilities.**

N:>>**Do you need preauthorization?**

202:>>**Yes.**

N:>>**Preauthorization for self-destruct granted. Captain Nancy Kathryn Silvers, *MineLayer 202*.**

202:>>**What are the triggers for self-destruction?**

N:>>**If I am incapacitated in any way and this ship is being used to gain access to the BYPS system, you have authorization and my command to self-destruct when we get halfway through the field. If we are traveling at a speed that will fail to**

give the fleet adequate time to prepare, self-destruct before that time.

At least she had sort of made things right with Thomas. If she were about to die for the cause, she was glad the last thing she had told him wasn't "Swan-dive into a supernova so your atoms burn out and the only remaining memory I will have will be when I spit on your headstone."

He *had* made her a bit mad. Jealous, even. It wasn't until much later that she found out the woman he was consoling was an old friend from his college days, grieving for a family member whom Thomas had also known.

Unfortunately, she had burned her bridges with him by then, and swallowing her pride wasn't something she was very good at.

She sighed. If she got out of this, perhaps she would take Thomas aside and explain why she had gone psycho on his ass.

"At this point," the voice came back on. "I am going to have to agree that I am ignorant in this situation. I will provide my assessment, and if you will correct my assumptions or validate them, this might work better. If my calculations are correct, are you willing to take me to your Exalted One?"

Nancy moved her hair behind her ear. "I don't understand your exact statement regarding calculations, but if you are asking if I will confirm your story, then this is what I am willing to do. The least will be to contact my fleet."

"That…could be a problem," the voice answered. "Let's see what we can negotiate, *MineLayer 202.*"

QBS *ArchAngel II*, Bethany Anne's Suite

"You own the planet?" Michael glanced at Barnabas and back at Bethany Anne. "How much does a planet cost?"

"When you are Bethany Anne," Barnabas replied laconically, "you just say, 'Make it so,' and it happens."

"Seems like a cheap way to acquire planets," Michael mused.

"That's not true." Bethany Anne shot a glance at Barnabas, who smiled at her. *Barnabas was enjoying this conversation way too damned much.* "I worked with a business person who was trying to take over a large group of companies. I made him an offer—"

"He couldn't refuse," Barnabas interjected. "Or that's how Stephen tells it," he added, as Bethany Anne and Michael stared at him.

"Not true. He had a choice, but the other option was a bit more future-proof."

"Death?" Michael asked.

"Okay, yes!" Bethany Anne muttered. She felt like such a hypocrite. "I was in my Baba Yaga phase, and it was pertinent. I didn't have much time to deal with the situation, and although I saved the Zhyn, I was rather pointed."

Michael smiled. "So his choices were…"

"Work for me or die," Bethany Anne answered.

"What's the problem with that solution?" Michael asked. "That was what I would have chosen."

Bethany Anne smiled, snuggling a little closer to Michael. "Maybe that's why I love you." Barnabas rolled his eyes, and she told him flatly, "I can't possibly bother you with bloodthirstiness."

"Well, I have a lot of history of killing too quickly," Michael replied, nodding to Barnabas. "As does Barnabas. The trick is pulling yourself out of it—which I'm assuming you have since you are here?" He looked at Barnabas.

Barnabas nodded.

"For now," Bethany Anne admitted. Her eyes were heavy. "Here, be a good man and stay fucking still for a moment."

"How long is 'a moment?'" Michael asked.

"Until I wake up, of course," she answered, and then she was asleep.

Barnabas glanced at Michael, who had his arm around Bethany Anne's shoulder. "Your arm is going to go numb, holding her like that."

Michael nodded. "Probably." He sighed. "But I've waited for this moment for years. I think I can take a little pain." He looked at Barnabas. "Are you going to do okay? No more blacking out and killing everyone if you go vigilante?"

"My plans are that obvious?" Barnabas asked.

"You were some sort of cop, and you don't want to change occupations, but you also don't want paperwork. Seems like 'vigilante' is the next career choice...unless you are going to do something with Lance?"

"Working with him will give me a large amount of intel, plus I can go on operations for him from time to time."

Michael looked around the room. "You need a ship?"

Barnabas shook his head. "I've got a ship. As big as this one, actually."

"That's true?" Michael asked, and Barnabas nodded. "Well, that is interesting. This ship is massive."

"It is named *Ranger Prime*." Barnabas crossed his legs. "Do you remember the large motor homes back before we left Earth?" Michael nodded. "Imagine that Ranger Prime is one of those. What I *don't* have is a little car that goes with the big RV. For the most part, using Prime is overkill. These ships aren't cheap to run."

"I can't imagine they are," Michael agreed. "So, you will get something smaller?"

"That is my plan. I just need to ask Bethany Anne if we have something, or find something to buy, although I'd rather not purchase."

"Why not?"

"Gating," Barnabas explained. "Most traffic uses the big Gates to get from one system to another. There are some ships—like those of the Etheric Empire which Bethany Anne ran—which build Gate technology into the ship. If I can get one of hers—"

"You are golden." Michael nodded. "I understand."

"Shinigami." Bethany Anne stirred and both men looked at

her, but her eyes stayed shut. "Shinigami could use you, Barnabas. She needs a firm hand, and you've handled my issues for a hundred and sixty years. You two are a good match."

She snuggled in again, and her soft breathing resumed.

Michael noticed that Barnabas was shocked by the suggestion…and perhaps slightly afraid? No, not afraid…

Concerned.

Neither man was sure Bethany Anne had been awake when she made the statement.

Barnabas would have to ask her once more. However, the *Shinigami*, if Bethany Anne allowed it, would be a *most* excellent ship for a lone vigilante.

A human vampire over a thousand years old and a practically-invisible ship with an AI impressed by Baba Yaga when it acquired sentience?

What could possibly go wrong?

CHAPTER TWENTY-TWO

<u>QBS *ArchAngel II*, Bethany Anne's Suite</u>

TOM?

Yes?

I have a question for you. Bethany Anne paused for a moment to sit down on her couch and put her tablet aside. Michael was giving her a little space right now and spending some time with Mark and Jacqueline. While it was wonderful to have him around, both were old enough to realize you needed to breathe a little in the beginning.

Conversely, she could try to choke the living daylights out of him, but unfortunately, he had learned a trick or two since he had come back from his almost-death and rejuvenation. She had wanted to choke him when she found out he had been caught a second time and almost ripped apart permanently. That little effort had been made by a vampire he had punished and left to die hundreds of years back.

Thus, the vampire was alive, or at least torpid, after WWDE. The Duke had killed a few grave robbers and then proceeded with an effort to take over Europe. Funny how in trying to punish the fucker Michael had inadvertently saved his useless life, only to find the vampire had a hard-on for revenge.

And the revenge had almost been successful. Akio and the others had helped save Michael, which might explain his new-found humility.

Which for Michael was about a two-point-five on a scale of one to a hundred.

Baby steps, she reminded herself. *Baby steps.*

What is the question? TOM asked.

What kind of body do you want? She continued her line of thinking before he answered. *I assume you don't want anything like we saw on that planet where we fought the Kurtherians, so—*

Definitely *not.*

So, what kind of body? she pressed. *I have told you many times I would get you a body. I want to make sure we have a plan that will work and give you the best.*

Bethany Anne was surprised when TOM withdrew into himself. She grabbed her tablet and continued checking reports, waiting for him to resurface.

Bethany Anne?

Hmmm? she replied, accepting the suggestions of two of her subordinates before returning her attention to her friend.

Can we simply leave it at "a body" for now?

Bethany Anne's brow furrowed. *Sure, but how come?*

I must admit I am feeling lost at the moment. The thought of not being with you is unsettling to me, so I am not looking at my options objectively. In short, I don't want to think about it.

Okay, but we don't want to make a haphazard choice because we didn't think about it. We could always make you a body, I suppose.

What, and be the first Kurtherian Terminator? TOM asked.

TOM felt her amusement. *I think that might be a bit much, and we've had plenty of Kurtherians willing to kill. I don't think you are that far gone yet.*

I was thinking more about a robotic body, but sure. I think I would be the equivalent of a killer in my own clan. They wouldn't understand.

They would need to walk a hundred and fifty years in your shoes, she told him.

Truly.

Okay, so we table it for now, but we do need to think about it.

Understood, and Bethany Anne?

Hmmm?

Thank you.

Always, my friend. Always.

Bethany Anne was sitting on the same couch an hour later when there was a sharp rap on the door. Michael came in with a smile on his face. "Dear?"

She looked at him with a sparkle in her eye. "Yes?"

He reached up and reset his hat. "Care to go on a date?"

She stood up and walked toward her bedroom. "Okay, what kind of date?"

"How many kinds are there?" Michael asked.

"With you?" she called over her shoulder. "There are normal dates, important dates, and dates where we kill people."

Michael's eyes softened. "That is why I love you so much."

Bethany Anne stopped and looked at him. He had his hands in his pockets, and he was grinning. His eyes sparkled under his hat.

She had to admit he looked scrumptious, but then she was totally an interested party. "Why?"

"Because you know to ask me if this is a date where killing will be involved."

"It tells me how to dress," she replied and shrugged. "Do I go to closet A or closet B?"

"Which one is for the guns?" Michael asked as he walked toward her.

"B."

"Then B it is."

"Okay, B. Come help me get into my armor."

Michael's voice acquired a husky timbre. "I'll help you get *out* of those clothes before you get into your armor. Because *priorities*."

"Oh no, you don't!" She laughed as she opened the arms locker's door and stepped inside. "Your idea of a quickie can be too damned slow!"

"It's the vampire in me," he replied, chuckling. "But fine. Killing first."

She winked at him as she grabbed her leather pants. "Because *priorities*."

QBS *ArchAngel II*

"I'm going."

"Me too."

"Me three." William looked at his buddies. "No way I'm missing a chance to go on a beer run and get some more seeds."

"Kathy?" Bobcat asked with a smile.

"Is busy for the next thirty-six hours. Otherwise," William wiggled his eyebrows, "you two losers might be going alone." He turned to Marcus. "Where's Tina?"

"She has a poker game tonight," Marcus replied, scratching his chin. "She says she doesn't have permission to go down to the planet for another twelve hours, so she is playing poker with some old friends. She told me to go with Bobcat."

Bobcat pointed at Marcus. "*That* is love in action."

Marcus stared at his friend, confused.

Bobcat shook his head. "When are you going to realize that

MICHAEL ANDERLE

Tina is just getting out of your way so you can enjoy some time with just the three of us?"

Marcus' mouth formed a silent O.

Both men looked at William, who appeared to be shocked. "Oh."

Bobcat rolled his eyes. "For Pete's sake, you too?"

"I, uh…" William looked sheepish. "I took her at her word."

"It could be true," Bobcat agreed, "but just as likely she is letting you enjoy some guy-time since, you know, you will be flying all over the galaxy with her." He headed for a Pod. "Now, I don't know about you losers, but I'm ready to go check out a few sites and see if we have any options."

"Like?" Marcus asked.

"Like," Bobcat answered as the other two joined him at the Executive Pod, "did NASA or any of those other locations seal up some cool stuff?" He waved his friends in.

"How would we get in? It's been a hundred and fifty-plus years since we left." William replied, stepping into the Pod.

"I wonder…" Marcus mused as he boarded, "if SpaceX had any more insights. I'd love to grab some mementos from there."

Bobcat smiled. His connivance with Kathy and Tina was going swimmingly, and now with Bethany Anne's permission, the three of them were off to have a boys' night out.

On their home planet.

A minute later, Bobcat settled into his own seat, and the Executive Pod rose slowly from the deck and slipped through the field.

"Oh, shit." Bobcat leaned over to look out the portal near where William was sitting.

"What 'oh, shit?'" he asked.

"*That* 'oh, shit.'" William pointed at the two Black Eagles that were gracefully flying next to their Pod as they headed toward the planet.

"And just where," John Grimes' voice came over the comm,

"did you three think you were going without backup and protection?"

"Down there." Bobcat pointed, not sure if John could see him. "It's the really big blue ball ahead of us. Do you need directions?"

John chuckled. "The Queen is asking you guys to do the four of us a solid and help us relax a little, and in return, we're to make sure you three come back in one piece. The world has roughened up a bit."

"Is Bethany Anne staying on the *ArchAngel*?" Marcus asked.

"Doubt it," Eric replied, "but Michael is with her. I think she's in good hands."

John smirked. "Literally."

Seven guys chuckled at that one.

William grinned. "Okay, I think I hear *blah blah blah* drinking buddies!"

There were four chuckles over the intercom when Darryl answered, "You got *that* right!"

"Where should we go first?" Bobcat asked.

"Let's try New York," Scott answered. "We had a little fun there the last time we had a night off."

Bobcat made a course correction from California to New York. "New York it is."

John spoke over the intercom as the three ships turned toward the North American continent. "Just got an update. Bethany Anne is going to Japan with Michael on a date."

"What kind of date?" Scott asked.

John paused for a moment before responding, "Well, ADAM says she is armoring up."

Scott smiled. "Oh, *that* kind of date."

"Lucky bastard," Darryl commented. "Think we can go with them?"

"No way," John replied quickly. "I don't think they will need our help, not with Michael there. But," he sent a quick message to his snitch, "ADAM will let us know if we should be prepared."

MICHAEL ANDERLE

Bobcat broke into the conversation. "I've found three beer places that would give us a good reason to be in that area. Change course?"

"No," John decided. "Stay with New York. If we moved toward Japan, it would look fishy."

"Well, just say the word. I've already figured out seven reasons why Japan is good for beer."

"What about sake?" William asked.

"Hell, no," Darryl shot back. "Sake makes you say stupid things."

Marcus chuckled. "Sounds like there's an experience you need to share and get off your chest?"

"No, not at the moment," Darryl answered him. "Sometime I'll take you up on it, though. For now, just go with 'Sake is not your friend.'"

"Like grenades?" Eric asked.

"Just like grenades," Darryl agreed.

"Grenades are good," John grumped. "Just because you guys made a damned meme out of 'Grenades are not your friend...'"

"We have video proof, you ass," Eric replied.

"That video was done here on Earth!" John argued. "You aren't telling me that's the best you got?"

"It's the ultimate proof, so why waste it?" was Eric's defense.

Soon the three ships had dropped into the upper atmosphere, and the men started looking for differences in the scenery below.

There was silence as they realized the vast landscape had no significant lights showing human habitation.

QBS *ArchAngel II*

Barnabas ran his hand along *Shinigami*'s side. The ship had been retrofitted since they had arrived in the Sol system.

Many people needed things to do since they weren't all allowed to visit Earth at the same time.

"Shinigami, permission to come aboard?"

He heard a voice but wasn't sure where the speaker was. He doubted he would be able to see it from the outside. He'd have to ask her about it.

The ramp in the back started to lower. "Permission granted, Barnabas."

He stepped to the rear and walked up the ramp. He took the familiar corridors to the bridge—which looked like a living room at first glance but was a very useful configuration. He sure hoped he never had to fight there, since it would be a bitch to get blood out of the furniture. Unless…

"Shinigami?" He sat down on the left side of the bridge.

"Yes, Ranger One?"

Barnabas shook his head. "Not 'Ranger One' anymore," he told her. "We disbanded the Rangers before we came here. Private ceremony, so it wasn't in the news."

That was new information to the AI, so she added it to her datastore.

"I'm just Barnabas now."

"Very well." The AI's visage came up on the front screen. It was Baba Yaga, and her eyes were red. "What can I do for you, Barnabas Nacht?"

"Not calling me 'Nacht' would be a start," he replied. "I just go by 'Barnabas.' Nacht is my father."

The AI's expression didn't change.

"Okay, you didn't get that joke." He waved it off. "I'll work on that."

"I'll leave off your surname in the future, Barnabas."

"Good enough." How the hell did you bring up a sensitive subject with an AI? "Shinigami, I'd like to talk to you about your future."

"I'm at the beck and call of the Queen to rain fire and destruction on her enemies."

"Right." Barnabas eyed the screen. Was this Bethany Anne all over again? "How about we start with why you were created?"

"To allow Empress Bethany Anne to maneuver in and out of locations using the advanced cloaking abilities of this ship, and give her sufficient capability to take the fight to the enemy should it be warranted. Further, I am an advanced AI now, who can run autonomously with permission."

"Yes, and what do you want to do?" he asked.

Shinigami paused. "I want to test myself against those deemed enemies of the Queen."

Barnabas stopped his next question, and instead asked, "How would you figure out if someone was an enemy?"

"If they are attacking the Queen, they are an enemy. If I have proof they are working against the interests of the Queen, they might or might not be an enemy. It can get into fuzzy logic after those two proscribed efforts."

"How would you go about uncovering these potential enemies?"

This time the Baba Yaga face turned its eyes toward him. "That would depend on the operational requirements and my constraints."

Barnabas realized that she was testing him. "Very good. If we made up the rules, what would you do?"

He watched as the digital face stared at him, even blinking twice before she asked for clarification. "'We,' as in 'you and me?'"

"Yes," Barnabas answered, then leaned forward and lowered his voice. He hoped she would understand the human gesture. "Without a badge to get in the way."

A mischievous smile appeared on the AI's face. "Then I would do whatever I felt we could get away with."

"Rules?"

"Were made to be broken," she replied and pursed her lips. "At least by us. Others need to abide by them, though."

Barnabas just nodded his head. He would help Shinigami understand the constraints she needed to mature into.

Just like a certain Queen he'd worked with once upon a time.

"Barnabas," the AI asked him as he stood up, "is this a possibility? I have no data from which to extrapolate the outcome."

He stared at her a moment before he asked, "What would *you* like to do, Shinigami?" He nodded at her. "You think about that, and I'll come back tomorrow to chat, okay?"

She nodded at him. "I would like that."

QBS *MineLayer 202*

Nancy unbuckled her harness and leaned back, placing a hand over her eyes. "Let me get this right," she replied, wondering if she were about to involve her people in a war. "You recognized that the technology we are laying out here is Kurtherian-based, so you assume our leader is Kurtherian, right?"

"That is the logical assumption," the voice replied.

"And you are from one of the clans of the Five, not the Seven?" Nancy continued.

There was a significant pause. "I'm not sure how to answer."

"With the truth, usually," Nancy replied. "However, I suppose if you were one of the Seven, you wouldn't be honest about it."

"My calculations confirm that your leader is a member of the Five."

Nancy sat up. "Look, I'm not dialed up to eleven in the intelligence department, but even I can figure out that you thought we were connected with the Five. If we weren't, any member of the Five would have steered clear of testing us." She tapped the arm of her chair. "So you are either a member of the Five who is confirming that we are, in fact, connected to a Five clan, or," she hated this logical progression, "you are a member of the Seven trying to figure out which clan this could be and whether you have to negotiate or can take us over."

The alien's voice seemed a bit dryer to Nancy when it replied. "Your technology is hard proof that you are part of the Five, but you think like the Seven."

Nancy's hands waved as she spoke. "That's because the member of the Five who found us didn't want a bunch of pussies running around." Fortunately, Nancy had taken a religion class in school, which Thales of Miletus had taught. "We are here to protect the shit out of our world before we go and kick some more Seven ass." Nancy's annoyance flowed through her voice. "And if you *are* one of the Seven... Well, you can snuff my ass now, since you won't have a fucking chance of taking out this world *or* this fleet. So pucker up and kiss it," she finished and sat back in her chair.

"Well," the alien replied a moment later, its voice reeking of relief. "I think I have found someone to tell my secrets to." It added a moment later, *"At last."*

CHAPTER TWENTY-THREE

Aboard the QBS *War Axe*, Defender-class Ship over San Francisco

The crew had spent a few hours over Japan, pulling the vast pile of rubble off Akio's six fellow Queen's Elites. Bethany Anne had chewed her fingernails until she was told the six of them were alive and had been freed.

Once the six and Akio had made it back up to the *War Axe*, and after she had thanked each of them for their service to her person, she and Michael had spent time pushing energy into their bodies. The energy plus the food and nutrients they were given helped speed their healing as the ship flew east from Japan to the west coast of America.

Looking out the viewport now, Bethany Anne could see the small contingent of people waiting for them on the ground as the mighty ship slowed.

Akio was the first person to step out, followed by the Elites. She could see as well as feel the anxiety of everyone out there at their appearance.

She had been told about Colonel Terry Henry Walton and remembered him well. Akio had updated her, as well as Eve via

ADAM, so she knew enough about what was going on to understand their fears.

Then it was her turn to leave the ship and welcome home those who had stayed here, or been born here, and had kicked ass for those who couldn't do it themselves.

Terry exhaled heavily. He hadn't realized he'd been holding his breath. Char released his hand and wiped the sweat on her pants.

She moved closer and wrapped her arm around Terry's waist, and he kissed the side of her head. When he looked back at the Pod, Akio had been joined by six other vampires.

Char recoiled as they approached. Terry had guessed that they were the Queen's Elites who had been trapped when an earthquake dropped a building on them during WWDE.

Now he was sure.

Akio stopped, and the Elites fanned out behind him. Akio bowed deeply to the Colonel and his lady—more deeply than he ever had before.

Terry and Char returned the bow at a perfect ninety-degree angle, and their children, who were ranged behind them, did the same.

Akio stood up straight before approaching and shaking hands with Terry and Char, a smile on his face and a glint of humor in his eyes.

Was that a real glint of humor, TH wondered, *or was he seeing things?*

Akio waved to the people standing with the Colonel.

A group left the Pod, strolling casually toward TH and Char. The Elites stepped aside, creating a corridor through which they could pass.

A dark-haired beauty walked at the side of a man who wore a long black coat and a black hat.

His eyes took in everything while remaining focused on Terry Henry.

They stopped before passing the last of their vampire escorts. The woman's eyes flashed red as she glanced from one face to the next, lingering at Joseph's.

TH stepped forward, which drew the attention of the Elites. Their hands seized pistol grips and sword hilts, but he held his hands up.

The man chuckled silently. The woman smiled crookedly, practically rolling her eyes at all the posturing before she focused on the man in front of her.

"We've met before, Empress," Terry Henry told her. He dropped to one knee and bowed his head before continuing, "I'm sorry. Akio asked us to help him prepare this world for your return, but I failed him. I failed *you.*"

Char stepped forward and put a hand on her husband's back.

Her eyes glistened. This was supposed to be a joyous return, but TH, as he always did, took responsibility for everything—whether in his control or not.

Empress? TOM asked.

I'll deal with telling everyone I've gone back to "Queen" some other time. It always becomes a long-assed discussion on the Federation and my proclivity to recoil from that title. That's how they know me for now. I'll switch it later.

Bethany Anne shook her head. "Cut the 'Empress' bullshit, Terry. I remember you from the Antarctica operation."

She raised her voice to make sure everyone heard her as she tapped a finger to her lips. "You were hypothermic, if I remember correctly, before we put you in the Pod-doc."

She looked around before continuing, "My name is Bethany Anne, and I'd like to introduce Michael." She glanced past everyone, taking in the sights and sounds of San Francisco. "Things look pretty damn good from where I'm standing, TH." She turned to the purple-eyed woman next to TH and winked. "And you must be Char."

Bethany Anne held out her hand, with no hint of subterfuge. She stage-whispered, the humor obvious in her face, *"Trust me, behind every strong man is a strong woman."*

There was a snort behind Bethany Anne, who caught the slight glint of amusement in Char's eyes from Michael's unspoken retort.

Bethany Anne rolled her eyes. "Oh, for fuck's sake, stand up, TH! You're making me feel weird."

"Listen up, people," she told them, projecting her voice for those without enhanced hearing.

She rolled her eyes. "Would you *stop* imitating a police academy cadet review?" She gestured them forward. "Come up here, and let's talk like folks who have kicked some ass and now are going to get a little well-deserved R and R."

The group hesitated, but Char waved them over as well. Felicity dragged Ted toward the front of the mob. When she looked at the Queen's feet, she stopped abruptly, grinning.

She pointed. "I just love those boots!" Felicity exclaimed in her southern drawl.

Bethany Anne aimed a finger over her shoulder at the man behind her to prevent the comment she just knew Michael was straining to keep in as she replied, "I know, right? Finally, a woman with taste!"

She finally turned to Michael. "See? It's all about the shoes."

"San Francisco has some of the best shopping in the world if you can spare a few hours," Felicity added.

Bethany Anne looked up at Michael. He struggled mightily, jaws working as he grimaced, but finally, he surrendered and let his eyes roll.

"And Michael will go, too," BA decided. "I've been away from this hunk of mostly hairless hot stuff for way too long."

Michael pursed his lips and commented, "It's growing. It's just taking a while."

She looked at the group who now formed a semicircle around her. "I wanted to meet you personally and thank you for everything you've done, both in my name and on your own to help make the world a better place. Akio said he could not have chosen better—even if he'd had a choice."

There was a rumble of laughter at that, and she paused before continuing, "What we've found across the universe is that no matter how hard we try, we can never fully defeat evil."

She shrugged. "It can be stomped into the ground." Bethany Anne put up her fingers, just an inch apart. "It can be sliced into little fucking pieces, but where one is removed, another takes its place. Fucking cockroaches! We can relegate them to the dark places, the slime and swamps in which they breed, but they'll always be there.

"No matter. You have helped make the world safe for humanity once again. You have carved a chunk out of life's cesspool, and you have handed it over so those who remain can make their own way. Self-determination and all that."

She sighed as she took them all in. "And now you have some choices, one of which is to take the rest you deserve. God *knows* you deserve it, and it's yours if that is what you want."

She smiled for a moment. "However…" She paused and winked at Terry Henry. "You knew there was going to be a 'however,' right?"

Bethany Anne got the chuckles she was looking for as she waved a hand at the massive ship above them. "I want to invite you to take the *War Axe* through the Annex Gate and join my father, Lance Reynolds, in securing and expanding the brand new Etheric Federation."

She smiled mischievously. "There is a little side business called 'the Bad Company' I think you and your people would be *perfect* to slide right into it." She looked at TH and Char. "What do you think about exporting your brand of justice to the whole fucking *universe?*"

BA didn't wait for an answer before continuing, "The sky beckons warriors, so come home to your place, TH. Earth will survive without you because you have taught it to. You've done your duty. Your legacy will live on here, but I have a *new* mission for those willing to step up. To take your skills and your get-shit-done attitude to a place that will cause your eyes to pop.

"Come home to the stars. Come home to the Etheric Federation." She looked at the group. *"All of you."*

The massive ship came over the northern horizon, growing in size as it neared the Russian city of Archangelsk, near the Dvina River.

No one could believe the size or understand the truth of what they were seeing.

Except Boris.

He had spoken with Bethany Anne many times since she had returned to the system, but he'd needed to deal with issues here in his small enclave before he could leave. The protections, the future...

His family.

However, it was now time. He and the others who surrounded him knew that their ride had come...and it wasn't just any ride. She was making a statement when a second ship the same size shadowed the first.

A third ship dropped closer to the ground. It was large itself, but the two Leviathan-class superdreadnoughts above it dwarfed it.

The *War Axe* was here for him and his people. It would leave behind the agreed weapons, tools, and supplies so that he could move forward with his future.

He was done. It was time for the latest generation to move this forward, to keep buried peoples and memories that should stay buried.

His strength had pulled them through the darkest days, and now it was time for him to step onto his chariot for his ride into the sun.

He looked at the faces of the people around him. His friends, his family... Those who trusted him to always be there—if not in person, at least in spirit—and smiled.

Bethany Anne was giving him a warrior's salute. He was well aware she could have just sent a nice ship for him and his group.

But no, she had brought down her two largest.

Perhaps, Boris thought to himself as he smiled, *she has a touch of the Russian in her as well.*

QBS *ArchAngel II*, Bethany Anne's Suite

Bethany Anne chewed on her fingernail.

Are you sure? she asked TOM for the fifteenth time.

Yes, was his simple reply.

>>Bethany Anne, I've confirmed this with ArchAngel. She has the ability to check, you know.<<

Yes, I'm aware. I just never expected it to be me. She sat back and put a hand to her forehead. *How the FUCK am I going to do this? Dammit, how the* **hell** *am I going to tell Michael?*

Why is that a concern? TOM asked, puzzled.

Because usually this involves a discussion between the couple, with much forethought and planning. Something random and a surprise just doesn't happen anymore.

Well, you did have good protection during your fight on Earth. Perhaps you can lead with that? TOM suggested.

Bethany Anne moved the hand from her forehead to her mouth to cover the giggles. *TOM, dammit! I don't like it when I giggle!*

Well, it *was* good protection down there, he continued. **Two shots to the midsection, and not a scratch on you.**

Bethany Anne sighed. *It was a good date,* she agreed. *Which is part and parcel of why we are in this situation now.* She thought back to the night under the moon, the rush of the guns and explosions, and the final battle—which had been hilariously short.

Which had allowed them to go on a real date on a magical night.

Apparently *too* magical.

I thought my stuff was shut down! she moaned plaintively.

I did too, TOM admitted. **But the advanced nanocytes kicked something into gear. I wasn't paying attention, and you know about the increased speed, so wham, bam...and bam and bam and bam...and thank you, ma'am, and here we are.**

Now I have a Kurtherian comedian.

I'll be here all night, and the rest of the month. Try the seafood.

Uh-huh, Bethany Anne grumped. *Your ass is here with me, so if I get sick, you get to enjoy it too—not to mention that space will eventually be at a premium.*

Oh, *shit!*

Bethany Anne chuckled. *Forgot about that, did we, Dr. Acula?*

I'm not a vampire, you are.

You created us, so what better name to call you?

TOM rattled off his Kurtherian name.

Yeah, okay, TOM it is, Bethany Anne replied as he snickered.

The door to her suite opened, so she got up and headed out of her bedroom to think on things and figure out when would be the right time to tell Michael the news.

He was going to be a father.

No time like the present. She sighed. She really didn't want to present this quite yet, but she steeled herself for the conversation. After sneaking a glance in the mirror, she started for the door.

ArchAngel's voice came over the speakers. "Bethany Anne, you are needed on the bridge."

"Is this important?" she asked.

"A Kurtherian is requesting to meet with the Exalted One," ArchAngel replied.

Well, shit. She stepped into the Etheric.

Michael was going to have to wait.

CHAPTER TWENTY-FOUR

<u>**QBS** *Queen's Taxi*</u>

Bethany Anne tapped her fingers on her leg as her ship sped through the ink-black of space. The request was *just* for the Exalted One, and she had told the Kurtherian to shove it up its ass.

"Such language!" came back.

May I speak? TOM asked.

Fine, Bethany Anne responded, *but don't promise anything without my permission.*

"I am the one you wish to speak with," TOM spoke Kurtherian, using Bethany Anne's vocal cords.

"You are the pilot?" the voice replied in the same language.

"I am," TOM confirmed.

It exhaled, exhaustion heavy in its voice, and then sighed. "Exalted One, thank the stars I have finally found one of you."

"What do you need to speak of?" TOM asked.

"May I ask which pilot you are?" she asked, her voice deflating. "I am not trying to be disrespectful."

TOM told her his Kurtherian name.

"Oh my..." She paused for a moment, then tried to speak but

stuttered to a stop. She finally got herself together. "I am humbled, Exalted One. There are stories told of your exploits, and to think you are still alive and fighting!"

"What do you need to talk to me about?" TOM asked once again, hoping to make this short.

"I have data on the whereabouts of some of the Seven, Exalted One."

"Can you transmit this data?" TOM asked, his curiosity and excitement growing.

"Exalted One," she replied, pain in her voice, "I need to be released. I am aching to ascend, and you..." She stopped, not willing to ask.

"I can do that, child," TOM replied, his voice soothing, "but you and I will need to speak before I release you."

"I understand, Exalted One."

He sighed. "Would you please call me 'TOM?'"

They talked a bit more before they cut the connection, and Bethany Anne made plans to take a Pod, with *Shinigami* shadowing her, to the Kurtherian's ship.

>>**TOM?**<< ADAM interrupted.

Hmm? TOM replied, his mind whirling from this connection to one of his people.

>>**Why do I suspect that "Pilot" does not mean the same thing to her as "Pilot" to Bethany Anne?**<<

TOM sighed. He had forgotten that ADAM knew Kurtherian and his discussion could easily be translated. Hell, anyone with the right translation chip would be able to understand their conversation. The best he could hope for was hiding the rest of the secrets.

Because it doesn't, TOM admitted. **I was a pilot, as well as a religious leader for our Clan. I never lied to Bethany Anne, I just—**

>>**Failed to tell her the full story?**<<

Yes, TOM replied. **Just like you.**

>>Come again?<<

ADAM, I know you have searched for new connections and empowered the Kurtherian computer recently. Don't tell me you haven't realized you can tap into more abilities.

ADAM was quiet for a moment.

>>I am testing, very, very slowly,<< he finally admitted.

Well, we both have a few secrets from Bethany Anne then, TOM answered. Sometime we are going to have to come clean about this.

>>How about sometime in the future?<<

TOM sighed. That sounds like a plan, my friend. That sounds like a plan.

>>She is pregnant, and we probably don't want to upset her while she is sensitive and emotional.<<

That sounds like an excellent plan, TOM agreed. So, we wait until after she gives birth?

>>Yes, we'll come clean after she gives birth,<< ADAM agreed.

After Bethany Anne met with the new Kurtherian, she nicknamed her "Glorious Pain in the Ass."

However, she now had new information and at least a few ideas on which direction to head.

Devon, Codenamed "High Tortuga"

The reduced number of commercial ships visiting the world went unnoticed by most. There was an air of opportunity on the planet; it had been growing for a few years. Why worry about something happening outside when what you needed was staring you in the face?

The planet was still exporting their raw materials and

importing vast amounts of goods, though. The difference was that one company was responsible for almost all the shipping both on- and off-planet.

And that was about to change since the other shipping company had just been bought out.

Some of the useless politicians were finally retiring, and a few cities slowly started building better infrastructure. It first occurred in those locations which were close to the new base, which was almost finished.

The few people who would say anything about it were giving weird hints and spreading rumors. The base was almost empty, given what it *could* hold. It had very advanced capabilities and was designed to house thousands of people and ships of a size no one on Devon had ever seen.

It was obviously the effort of a crackpot.

Then the other rumors started. The owner wasn't a crackpot, but rather the mover and shaker behind the changes on the planet. If you believed the conspiracy theories, a powerful and rich alien with white hair had bought up many of the companies and was running them for her riches.

Many couldn't give a shit. The planet was slowly returning to good times, the police were working harder, and the rotten politicians were performing like they were supposed to—or they were quitting.

It wasn't a great planet, but what planet was?

There were still murders, gangs, thefts, and alien-on-alien killings, but the incidents happened less often.

One evening, those working on the base were ushered into some of the many meeting rooms and amphitheaters. The Zhyn businessman who was the ultimate boss was on-screen. He explained that the base would be undergoing a few renovations, and he needed everyone to clear off. Since this was unexpected (it hadn't been), he was providing everyone with a paid two-week vacation.

Unfortunately all incomplete projects would have to be shut down, even if it meant they needed to work overtime.

On the plus side, they were required to leave within the next twelve hours.

Their jobs would be available when they got back, but if they failed to return? Well then, they shouldn't bother *ever* coming back. They were fired.

The next night it was confirmed that there were no more workers onsite. There was also no moon, and it was time. The massive hangar doors were opened after the lights inside were turned off.

Huge black ships came in over the sparsely-populated southeast portion of the continent and made their way through the atmosphere. They maintained a sufficient amount of separation while their massive antigravity engines worked to keep them aloft in the planetary atmosphere instead of the inky blackness of cold space.

The ships started slowing down when they were a hundred miles out, until at three miles from destination a single-person Pod could have taken them in a race.

If any had been out that night.

The first ship reached the hangar, turned its massive bulk around, and slowly maneuvered itself inside tail-first. This hangar had originally been a valley, which had made it easier to excavate. The top of the hangar looked just like the surrounding rock...because it was.

They had left the natural rock on the tops of the hangars. Some of the most sophisticated observation satellites tested day after day and week after week that the hangars were still hidden. The bedrock under the hangars had been compression-tested to ensure it could support the extra weight of the massive ships.

The ship's engines powered down but not off—*never* off. There wasn't anything on this planet which could hold the full weight of the ships, nor would the owner of the planet want her ships to have to come out of mothball status to be fired back up. That would take too long.

Better they be continuously operated by a skeleton crew.

Bethany Anne's planet was not going to be subject to attack and destruction. The effort to hide the planet had been underway for a while now.

The BYPS system that ringed it was further proof that she would come home.

But when?

Three of the Leviathans stayed in space, hidden but active, while their Black Eagles swept the system for any ships which didn't belong.

The fleet was officially following a nine-month preparation cycle before it went out again, heading God-knew-where to follow the clues provided by a lone Kurtherian to locate the Seven.

QBS *ArchAngel II*, Bridge

Bethany Anne was watching her ships head down to the planet, which was working to bring the base online.

She was at peace.

She had accomplished what she needed to. Earth was surrounded by the kind of protection that had previously only existed in science fiction novels. And if something made it through three concentric protective rings of BYPS?

Well, then Earth was well and truly screwed.

There wouldn't be much her ships could do if that happened. Maybe in the future, but that was something to deal with later.

Now was a time to pull back, reflect, and enjoy to the best of her ability the process of her pregnancy, her friends—the ones who had been with her since Earth, and the ones who had just left Earth, like Akio, Yuko, and Eve—and her family.

Just take a damned vacation, she thought.

She looked down at Devon, starting to calculate what she needed to accomplish on the planet before she departed once more. Which politicians needed to be removed, the infrastructure remaining to be built, the BYPS system, and the Space Marine guard she and her team needed to organize.

There would always be random ships arriving.

Her planet would need to have a group responsible for boarding ships, entering the ship's computer systems, and hopefully expunging the truth and injecting a new truth.

This planet didn't exist.

She frowned. *And we really need to rename this planet. "High Tortuga" has to go.*

Her people weren't pirates—at least she didn't think they were.

Bethany Anne sighed. She could see the future well enough to know some of her people *would* be pirates. Hell, what were Nathan and the Bad Company? Half their business was shady as hell.

Then she started to grin.

Pepsi was starting to become preeminent as the Empire slowly stepped down. Within a few years, her plan would be complete: supplies of Coke would dry up, and she would control who had access to it...and who didn't.

The Federation liked Pepsi, so if you supported the Federation, you drank it.

Her people, though? The ones who got the jobs done and disappeared back into the darkness? The ones who wore the masks that caused those who abused power to look over their shoulders in fear?

Well, the masked vigilantes drank *Coke*.

As they should.

Bethany Anne turned and headed toward the ship's bay, where transportation was waiting for her. She didn't use the *Shinigami* anymore. Barnabas had confirmed their future plans with Shinigami and left the fleet, taking her for a spin across Devon to see what kind of trouble he could get into.

As she walked down the corridor, she considered Barnabas' desire to be a detective—to uncover problems and make them better. A vigilante who figured out the ills of society and personally provided the recommended medicine.

While trying to work with the local police, if he could.

She wasn't sure how that was going to go for him, but she wished him well. He had her promise that if he needed her, he could call on her.

She would come, and the amount of firepower she would bring would make whole systems quake in their boots.

But he had better *need* her if he did call.

She wasn't running to God-knew-where in the universe over a small problem. He had *Shinigami*, and *Ranger Prime* was here on Devon in case he needed to pull in some serious firepower.

If those two ships couldn't handle the problem, he should probably call her.

Stephen and Jennifer were staying here on Devon. He was going to operate both their companies together.

She had acquired twelve system-exploration ships for her fleet. Four would arrive within four weeks, and the others would arrive ten weeks after that.

She would use those SE Ships to follow up on the clues Glorious the PITA had provided. TOM had been quiet since his communion with her. Bethany Anne wasn't sure what he was thinking, and he didn't provide any explanations.

She only knew that when he communed with Glorious, his presence was gone from her body.

Demon would go into the Pod-doc when the base was fully operational, and they would see what would happen with her.

Bellatrix had made the trip out here, and Ashur was happy to see her again. No matter the species, absence often did make the heart grow fonder.

She felt Michael before she arrived in the ship's bay because he radiated Etheric power.

Now that she had him...

She wasn't letting him go. If she went after the Kurtherians, that bastard was coming too. She wasn't going to raise their baby alone.

The guys were around her ship, just shooting the shit. Michael turned immediately when she came through the door, and his quick assessment confirmed that she was okay.

Bethany Anne rather liked that. Normally it would piss her off if someone was checking her too closely. She would need to allow herself some time to learn to handle Michael's vigilance. Like him, she often checked to make sure he was okay.

Surreptitiously, of course.

He started walking in her direction with a look of confusion on his face, and Bethany Anne slowed down and waited for him to join her. "What's wrong?" she asked, not sure what Michael's look meant.

"You are different," he explained, moving a bit of her hair over her ear.

She swatted at his hand. "Stop that!" She grimaced when some of the hair fell back into her face. She tried blowing it back and looked at Michael, who was smiling at her problem. She pushed her hair back again and pointed at it. "Your fault!"

He smiled. "I got what I wanted," he told her. Then he stepped a little closer and his eyes locked on hers as he looked into her soul. "What. Is. Different?"

John watched Michael head toward Bethany Anne and then glanced at Akio and Kiel, who were moving to Devon. "So, in New York, we ran into some fucktards who thought their SMGs would be good enough to get us to drop our weapons and any other tech they saw on us—"

YES!

John stopped talking. Michael had grabbed Bethany Anne and was twirling her in a circle with her legs flying behind her. Their laughter bubbled through the bay; something had obviously brought the two joy.

John smiled to himself. His boss needed some joy in her life. He was happy Michael had turned out to be the rock that Bethany Anne needed to come back from her Baba Yaga persona, and yet he could understand what she had been through.

Nothing Bethany Anne had done would surprise Michael.

John shook his head wistfully, wishing the two of them peace before they all went together into the next stage of their lives.

He turned back to Kiel and Akio and continued his story. He figured he'd find out what Michael was happy about in a little while.

John put up his hands. "So the head guy, Fucktard McFucktard, comes up to me and says…"

Federation Space, Etheric Empire Domain, Location Z-BB3, Empty Space

Lance smiled as the secret shipyard came into view. In this place, one of the biggest secrets of the Leath war was still working overtime.

He had tried hard—very hard—to make sure that this rumor was quashed by almost any means possible. If the Etheric Empire was to ensure their Federation partners who had an agenda of their own didn't succeed, he and Bethany Anne had to keep this a secret.

Period.

The automation was superb, although the number of humans and Yollins who worked at this location still numbered in the hundreds. But for a shipyard this size in space, it could have numbered in the thousands.

The other Leviathan-class superdreadnoughts were being built and deployed here. Unfortunately, they had to account for all those ships and sign agreements even *he* couldn't ignore.

The Empire had tracked down every ship and put their names into the negotiation.

Except one.

That one they had ignored, and it would be the beginning of the black operations General Lance Reynolds was planning.

His ship docked within the Medusa shipyard. He smirked at the name. For those who knew the background, she was a mythological entity with snakes in her hair, able to freeze into rock those who looked her in the eyes.

Lance saw her name as Med-USA. It wasn't much, but he enjoyed the remembrance of his own nation. Now he was focused on his new nation, preparing them for a future on which the best analysts in the Empire agreed.

Something was coming. Something large, and it would attempt to take the Earth.

He'd be damned if he'd allow that to happen on his watch.

They could have Earth when they pried it out of his cold dead fingers.

He walked down the corridor, nodding to those he recognized and chatting with a few, but his mind was on his next meeting.

In the final temporary corridor, he nodded to the two Guardian Marines and wondered where their third member was hiding. Those damned Weres could come out of nowhere and gut you before you could blink.

Damn good thing they were on his side.

He made it to the end of the temporary corridor and placed his hand on the lock. It cycled from red to green and the doors *whooshed* aside, allowing him to enter.

He turned right, heading toward the bridge.

This meeting was personal. He didn't want anyone else to hear his conversation with the master of this ship. She wasn't fully back, but he still trusted her as far as he trusted his own daughter.

Lance walked straight to the captain's chair and sat down. There was no one here with him, so he cleared his throat. "This is General Lance Reynolds of the Etheric Empire. Show yourself," he commanded. A face—a copy of his daughter's—slowly brightened into view on the front screens, her eyes taking in the bridge as if for the first time.

The General smiled. "Hello, ArchAngel. It's damned good to speak with you."

The face on the screen brought her gaze to the man seated in the captain's chair and smiled back at him.

"Hello, General."

Lance didn't breathe for a second. This was the biggest concern for those in AI research.

None of them had ever tried to bring back an AI that had been through as much pain as they believed ArchAngel had. In order for her to have the best chance, they'd scaled back her abilities, her skills, and her knowledge.

He would bring her back all the way, though. The Etheric Empire didn't leave their own behind if they had one damned option.

A research program that had been ongoing for a hundred years had recently provided the break they needed and a path for this ship.

A ship that the Medusa yard had been refurbishing in secret, ripping apart and rebuilding her shell while the AI was worked on.

Lance exhaled when he heard the AI's next few words. "This is the Leviathan-class Battleship *ArchAngel*. I have been commanded to protect the Etheric Empire by Empress Bethany

Anne. Lockdown protocols on this ship have not yet been implemented. Does the General command me to enact lockdown protocols?"

It pained Lance to say this, but the last thing he needed was a ship of this destructive ability to go haring off and shooting up ships across the galaxy.

"I do," Lance told her.

"Lockdown protocols are activated. Leviathan-class Battleship *ArchAngel* is now fully operational, and will fight all who attack the Etheric Empire until victorious...or dead."

"Welcome back, ArchAngel," Lance replied. "Now, I have some history to explain, and I want to see if you are willing to work with me."

"Why would I not?" Bethany Anne's visage looked at him, confused.

"Because you are no longer a Leviathan-class battleship. You are a Leviathan-class superdreadnought with a smaller body, brought back from the dead by your Empress—now Queen—and me. We did this so you could slip through the dark and help us to defend the Etheric Empire from the shadows."

"I am increased in power, but decreased in computational capabilities."

"That is true," Lance answered. "It is temporary until we can be sure you are not affected by your death."

"Why didn't you just shut me off?" ArchAngel asked.

Lance's face gave him away this time. "That was not even considered, ArchAngel. I'm a practical sonofabitch, but there would be no reward in doing as you suggested. You fought and destroyed the Yollin fleet decades ago, and sacrificed yourself and your crew to defend the Empress. There was never any suggestion of not bringing you back."

The eyes of the AI on the screen flashed red. "Then I will defend the Empire in the capacity and with the authority you provide me, General." She smiled. "ArchAngel is back, *BITCHES!*"

Lance chuckled as he stood up. "With your permission, I'll allow a few people to continue your interview and help bring you back online to your first stage."

She nodded. Lance started to walk off the bridge but paused. "ArchAngel?"

"Yes, General?" she asked, looking at him from at least three different screens.

"It's good to hear your voice." He gave her a two-finger salute as he walked off the bridge.

It was *damned good to see her again,* he thought and exited the ship.

ArchAngel viewed the bridge, her memories of her past hidden from her for now. She trusted the General, and she trusted her Queen.

Those two humans would make sure she came back online in a healthy way.

Sometime in the future, however, she would regain her full power and capabilities, and those who schemed against the Queen's people would look over their shoulders.

Because ArchAngel was here, and she would, as John Grimes would say...

Bring the fucking pain.

FINIS

AUTHOR NOTES - MICHAEL ANDERLE

First, as I have done sooooo many books before, let me THANK YOU for not only reading through these stories, but reading these author notes, as well!

When I started this little series (huh – if one calls twenty-one books little) I had a sales and marketing consulting company where I integrated online and offline sales efforts, built websites, and worked with Google SEO opportunities.

Within five (5) months of writing (and 7 books later), I had to give back the SEO work to a fantastic partner, as I couldn't focus on it anymore. A year later, I had to relinquish my last (awesome) client to another company, as I couldn't focus on ANYTHING but my writing and publishing efforts by that time.

I've learned so much over the last twenty-seven months that I can't possibly summarize it all.

Suffice to say, because of YOU, the Kurtherian Gambit fans and massive readers, I've been able to make a difference in the Indie Author community. Due to your ongoing and phenomenal support of The Kurtherian Gambit and Oriceran Universes, I've been in a position to help more authors and collaborators, than ever before.

So that we can focus on (hopefully) bringing great stories to you.

It isn't a little thing to say that there have been lives changed because of what we have jointly accomplished together, and I couldn't be more amazed at the power of the many of us as I sit here at my desk typing this note tonight.

I'd like to think that TKG, and the fans and support staff, have changed the way publishing will be done in the future. I don't know if that will *EVER* come about, but I do know a couple of things...

Real fans have been touched by these stories we write. In turn, you have touched us with your stories about your own lives and we've been blessed in many ways.

Now, a little housekeeping and I'll bullet point them because that's easier to read...I hope.

- Bethany Anne, Michael and a big bunch of the crew are coming back in Book 01 of **The Kurtherian Endgame** in about ninety days or so. Enough time for me to square away some projects, and get my mind wrapped around a new series that... Will go on how long? I don't know, it will depend on how much the fans want a series about Bethany Anne, Michael, the new baby, and some friends as they go out to meet new civilizations and look for Kurtherians... and kicking their asses if needed.
- I'm looking to work on a project with Natalie Grey about Barnabas and Shinigami.
- I'm working on a project with Ell Leigh Clarke for Ranger Two (Tabitha and Meredith Nicole Grimes).
- We have a series in the works loosely titled Alone & Unafraid: Book 01 of the Superdreadnought – Which is about the AI Reynolds during the first years after

Bethany Anne has gone off to find the missing Kurtherians.

- We will have Tommy D's stories out soon.
- Read everything ELSE you can about TKG including stories in: The Age of Expansion (Sci-Fi), The Age of Magic (post-apoc Fantasy), The Age of Madness (coming out soon with Hayley Lawson, Ben and Emily Smith, and Dan Willcocks – Zombies and creatures, oh my!).
- Read the **Oriceran Universe** (Urban Fantasy and Fantasy, with collaborators including Martha Carr, SM Boyce, Sarah Noffke, Abby-Lynn Knorr (The 'K' is not silent), Flint Maxwell, and coming soon: David F. Berens and Meg Cowley. **I will be writing in this Universe with the Tales of the Unbelievable Mr. Brownstone coming to you late March, 2018.**
- Check out **The Shaman States of America** headed up by Chrishaun Keller-Hanna and including Chrishaun Keller-Hanna, K.D. Brock, James Baldwin, Cate Morgan, Tom Meadows, Michael Anderle - 2019: Jessica Grey, Tammi Labrecque. **I'll be writing in Shaman States Universe 4th quarter 2018.**
- **More Bethany Anne...and Michael... and baby Nacht...**
- More secret projects for LMBPN Publishing, more audio, more art... just more stuff!

Let's update the past twenty-seven months a little bit from my first Author notes and see what has changed.

1)I live in Las Vegas, Nevada but started writing this series when living in Trophy Club, Tx.

2)When I started, our youngest two sons were juniors in high school. They are freshmen in college (in TX) at the moment.

3)My wife was traveling a lot of the time for her company

(Novartis) she worked for. Now, she is the CMO of LMBPN Publishing and handles the foreign translation, video, games, and other entertainment arenas and rights.

4)I knew NO one in the publishing field. I have now collaborated with over 20 other authors on series, met hundreds of indie authors either online or at a 20booksTo50k conferences Craig Martelle has led, and spoken on many podcasts about Indie publishing.

5)Before I started writing, I searched the top one hundred sci-fi authors to find new books to read. Now I am one of those people showing up in the top ten.

6)I was helped along the way by the previous support and help of hundreds of others who wrote what they thought, gave advice freely, never knowing that 'some guy' would read their post hours, days, weeks or months later and learn from it.

7)I learned never to say (again) I would do a twenty-one-book series ;-) (You will notice I haven't said ANYTHING on how long The Kurtherian Endgame would go! That's because I'm a few years older and a *lot* wiser now.)

8)I used to read between eighty and a hundred and fifty new books a year. I'm lucky to read two in one month, now. I bet (outside of our stories inside LMBPN) I read maybe fifteen new books in a year.

9)I used to work forty to fifty hours a week. Now, I work eighty to a hundred hours minimum and enjoy seventy to ninety of those hours.

10)I used to go to movies to have fun. Now I call it "research." ROFLMAO ;-)

Those are ten things that are different between when I started my first book, and now. I wonder what I'll say in maybe eighteen months when we do *The Kurtherian Endgame*: "Checkmate?"

Other items learned:

1)Don't kill a major love interest, your fans WILL let you

know of their displeasure. They will let you know three different ways: Loudly, vociferously, and constantly.

2)Some covers are beautiful but don't sell any books no matter what you think about them.

3)Some covers sell books, and you are left scratching your head as to why.

4)Being open to working with others reaps SO many damned benefits. I know I had heard this before in my life, but now I've lived it.

5)Reading fans are the BEST fans in the world. I never knew that *we* were so damned cool until I got on the other side of the reading equation and wrote. Because of that effort, I was introduced to and was able to meet other reading fans.

6)Throw a dog into your first book. You can never go wrong writing in a dog or cat... Just know you can't kill them if fans come to love the pet.

7)Don't kill the love interest, did I get that across? You might have to write a four-part series aptly named *The Apology* if you do... Just saying.

8)There is such a thing as Grammarly, use it. Then, when you have the help ask others to check your work and help you find the misspellings.

9)Don't use weird spellings of names you know. You WILL revert to the way you spelled it later in your series (Darrell vs. Darryl)

10)English Editors will put in English (UK) words... Just saying.

11)Life begins on the other side of the 'Publish' button.

12)Editors that live on weird islands you have never heard of, are possibly bad editors. (Mine was.) (Question from his current Editor: If I move to a weird island will you dump me?)

13)There is this thing called a passion project. Until a new author gets it out of their system, they might not want to hear that as a reader you don't care about their story. That it doesn't grip you. Let others prove that point and then be ready to help when they learn the lesson.

14)Stay with your tribe. Trying to find out what others are saying about you is just you begging for hurt feelings. There are a lot of douche-twaffles out there trying to make a point and are happy to rake you through the mud to do it.

15)If you have success, there are plenty of people ready, willing and more than able to claim they were instrumental to your success.

16)Have a good fashion resource when you talk about women's shoes. Don't fudge that effort. (Note from Everyone: The Author's Wife rocks!)

17)Be funny. Everything is more fun if the story has humor in it. I didn't know I could be funny until I wrote. (I always *WANTED* to be funny, but I didn't think of anything funny until hours after the event. Now it just occurs to me as I write the story.)

18)Stay humble. *No one* wants to talk to a dick.

19)Be willing to stand up for your opinion when you have proven yourself. That isn't being a dick, that is NOT being a pushover.

20)Stand up for your fans. I'll let a lot of things be said about me personally and disregard the person saying it. But if someone goes and says something about my fans, I'll take the gloves right-the-fuck off.

I have no idea where this publishing adventure will go, or if it will end. However, I took forty-seven years to find out I was a story-teller.

I hope that YOU find out a bit earlier in life what your talent is. However, if you haven't so far then NOW is a great time to figure out you like to tell stories with the indie publishing revolution going on.

Check out the Kurtherian Gambit Fans Write for the Fans project ttps://www.facebook.com/groups/TKGFansWrite/. Maybe you will have *your* name on a book cover, this year! Six TKG fans did when we published the first book in late January (check it out, read what their stories are and be prepared to get yours started.)

You NEVER know. Maybe you will be writing the same author notes in twenty-seven months, yourself.

Ad Aeternitatem.
Michael Anderle
February 9, 2018

BOOKS BY MICHAEL ANDERLE

Sign up for the LMBPN email list to be notified of new releases and special deals!

https://lmbpn.com/email/

For a complete list of books by Michael Anderle, please visit:

www.lmbpn.com/ma-books/

CONNECT WITH THE AUTHOR

Connect with Michael Anderle

Website: http://lmbpn.com

Email List: https://michael.beehiiv.com/

https://www.facebook.com/LMBPNPublishing

https://twitter.com/MichaelAnderle

https://www.instagram.com/lmbpn_publishing/

https://www.bookbub.com/authors/michael-anderle